I0730148

VEIL

a novel

JEFF CLULOW

THIRD EYE PRESS

Copyright © Jeff Clulow 2025

The moral right of Jeff Clulow to be identified as the author of this work ('Veil') has been asserted in accordance with the Copyright Amendment (Moral Rights) Act 2000.

All rights reserved.

No part of this publication may be copied or reproduced in any form without permission of the author other than excerpts for criticism or review purposes.

AI training expressly prohibited. No part of this publication may be reproduced or uploaded to help train generative artificial intelligence (AI) or learning language modelling technologies.

This is an AI-free book. No AI has been used in the creation of this work, including cover design, audio recording, research, editing or creative content.

This book is a work of fiction. Any resemblance to actual persons or events is coincidental.

Cover design by Jeff Clulow.

Cover photography of bride by Lorenzo Gulino (captblack76), courtesy of 123RF.

Forest background photography by Ryslan Бойко, courtesy of Pexels.

Proofread by Liz at Elizabeth Bird Proofreading Services.

Caution: this work contains adult themes, mental illness, self-harm and horror.

ISBN (ebook): 978-1-7641397-0-0

ISBN (paperback): 978-1-7641397-1-7

PRAISE FOR 'VEIL'

'Atmospheric, compelling, and gorgeously written.' – *Brent McGregor, prizewinning author of 'Strange Murmurings' and 'Blood Tide'.*

'Gothic horror at its best. Clulow intrigues from the outset, crafting characters and a story that cannot be put down.' – *Alister Hodge, bestselling author of the 'Cryptid Killers' and 'Plague War' series.*

'A gripping tale of loss and redemption...terror balanced finely with life's beauty. A brilliant read. More please.' – *Clare Rhoden, author of 'The Chronicles of the Pale' series.*

'His [Clulow's] writing style is lush, descriptive, and beautiful, and through his deft narrative, Aeolus House comes to life in minute detail...Clulow is a new writer to me, but one I'll seek out again. – *S.E. Howard, author of 'The Vessel'.*

'Veil is beautifully written and atmospheric, bringing not just the characters but also the setting vividly to life.' – *Paul Sheldon, the Australasian Horror Writers Association.*

'I tore through Veil like it was a cursed love letter I wasn't supposed to read. The vibes are spooky, the romance is tragic, and the drama? Top tier! It's romantic, twisted, and totally addictive.' – *Sue. Goodreads.*

'Gorgeous, literary writing with a sharp emotional edge...Veil delivers a beautifully written, heart-wrenching experience. It's introspective, eerie, and quietly unforgettable.' – *Teneil. Goodreads.*

'[A] very enjoyable, atmospheric, and detailed story that will stay with you.' – *David-Jack Fletcher, editor and award winning author of 'Raven's Creek', 'The Count' and 'Indentured'.*

'Veil is a haunting exploration of legacy, trauma, and the ghosts we inherit — both literal and metaphorical. Gothic horror aficionados will find much to admire in Clulow's work, and new readers to the genre may find it an ideal introduction.' – *Samantha Seay. Netgalley.*

'A beautifully dark, tragic story. I think Clulow does subtle, creeping horror excellently and this story left me thinking about it long after I'd already set it down. A strong female character, excellently developed plot and decadent writing style leaves me excited for what else Clulow has in store.' – *K.B. Goodreads.*

'This isn't your average haunted house story. It's a slow, graceful unraveling of one woman's broken spirit tangled in the tattered threads of memory, grief, and legacy—and I devoured it like a whispered secret I wasn't supposed to hear...Jeff Clulow doesn't just write a story—he paints it in fog and fragments...And no spoilers, but the final few chapters? Poetic. Painful. Perfect.' – *Rebel. Goodreads.*

'I have absolutely nothing but praise for this book. Seriously. The storytelling was beautiful, the pace was perfect, and the end was rounded off flawlessly.' – *Robyn. Goodreads.*

'I loved how the suspense kept building with every flicker of the veil's visions—it made me feel like I was right there in that crumbling house, desperate to know the truth. This was one of those reads that stayed with me long after I turned the last page.' – *Abigail L. Goodreads.*

'Just be ready for the deep emotions. The book mixes trauma and romance in a powerful way.' – *Abby. Netgalley.*

'This book was really, really good...It was a short, enjoyable, and somewhat heartbreaking read.' – *S.H. Gray (The Fanged Librarian). Goodreads.*

'Wow. What an unexpected gem this book turned out to be! I honestly have nothing but good things to say...This was the perfect little dose of gothic horror, in all the best ways.' – *Gabzreads. Netgalley.*

'Such an intense and emotional read, and Clulow writes in such a way that you feel the tension, anguish, and the heartbreak. The story pulled me in from the beginning, and found myself lost in...until the very end.' – *Jazmyn R. Netgalley.*

Acknowledgements

Thanks to my patient family for living with this story for far longer than reasonable.

Gratitude also to my friend and fellow dark scribbler Brent McGregor for guiding this story along. You are the demon at my shoulder.

I'm grateful to Alister Hodge as friend, writer and health professional. Al, your advice in both storytelling and the field of medicine makes this story ring true.

Thank you Georgina Ballantine for your experience and wisdom both as writer and therapist. Without your help I would not have navigated the minefield that is mental health. You put me right and made my characters real.

Lastly, thanks to Liz at Elizabeth Bird Proofreading Services for making sure my work is fit to be seen in public.

For Ivy and Ray

CONTENTS

1

THE END

SHE WAS OLD. And this was her wedding day.

As it always was.

A day of devotion and promises.

A day of endings and beginnings.

She only had to make it to the rock.

The bright isle.

She wore her dress as before, the veil across her face. Silk voile, translucent, moved against the dryness of aged cheeks.

When she was young she walked upon moors like these.

When the thorn trees bloomed like cherry flower; when the sun shone and the winds were mild.

She had walked in the shadows of ancient tors and marvelled at the empty sweep of rust-coloured downs, her head against another's shoulder. Now, this was no landscape she recognised.

It was a corruption, a nightmare that might drag a devil from its sleep.

Above, the sky churned; blood stirred into boiling pitch. It swirled in maddening eddies of purple, crimson and black.

Stunted trees of wych-elm and hawthorn, bent and beaten by the wind, hung uprooted in the air, revolving slowly – dark shapes trailing dark roots.

Behind the brooding clouds the lightning flashed.

The wind was filled with whispers. A chorus of the damned hissed curses in her ear.

She lifted a leaden foot in the direction she must go.

Sharp fingers of gorse and briar clutched at her hem of white silk.

Her bare feet slid in cold mud, her soles numb and bleeding.

Then, through the mist of the veil, she saw it gleam in the distance. From a sapphire sea the island rose. Towering cliffs of dark granite glistened, slick with seawater. At the very top a rounded space of thick grass shone in blinding sunlight.

There her love, her betrothed, waited. A hand beckoning.

There it was, the holy place. She saw the tumbled stonework and the altar of the Anchorite. The place of joining.

How far? One mile? Ten?

From her throat she hitched a sob, stepping onward.

'I follow,' she said. Her eternal promise.

From behind, a voice called her.

'Emma!'

She stumbled forward and the world tilted. Rearing up, it struck her hard against the head and shoulder. She lay on her side in the wet briar and marsh grass while energy, strength and hope ebbed.

'Emma!'

It was a voice she knew and trusted. A kind voice. *Dr Passmore?*

She felt warm hands around her own. Comforting hands. Electric torchlight flickered all about. More voices.

'Dear God Emma, what have you done?' begged Dr Passmore.

She lifted a finger towards the shining vision in the distance.

'I follow...' she said.

Her final words were stolen by the cold night. Her last breath escaped her in a long, low susurration.

Then, in her ears and on the moor, the whispers in the wind fell silent.

2

'THERE'S SOMETHING WRONG WITH YOU'

SETTING DOWN her book, Suze looked towards the ceiling.

They must be asleep by now, surely?

She was half-asleep herself.

Please let them be asleep.

She rose from the sofa and crept upstairs in bare feet. Opening James's door, she saw the boy sprawled across his bed, the covers pulled back. She tiptoed inside and arranged the sheets and blankets over him. Leaving him, she walked along the hall, straightened one of the limited edition Hockney prints on the wall, and peeked inside Juliet's room. The little girl's doll-like face was framed by ringlets, her eyes closed. She was fast asleep.

Further along the hall was the master bedroom. Suze slipped inside and thumbed the light switch. The immense, walk-in wardrobe was filled with hanging gowns and dresses. She leafed through them and selected a simple, long-sleeved dress in greys and blues. Draping it across the bed, she spread the sleeves wide and smoothed out the creases. She pulled the hem towards the foot of the bed. It looked for all the world as if a woman had lain there spreadeagled, then had somehow been spirited away from inside her own clothing. Suze studied the arrangement for a moment, brows gathered. She could add something more. *Stockings perhaps? Jewellery?*

No.

This was enough.

Just a few minutes. That's all she needed.

With care, she crawled onto the bed and into the middle of the dress. She lay on top of it, letting the dress's outline frame her own.

She pulled the long arms around her, curling up in their embrace.

Then she closed her eyes.

———◆———

The slap landed hard across Suze's face, waking her in an instant.

Panic clawed at her.

She'd fallen asleep. How could she be so stupid?

The woman's face hovered above, purple with fury. Suze could make out the swollen veins in her neck and forehead, the dishevelled curls of her coiffure, matted and stiff with hairspray. Her breath stank of wine and cigarettes.

Suze's ears rang from the searing impact of the blow. The woman above her was screaming. Her mouth moved and Suze felt the spray of spit, yet the woman's voice was elsewhere, raging in a vacuum of silence.

Another blow landed. Sound rushed in, a runaway train, a meteor falling from the sky. It exploded in Suze's hearing.

'Get off my dress, get off my bed, and get the fuck out of my house!' screamed the woman, stabbing a scarlet fingernail at the door.

Suze sprang from the bed, cheeks burning. In her periphery she saw James appear at the bedroom door, dressed in his pyjamas. He rubbed his eyes.

'What's all the noise?' he asked, his voice thick with sleep.

'Back into bed, darling...' said the woman with feigned nonchalance, then, lifting her voice to the ceiling she shouted, 'Harv, get up here, now!'

There was a clumping of footsteps on the stairs and a man wearing a tuxedo and an expression of alarm appeared in the doorway behind the boy.

'Harv, look after the kids!'

'But what's *happening*?' insisted the boy.

Harv swept James up, explaining. 'Nothing sport. Just grown-up stuff.'

As they walked away, Suze saw the boy grin over the man's shoulder. 'Has Susanna done something *bad*?'

The woman waited until the boy's bedroom door closed, then she came at Suze in a storm of bristling chiffon and vehemence. Suze felt a hand grip her wrist, fingernails like a dog bite. She was dragged from the master bedroom along the hallway, past more Hockneys and hauled from landing to landing down the staircase. She stubbed her toes against the Poggenpohl kitchen and ran her shins against Parker Knoll furniture all the way to the front door. The woman released her grip to struggle with the locks, giving Suze time to gather up her coat and boots. The front door was flung open to reveal the cold night beyond. 'Out!' commanded the woman.

Suze escaped through the doorway.

'Stop!'

Suze did as she was told and turned back. The woman retrieved her handbag from an antique lowboy beside the door and rummaged through it. She produced a purse and began pulling out banknotes, one at a time. Each of these she screwed into a ball and threw at Suze.

'I'm paying you for looking after the kids tonight because I want everything square,' spat the woman.

With her coat and boots in one arm, Suze caught a five-pound note and a couple of ones. The rest were snatched away by the chill October wind.

'But I'm calling the agency first thing Monday,' declared the woman. She stood for a time at the threshold with a judgemental expression, chin lifted, eyes narrowed in scrutiny. 'I never liked you,' she said. 'I always knew there was something *wrong* with you.' Then she slammed the door so hard that the Hockneys rattled.

Suze padded down the stone steps of the terrace in bare feet. She crossed the road, splashing in shallow puddles. The wind cut through her thin T-shirt. The sharp crescent of a new moon was a grin in a cold, cloudless sky. She'd put her coat and boots on later. She just wanted to be out of range. She'd avoid the exposure of streetlights and hug the shadows all the way to the Edgeware Road. From there she'd take the night bus home to her draughty attic flat in Finchley.

And to consequence.

3

'WE WERE NEVER THERE'

THE *LITTLELANDS Crèche and Babysitting Agency* was located in a converted house in Bayswater, its sole owner, architect and administrator being the deportment-schooled bundle of propriety known as Odette Mason. Odette had spent years and a great deal of her own money in building her business but, with the Falklands War over, the trade unions brought to heel and Thatcher firmly ensconced in Downing Street, Britain had seen the rise of a new middle class. The yuppies and muppies had poured into West London. Perhaps they'd always been here and it was just the tax cuts and the widening divide between the haves and have-nots that put more money in their pockets and made them more conspicuous. Whatever the reason, they needed somewhere to shelter their entitled offspring while they worked and played. Littlelands appealed to their newfound sense of snobbery. The crèche now had a waiting list and the mere mention of its name was a valuable credential in gaining admission to many desirable prep-schools.

Littlelands was a *cause célèbre* and Suze knew that Odette would fight tooth and claw to protect its reputation.

'We should count ourselves lucky that the Crawfords won't take this any further,' said Odette. She was bouncing a distraught little boy on her knee, perhaps a little too physically. She could bounce a toddler on her knee while she interviewed new staff, took a phone call or completed her tax return. Odette was a paragon of multi-tasking. 'Bad press could ruin us,' she added.

Odette's eyes bored into Suze. Her eyes always protruded slightly. They had a bulbous quality. Together with her high, pencilled eyebrows it gave her the appearance of being continuously appalled by everyone and everything she encountered. 'They've agreed to let their children stay at Littlelands. On one condition.'

Suze knew what was coming. The Crawfords needed the kudos Littlelands would bestow on their progeny. Littlelands needed this whole thing swept under the rug. A deal had been struck.

'I can't keep you on my books,' said Odette. 'Not after this. I'm sorry.'

'I know,' said Suze.

'Do you have anything to say?'

Suze didn't answer.

'Anything at all?'

'Not really.'

'How many times have I told you all? We sit on their sofas, we watch their TVs, and use their toilets if we have to. Then we leave everything as it was. We leave no trace of ourselves, *we were never there*.'

Suze had heard this mantra before. All Odette's babysitters had.

'What on earth possessed you to do such a thing? And with one of our regular customers? After everything I've insisted upon, after all I've tried to teach you, why would you do this *now*?' Odette's eyes narrowed. 'This *is* the first time?'

Again, Suze didn't answer.

The bouncing stopped. Odette gave a laboured sigh and closed her eyes. When they opened, she turned them to the child on her knee. 'Alexander, I think you're all right now, and I want you to go play with Evelyn.' She placed the boy on his feet. He stopped blubbing, sensing the force of her will. Dutifully, he turned and ran off. Odette's gaze now fell on Suze. 'How many times?'

Suze shrugged. She hadn't been counting.

'My God.' There was no judgement in Odette's voice. Only shock.

'I don't do it to hurt anyone,' said Suze.

Odette drew a long breath. 'Then why? Why do you do it Susanna?'

Suze remained tight-lipped. The explanation lay buried deep inside her. To her it was a simple hurt, a simple need. Yet for others it was such a hard thing to understand. To speak of it would make it trivial, stupid.

Odette leaned forward, her voice calm. 'Look, I know, I *understand*. You were raised as an orphan...'

'A foster child,' corrected Suze.

Odette's eyes bulged. 'Either way, did you know your parents?'

Suze shook her head.

'That's very sad. But it doesn't give you permission to live vicariously through other people's families.' Odette sat back. 'Is that why you work here? Why you want to work *with children*? Is it because you never had a childhood yourself?'

This was the kind of amateur psychoanalysis that irked Suze. It was true in a way, but not conscious or premeditated. She hadn't planned her life to be like this, it wasn't a scheme. It was something she was drawn to, a deep-down longing.

'I think you should seek out help, Susanna. This kind of behaviour, well, it's damaging.' Odette's bulbous eyes rested on Suze. 'And, for your own sake you probably need to reassess, to step back and think about whether this is the right kind of work for you.'

Suze frowned in question. 'But this is the only job I ever wanted.'

Odette's expression saddened. 'I don't think it's for you.'

'I like looking after children.'

'Perhaps, but frankly, they find it hard to relate to you. Look, you've been great with the day-to-day stuff. But with the finger-painting, the storytelling, and the games – well, you don't laugh, you don't smile or display any kind of joy.'

'Is that so important?'

'Children *need* these things. In truth, they find you – *scary*.'

Suze felt herself falling into a familiar abyss of self-doubt.

'Susanna, what happened? Why don't you smile?'

Suze stayed silent. She could never explain. The answers were too many, too complicated.

'Open up for once. Tell me. What's this all about?'

Suze shrugged again.

'Do you ever cry?'

Suze shook her head.

'You should try sometime. It helps.'

Suze knew that Odette had a good heart and that her advice was well-intended. But for people like Odette it was always easier to give advice than try to understand. They only saw things from *outside*. If they ever saw things from Suze's side, from *inside*, then they'd realise no advice in the world could help.

'Are you going to be okay?' asked Odette. 'Do you have enough to get by?'

'Sure,' lied Suze. 'I'll be fine.'

Odette stood and crossed the room to a filing cabinet. From this she produced a petty cash tin. She counted out three twenty-pound notes and handed them to Suze. 'Here,' she said, 'this'll help until you find something.'

Suze nodded in thanks.

'You'll need this, too,' said Odette, holding out some paperwork. 'Your P45. If you want to sign on.'

Suze took the documents. The government form was her admission to the ranks of the unemployed. Her ticket to the dole queue. There was a letter too, addressed to Suze, care of Littlelands. Printed on the envelope was a government seal and the sender's address: *St Catherine's House, Aldwych*.

'That arrived this morning,' confided Odette, nodding at the envelope in Suze's hand.

'What is it?' asked Suze. The government seal looked ominous.

'Haven't the foggiest,' said Odette.

4

A SUITCASEFUL OF SORROW

EVENING PULLED its autumn gloom across London while Suze sat in her draughty attic flat.

She was counting out her hurts at the tiny kitchen table. The place was just a single room big enough for a single bed and a single window above the kitchenette sink, with a shared bathroom one floor down. In winter the plumbing would freeze and the lack of insulation in the roof made the place impossible to heat. The plates and cutlery on the sink buzzed and rattled from the persistent drone of traffic on the North Circular. As cold and comfortless as the place was, she'd always considered it her own. Now she didn't recognise it. It wasn't really hers. Never had been. And now she had no idea how she'd cover the rent. Tomorrow she'd trudge to the DHSS, stand in queues, fill out their forms and place herself at the mercy of all the usual inquisitions. How quickly you could move from gainful employment to poverty. From taxpayer to burden.

She hadn't claimed the dole in over eight years. She'd been a model citizen of sorts. Of course she'd look for work, but without a reference from Littlelands, from Odette, it would be hard to prove any kind of consistent record of employment – at least, one where her work had been valued. She might have to put childcare behind her and look for something else. This grieved her. It's all she'd done since leaving school. She needed it in a way, it kept her in one piece. Now, at thirty years of age she'd have to retrain, start over. Back to square one.

Suze sighed.

The most painful thing was that Odette was probably right.

Suze didn't laugh.

She didn't cry.

She was probably unsuited to the work.

She'd lived a life of constraint, of numbness. She'd hid herself from the world because the world hurt.

And where had that got her?

What did she have to show for it?

She had nothing. A flat that wasn't hers, a job she couldn't go back to. She'd never been in a real relationship. Her only experiences were a few clumsy, fumbled encounters. She'd never had the time or energy for another person. She had no friends, no social life to speak of. The world had gravitated away from her, away from her inability to laugh, to smile, to cry. If she suddenly dissolved into atoms, melted into the universe right here at this table, there'd be no record. No one would know.

She counted out each little hurt. She knew where to put them, where to hide them.

In her memory was a suitcase. It was a cheap one made of some compressed cardboardy material. Outside, it was a glossy aquamarine colour that creased and scuffed easily. Inside, it was pale grey, adorned with motifs of soaring aeroplanes and ocean liners cruising through tropical waters. It had a single, turquoise handle with fake stitching moulded into the hard plastic and silver latches freckled with rust. The locks were always difficult to close but, if she sat on the lid long enough and reached down, she could click them into place. Then she'd lock them with a pressed-metal key.

Suze couldn't remember who'd given her the suitcase. The Children's Home? One of her foster families? She could still picture her first surname written on the surface in permanent marker, then crossed out and another surname written below. Paper stickers with different addresses had been pasted on top of each other: her different homes. Her different pasts. Her different lives.

She'd pushed that suitcase beneath so many beds. Everything she'd ever owned was inside it. To open it up was to see her for who she really was. But she kept it locked and hidden from everyone.

What happened to that suitcase in the end, Suze couldn't recall. Had the flimsy locks given up? Had the hinges failed or the compressed cardboard torn? Somehow she'd been parted from it.

Yet it was still with her, still in her mind.

Inside it lay all the secret stuff she never wanted the world to see.

All the bad feelings, all the bad memories.

She'd taken each one and, in her imagination, she'd placed them inside. Then she sat on the lid, reached down and pressed the rusty silver latches into place. She locked them away so they couldn't hurt her. And she'd never let them out.

Now, she'd take the memories of her dismissal, Odette's parting words, the slap from Mrs Crawford, the disgrace, the shame, the desperation and the loneliness, and she'd lock them in the aquamarine suitcase of her childhood. If the Odettes and the Crawfords of the world could only see the hole inside her, the one begging to be filled, they'd never regard her as damaged or perverse. She wasn't wicked. She'd done no harm. She was just a person in pain.

Lock it away, Suze.

Lock it all away.

The suitcase was already filled to bursting.

But it wasn't a real suitcase after all.

And there was so much more Suze could hide inside it.

5

A GREY AREA

THE DHSS WAS as tortuous as Suze expected. She spent the entire morning standing in lines and talking to people behind glass screens. A prison visit. The place was unheated and smelled of vagrancy and despair. She filled out the last of the forms and slid it through the gap at the bottom of one of the screens. It was checked and double-checked, then grudgingly accepted. With relief, Suze headed straight for the kicked-in doors and out into the cold, clear air.

It wasn't far to the bus stop but she strayed into suburban streets just feeling the need to walk awhile. Time was no longer a concern for her and there was nowhere she had to be. She walked without purpose along a path through a neighbourhood park, a square expanse of grass bordered by the fences of back gardens. Patches of mud marked out the goal mouths and centre spot of an impromptu football pitch. Elm trees stood bare, their autumn clothing piled in browns and yellows on the ground beneath them.

In one corner was a fenced playground where toddlers played. Suze found a bench and sat to watch. The children stumbled about, overdressed in layers of warm clothing, hats and scarves. They seemed less at the mercy of the weather and more at the overprotective nature of their mothers. Dads and mums pushed their offspring on swings, or sat on the opposite ends of seesaws, hamming up their excitement and overacting to every little laugh or squeal. Suze always found such scenes magnetic. They brought her comfort, but also pain, and a longing that bordered on jealousy. She was looking at the foundation of all life and it fascinated her: the family unit, that self-replicating, base building-block of creation. Each little family had its own language, its own way of doing things, its own likes and dislikes. At each family's core lay its own kind of strength; they were better together than on their own, more resilient. They looked after each other, protected each other, and closed their lives to all but a few outsiders. *It's us against the world,* each family seemed to say. *Family first, everyone else comes second.*

What would happen if she got up right now and made her way over to the fenced playground? What if she opened the gate and walked inside? How would they react? She'd be treated with suspicion and even hostility. There's no place for a single woman on the other side of that fence. It's a no-go area. For families only. That's the reason the fence is there. It's not to keep the children inside, but to keep the orphans, the loners and the unloved out.

She'd been on the wrong side of that fence all her life.

Suze frowned and thrust her hands deeper into her pockets. Her fingers closed around an envelope.

Pulling it out, she read the sender's address once again: *St*

Catherine's House, Aldwych. It was official and it worried her. But she drew a breath and tore it open.

On a single leaf of paper was the heading: *Registry of Births, Marriages & Deaths, St Catherine's House, Aldwych.*

The letter was addressed to her. Below was written: *Notice of Intestacy – Estate of the Late Emma Geraldine Lacey.*

Her brain was a muddle. The letter made no sense. *A mistake perhaps?*

She looked around for a litter bin.

What if it wasn't?

She sighed and glanced at the address. Three changes on the Tube. She could be there in what, forty minutes?

Suze pocketed the letter.

It wasn't as if she had anything better to do.

————◆————

St Catherine's House was a short trudge from Holborn Tube station to the corner of Aldwych. The building had an official stateliness to it, but lacked the grim overtones and unsightliness of the DHSS offices.

The queues were shorter, too.

'I received this. But I think it's a mistake…' said Suze, handing the letter to a studious young man at the reception counter. Over his shirt and tie he wore a colourful, chequered tank-top as if in quiet rebellion to his surroundings.

The studious young man seemed sceptical. This wasn't a place where mistakes were made. 'It's just a form letter. They get sent out to notify people of intestacy,' he explained.

'What does that *mean*, exactly?'

'Well, intestacy occurs when someone passes away without leaving a will.'

Suze shook her head. 'So?'

'So, without a will, their estate passes to the Crown unless relatives or beneficiaries are identified. Once the death certificate is filed with us, we search our records and contact any interested parties who may wish to make claim to the estate under law.' He looked at both sides of the letter, then back to Suze. 'That's why you got this.'

'But why me?' pressed Suze, pointing at the paper in his hand. 'I've never heard of this person.'

He glanced at the letter again. 'You're saying you're no relation to this *Emma Geraldine Lacey*?'

'Not that I know of.'

The young man flipped the letter over in his hand, as if looking for something he'd missed. 'How odd,' he said. His scepticism seemed to fade a little as if something had just occurred to him. 'I wonder, would you mind waiting?' He asked his colleagues at the counter to cover for him, then he locked his drawer, swept up his papers including Suze's letter and disappeared into the bowels of the building.

Suze looked around for somewhere to sit. There wasn't a stick of furniture. She paced, she walked outside until a thin mizzle of rain forced her back into the dry. She loitered by the door, she leaned against walls. After almost an hour she decided enough was enough. This was never going to be important. It was a glitch, a case of mistaken identity. She'd be told it was an error and there might even be a short, insincere apology. Nothing worth waiting for.

She lifted her head, letting a long sigh drift up towards the ornate plaster of the ceiling. Then she turned for the exit.

'Miss Newman?' The words carried a degree of urgency.

She turned. A door from the waiting area now stood open. She hadn't noticed it until now. The same young man stood on the threshold, a manila folder tucked under his arm. He beckoned. 'This way, please.'

Intrigued, she followed him down a long corridor into a windowless interview room. He motioned for her to sit, then closed the door and deposited himself into a plastic chair on the opposite side of the narrow desk. He placed both hands on the folder and eyed her with concern. 'I understand you were adopted?'

'Actually I was fostered – from when I was very young,' admitted Suze.

'Sorry, yes. Your name is Newman?'

'Yes.'

'This surname was given to you by your first foster family, the Newmans,' explained the young man. 'They even applied to adopt you.' He paused, uncertain. 'Although they later withdrew that application, I don't know why, but not before changing your name by deed poll.'

'How do you know all this?'

The man kept his hands over the manila folder. 'It's all here,' he said. Then he flipped the folder open, selected a leaf of printed paper and slid it across the desk towards her. 'This is your birth certificate.'

Suze read the document. 'But this isn't me,' she protested.

'Afraid it is.'

'*Celeste Dorothea Lacey?*'

'Your birth name,' said the man.

'But how do you know this is me?' argued Suze.

'As I said, it's all here. Here's the deed poll recording your change of name.' He slid another piece of paper towards her. 'It gives your original name and the subsequent name your foster parents chose.' Suze studied the document, open-mouthed, while the young man went on. 'With your new name and NHS number it was easy to find your current place of employment.' He inspected another leaf of paper. 'Littlelands Crèche and Babysitting Agency, am I right?'

Suze nodded, dumbfounded.

'If you pay tax, we can find you.'

Suze looked up. 'My birth name is *Lacey*?'

The young man gave a brief nod in return.

'Then this woman...' Suze was struggling with the implications.

The man offered a sympathetic smile and drew her attention back to the birth certificate. He placed a finger next to the words *Mother's Name*. Here it read: *Emma Geraldine Lacey*. The same name as in the letter Suze received. On the birth certificate, the column next to *Father's Name* remained blank.

'This is my *mother*?'

'This must be a shock.'

Suze's gaze rested on the documents, but her mind was elsewhere. 'Why now?' she asked.

'I'm sorry?'

Suze looked up. 'Do you know how many years I've been looking for her? How many phone calls I've made, how many forms I've filled out, how many queues I've stood in?'

The young man shook his head.

'I've been bashing my head against that same wall of bureaucracy all my life. And in the end, it's just, what, three or four pieces of paper that connect me to her?' She waved a hand at the contents of the folder. 'Why am I being told this now?'

'Well,' said the young man, clearing his throat. 'When a child is given up for adoption...'

'Fostering...' corrected Suze.

'Yes, well, in such cases the privacy of the parents is usually respected.' He placed his hands back over the documents. 'But this is a different matter, it's about inheritance now, and different rules apply. I'm sorry, but it's a bit of a grey area.'

'A grey area?' Suze felt the aquamarine suitcase strain at the clasps. 'The only reason I wanted to find her was to look her in the eye and ask her why she gave up on me, why she gave me away. I wanted her to know the shitty kind of life I've had just because she was too selfish to care.' Suze threw up her hands. 'And the moment I find her, she's gone. So I'll never really know the truth. How's that for a grey area?'

The young man fiddled with the manila folder. 'I'm very sorry. As I said, it must be a shock.'

Suze's finger strayed back to the birth certificate. 'And why is my father's name not here? Was she married?'

He shrugged. 'We have no details. And no record of her ever being married.' He offered another sympathetic smile. 'These are certainly unusual circumstances and whether you have any claim to your late mother's estate is now a legal matter. No other relatives have come to light, so I'd say you stand a good chance.' He slid a final document across the table. 'The first thing you need to do is contact the solicitor who filed the death certificate.'

Suze read the solicitor's name on the death certificate aloud. *'Carfax and Bell, Storm Bay?'*

'It might be worth giving them a call.'

'Where the hell is Storm Bay?' asked Suze.

'You've never heard of it?'

'Should I?'

The young man tapped Suze's birth certificate one last time. 'Well, perhaps you were too young to remember…'

Suze's eyes found the words *Place of Birth: Storm Bay.*

'It's where you were born,' he said.

6

'WE HAVE NO RECORD
OF A CHILD'

THE WALL OF THE PHONE BOX was covered in vulgar graffiti and written offers of promiscuity. It smelled of urine and the phonebook appeared to have been used as toilet paper.

Suze placed the manila folder on a metal shelf beside the payphone and pulled out the death certificate. The studious young man at St Catherine's House had been kind enough to give her copies of everything.

She dialled. Suze reached for the first of the 20p coins she'd stacked on top of the grey enamel phone. She pressed it into the slot and the call connected.

'Carfax and Bell,' chirped a young female voice.

'I'm calling about the estate of Emma Lacey?'

There was a pause. 'And you are?'

'I'm, ah, I'm her daughter.' Suze still hadn't come to terms with this development.

'Name?'

37

'Suze Newman. Actually, it's – never mind. Look, is there someone there I can talk to?'

Another pause. 'One moment.'

Suze heard the sound of muffled conversation. She guessed that a hand had been placed over the mouthpiece, the conversation was not for her ears. 'Your name again?' came the sudden question, loaded with suspicion.

'Susanna Newman. But my birth name is Lacey.' The name felt clumsy in her mouth.

Again, she heard muffled conversation, then the sound of the receiver being manhandled and another woman's voice on the line. It seemed more mature than the first but was edged with the same mistrust.

'Yes?'

'Hello,' said Suze.

'This is Ava Carfax. Who are you?'

Suze sighed and gave her name again. 'But the name on my birth certificate says Celeste Dorothea Lacey.'

'Your point being?'

'My mother is – was, Emma Lacey.'

'We have no record of a child,' came the reply.

'It's here on my birth certificate. She's listed as my mother.'

There was a long, unnatural silence. 'Look, documents can be forged and there are people in this world who'll stop at nothing to commit fraud.'

'But I've been given this by, by...' Suze held the receiver in the crook of her neck and rifled through the paperwork in the folder. She read out loud. '*St Catherine's House in Aldwych*. It's the office of the Registrar of Births, Marriages and Deaths. I've also got a copy of my change of name by deed poll. I'm a foster child, you see? Emma Lacey is my real mother.'

Another pause. 'Are these certified copies?'

'I don't know,' said Suze flipping the documents over. 'There's a stamp and a signature on the back.'

'And how did you find out about them?'

'I was sent a letter, a *Notice of Intest...*'

'Intestacy?'

'Yes, from St Catherine's.'

'Well, the letter should explain everything. Our client's estate will become intestate unless a beneficiary or heir is identified.'

'And I'm telling you that I'm that heir.'

'We don't have any evidence of a child.'

'Well, how about I come show you this – *evidence*?'

A long sigh sounded down the line. 'Very well. If you must.'

'Well, I will. I want to know more about my mother, and her estate. What's in it exactly?'

'I'm not prepared to discuss this over the phone. And I won't discuss it at all until I'm convinced you are who you say you are. Come to my office. I'd like to see these documents myself.'

7

THE THROWAWAY GIRL

IN THE DUSTY, echoing cavern of Paddington Station, Suze placed one of Odette's twenty-pound notes on the teller's counter. 'Single to Bodmin Road,' she said. The teller pushed a ticket and a few coins towards her in exchange.

Suze groaned. If she'd known how far away Storm Bay was, she'd have thought twice about meeting Ava Carfax. At this rate she'd be sleeping rough, or starving. But she was driven by the faint hope of finding out more about her mother. If she didn't go to Storm Bay now, she might regret it forever. Then there was also the promise of an inheritance. If there was a pot of gold at the end of this dismal rainbow then she'd count it as fair payment for a life of exile.

'Ten thirty from Platform One,' instructed the teller. 'The Riviera Express.'

Suze was relieved she hadn't missed the train. Her journey from

Finchley had been a challenge. The Hyde Park and Regent's Park bombings were still fresh in every Londoner's mind. Whether the IRA had stepped up their campaign or whether the authorities were just being more cautious was anyone's guess. Whatever the reason, there was more fear, more security, and more delays. Today's discovery of a forgotten school bag on the Central Line had brought the whole of London to a standstill. Services stopped, stations closed, and impatient commuters waited until the bomb squad moved in and blew up some kid's homework. But, by a series of unplanned detours, a bit of jogging, and sheer good luck, she'd made it in time.

Paddington Station was one of London's great nexus points, a place where the city's population in all its glorious forms crossed paths; a crucible of human diversity. The sounds of a busking West Indian couple rose up from the Tube station tunnel. Middle-aged businessmen with office tans hurried about with newspapers tucked under their arms and attaché cases in gloved hands. Dark suits and ashen faces. Young people were kissing their goodbyes at the platform gates: boys with long fringes and Oxfam trenchcoats; girls with chunky plastic jewellery, pixie boots and stiff, back-combed hair.

Suze climbed into a carriage and found a quiet seat by a grimy window. She searched inside her bag and pulled out her Sony Walkman, then searched again among the handful of cassettes she'd grabbed in a hurry while leaving her flat. Most of them were bootleg copies she'd bought at Camden Lock. They sounded fuzzy with fraudulence, but Suze didn't mind. She slotted one into the Walkman, pulled on her earphones and hit *Play*.

The train pulled away, under dirty bridges, through tunnels filled with diesel smoke and past sooty, trackside houses. In her headphones the scratchy, muffled music provided Suze with the perfect soundtrack.

The train gathered speed and intermittent sunlight burst into the carriage. Soon she was flying past the too-close streets and carbon-copy houses of the suburbs. Then factories, haulage yards, warehouses and depots busy with industry.

As the train pulled into Reading, the batteries in Suze's Walkman died.

From here, she'd have to be content with the view through the dirty window as cities and towns gave way to countryside. The train was pulling her westward towards a life she couldn't remember. A past that was hidden, a future that was unsure. In the depths of her mind Suze knew that she should be excited, that discoveries might be made and long-held questions might be answered. But she was fearful, too. She had no idea what she was going to find, and some of it might be painful to face.

Memories jabbed at her like pinpricks.

She was a child of six or seven once more, looking up into the brooding face of Paula, her first foster mother. Suze's surname was Newman back then, the first surname written on her aquamarine suitcase in permanent marker. Family after family her surname changed, but later in life she took it back. It suited her and she liked the way it sat with her Christian name. It also made paperwork and formality easier.

'You like playing with your dolls, don't you?' Paula had asked.

Suze nodded.

'What do you play? *Mummies and daddies*?'

'There's no daddy,' explained Suze with childish candour.

'Of course, so you just play *mummies* then?'

Suze nodded again.

'Do you love them?'

'Yes.'

'Do they love you?'

'Yes.'

'Do you ever think they love you *a bit too much*?'

Suze frowned, unsure where this was going.

'Do they want to sleep in your bed all the time? Do they steal your clothes to wear? Do they always follow you around and bore you with their stupid requests? Do they ever give you a moment's peace?'

Suze didn't know what answer she should give.

Paula had crouched then, holding Suze by the waist and poured her burning gaze into her. 'Susanna, I'm happy to look after you but I'm not the kind of mother you want me to be,' she said. 'I need you to stop being so – *clingy* all the time. Do you understand?'

Suze didn't. She couldn't. It made no sense, like a sum that didn't add up. The calculation was beyond her.

Paula Newman was elegant, attractive and Suze had loved her from the first. She'd loved her as only a daughter could love her mother. Perhaps Suze had imagined their arrangement differently. Perhaps she'd ignored the colder reality that Paula would never be her real mother and never saw herself as such. Paula was just stepping in and Suze had created a family that didn't exist.

Suze needed a mother to love. A mother to heal the loneliness and the hurt. But Paula would never be that woman. Although Suze would take their name and live under their roof, she was an interloper, an uninvited guest, someone to be tolerated.

It wasn't until she was much older that Suze began to understand Paula. Her husband, Suze's foster father, was emotionally distant. He was distant physically, too. He travelled on business a great deal and was seldom home. The only other member of the family was their son Raif, an eleven-year-old tearaway who shouted at his mother and made demands. With an absent father, Raif had no reason to fear discipline. Paula forgave his transgressions too readily. Raif grew petulant and self-centred. Paula doted on him and he threw it all back in her face. Suze could see that Raif was the real object of her affection. But he didn't want his mother's cloying attentions. He was pining for a father who was never there.

The house was the arena for an emotional tug of war.

Why they'd brought Suze into their family was a mystery. Perhaps they'd always wanted a daughter. Perhaps they'd tried for one. Perhaps Raif was destined to be their only progeny. It felt to Suze as if she'd been brought in to plug a gap. To be the daughter they'd longed for, to prevent Raif from being an only child, to moderate his selfishness. In the end it was Suze who'd been relied upon to foster each family, not the other way round. It was *she* who'd been brought in to fix things, to fill the holes and heal the pain. Was it ever about *her*?

Six year old Suze had looked back into Paula's eyes and struggled to understand why a mother, any kind of mother, wouldn't love their child unconditionally. It hurt – and it was the first great hurt that Suze had hidden away inside the aquamarine suitcase. 'Can

I bake my dolls a cake?' she said instead.

Paula stood. Her sigh was careworn, as if she'd used it too often. 'Of course.' She pulled on a thin smile. 'What about angel cake with hundreds and thousands?'

'Yes,' said Suze.

'You can break the biscuits for the base.' Taking Suze by the hand, Paula led her into the kitchen to look for ingredients. She pulled out a cake tin and produced a packet of digestives. Then, from a kitchen drawer, she handed Suze a metal mallet for tenderising meat. On both faces of the mallet was a chequerboard pattern of raised points. The mallet felt heavy in Suze's hand; something medieval, a blunt instrument – a weapon.

There was a little wooden Wendy house at the back of the Newman's garden where Suze often dragged her dolls to play. That day, she arranged them around the tiny table and broke the digestive biscuits with the tenderising mallet. Then came the sound of Raif returning from school with his friends to raid the fridge and watch *Crackerjack*. Suze heard the clatter of their bikes on the path and against the Wendy house.

'Give us those biscuits,' demanded Raif. Suze looked up to see him crouching in the doorway of the Wendy house.

'Mum gave them to me,' replied Suze.

Raif reached forward and grabbed a fistful of crumbling biscuits. 'She's not your mum,' he said, cramming the crumbs into his mouth.

'Is this your *sister*?' said one of Raif's friends with disgust, sticking his head through the small window.

'No, thank God,' replied Raif. Then he gestured to the biscuits, speaking to his friend, 'Go on, take some. She won't do anything.'

'She won't?' asked Raif's friend.

'Nah. She's too frightened. She has to be nice or we'll kick her out.'

'You can do that?' asked Raif's friend.

'Yeah, she's an orphan.'

The boy at the window reached in and scooped up a handful of biscuit crumbs.

'Watch this,' said Raif. Then he struck Suze across the face, turning her head. She met his eyes with a hateful glare. 'See? Told you. She won't do anything.'

'Jesus, Raif,' said the boy in the window, spitting crumbs.

Raif raised his hand at her again, and stared in wide-eyed challenge. Suze didn't cower. Her grip tightened on the metal mallet. Raif glanced at the dolls seated around the table and gave a derisive laugh. 'Look, she's playing *mummies and daddies* again, what a loser!'

'*Mummies,*' corrected Suze.

'*Mummies and daddies, mummies and daddies,*' sneered Raif in a sing-song voice. 'What do you know about mummies anyway, you never had any.'

'Paula is my mummy,' said Suze, flatly.

'No she's not! She's *mine*, you never had one!' Raif sat on his haunches, scowling. 'You're just a freak who never had a real mother!'

Something inside Suze broke. Hurt and pain tumbled out as the metal mallet wiped the scowl from Raif's face. Suze struck him in the mouth, splitting his top lip wide open and knocking out a front tooth, an incisor and a canine. The Wendy house was filled with his high-pitched, whinnying scream. He crawled outside, across the muddy garden on his knees, then stumbled to his feet and into the house. Suze looked down at the mixture of biscuit crumbs and blood. In its midst lay several gleaming teeth.

After that, Suze's feet hadn't touched the ground. Within hours, it seemed, she was pushing the aquamarine suitcase under a bed in the Children's Home once more. Raif had been right: she was a freak without parents, a person without ties who could be disposed of, rejected at will from the family unit. A temporary daughter. A throwaway girl. The Newmans had closed ranks, the way families always did.

Family first, everyone else comes second.

She spent time with doctors who asked her questions loaded with moral and philosophical choices. They showed her pictures and asked her what she saw. They made her draw pictures of her own and then questioned her about them. Suze never knew what they were digging for. She remained non-committal; she hid. She resisted being the kind of person they wanted her to be. She knew she'd made a big mistake but her mistake hadn't been striking Raif with the mallet. Her mistake had been that she'd lost control. What she'd been so careful to hide had spilled out. It was a slip, a fastening that'd come loose.

From then on, she resolved to keep her feelings locked down. She'd hide her hurt and loneliness. She'd never express her love again because love could be turned against you. It was best not to lay yourself open, to make yourself vulnerable. Don't let people think you're weak. Don't let them see you bleed. Don't show them what's on the inside.

Lock it away, Suze.

Lock it all down tight.

She was given medication she didn't need. It blunted her feelings, made her dull and lethargic. All the while she was passed from family to family, never showing affection or happiness, weakness or need. She became a *problem child*, constantly disappointing, never living up to anyone's expectations. She was closed, unreachable, a vacuum of emotion. The aquamarine suitcase was pushed under more and more beds, and became more and more filled with the hurt she had to hide.

Much later, in her twenties, Suze learned that Raif had made a name for himself in the city – a trader or stockbroker at Solomon's. He launched million-pound IPOs and lived in Chelsea on the commission.

She wondered how he explained the livid scar on his top lip.

She wondered if he ever thought of her.

The girl who always wanted a family, a mother.

The girl who still did.

⟵ ● ⟶

Bodmin Road Railway Station was nothing more than a clapperboard waiting room and a red-brick signal box. It stood on the main line like some kind of mistake, surrounded by a gloomy forest of tall pines. Suze waited forty minutes for a bus. Cornwall wasn't London. Things happened slowly here. If at all.

The bus took her north to Wadebridge where she caught another bus that skirted the coast. By the time she reached Storm

Bay it was mid-afternoon and she was the only passenger left.

The road into the town was fringed by low, flat bungalows with pebble-dash walls and PVC double-glazing. Further along, the buildings became older – stocky dwellings of grey granite with slate roofs stacked on either side of a narrowing street that wound down to a small stone harbour. In summer, Suze guessed the place would look pretty as a postcard but in autumn's bleak light it scowled like a cold welcome.

Lugging her holdall, she walked from the bus stop in the direction of the harbour. She passed a fish and chip shop gaily painted in blue and white, a Spar mini market and a camping shop. There was an old pub with whitewashed walls and a low door. She stopped outside an early century house of neatly-dressed granite. To one side of the door was a polished brass plate that read *Carfax & Bell*. Suze opened the heavy gloss-black door and stepped inside.

Ava Carfax was a tall, robust woman in her forties with short brown curls and a square face. She was bedecked in tweed, thick stockings and ladies Brogues. She looked prepared for a strenuous cross-country ramble or a grouse-shooting contest. She greeted Suze without warmth and led her into a small office. Suze noticed that Ava made the floorboards creak as she walked. The office was piled with paperwork and cardboard filing boxes. The shelves on three sides were crammed with legal manuals. When Ava sat behind her desk she made the room look smaller than it already was.

Suze produced the manila folder and slid it across the desk.

Ava read. She seemed unimpressed. Her brows lowered. She flipped a few of the documents over and checked the certification stamps on the back. At this, her eyebrows raised a little. Suze decided they were in need of a ruthless pluck.

Placing the paperwork back in the folder, Ava said, 'Well, these *appear* to be genuine.'

'Good,' said Suze, 'so, as I mentioned, I'd like to know more about my mother, who she was, what she was like, and the estate she left.'

One of Ava's untamed brows lifted in suspicion. 'As I said, these *appear* to be genuine. I'll discuss nothing further until I'm convinced they're authentic,' she said. 'I'll hold onto them for now.'

'I noticed you have a photocopier,' said Suze. 'I'd prefer you take copies.' *Suspicion cuts both ways*, thought Suze.

Ava remained silent for a while. She blinked. 'Very well, I'll take copies and we can talk again tomorrow.'

'*Tomorrow?*' Suze hadn't planned on staying the night. Her ill-conceived idea was to get the sleeper train back to London. Her draughty flat now seemed luxurious, and a long way away. 'But I've nowhere to stay.'

'Tomorrow,' repeated Ava Carfax.

— ◆ →

An early darkness was crawling over Storm Bay as Suze made her way back up the main street. The front window of the Spar mini market lit the incoming sea mist with its warm, electric glow. She stepped inside, hoping to find a notice board or advice on a cheap bed-and-breakfast for the night. The shopkeeper was a ruddy-faced, middle-aged woman with a talkative nature.

'Well, 'tis the off-season. Place is mostly closed down now,' explained the shopkeeper, her accent a Cornish burr. 'Best bet would be the caravan park. It's on the road behind the library. Just knock on the first caravan near the entrance.'

Suze thanked her and was about to leave when she caught sight of a solitary pasty in a glass-fronted food warmer. Her stomach groaned.

'Been there since lunchtime,' admitted the shopkeeper. 'But you can 'ave 'un if 'ee want,' she added with a smile.

Munching on the pasty, Suze trudged along the road breathing flakes of pastry into the dusk. The pasty was hot, peppery and good. She turned at a junction, following a signpost to the town library. Passing it, she kept walking, away from the street lights until the gate to the caravan park loomed out of the dark. Just as the shopkeeper had said, there was a caravan near the entrance, and there was a light inside.

Suze felt for her thinning purse, weighing her options.

The bus shelter was a possibility, but she'd freeze.

Biting her lip, she walked towards the lit caravan.

They'd better have something, she thought. *Something cheap.*

◄—●—►

The caravan was only slightly warmer than the bus stop might possibly have been.

There was no duvet and the blankets were thin, as were the caravan's walls. It was furnished for summer holidaymakers, not out-of-season itinerants like Suze.

The light of a bleak, misty morning filtered through the curtains preventing further sleep. Suze rose and inspected the tiny kitchen. There was no milk in the bar fridge but there were teabags and a kettle.

She drew back the curtains and sipped from a steaming mug. The mist lifted, revealing farmland.

Framed in the caravan's window was an empty field, stripped of its late-summer harvest and now ploughed in parallel furrows. Crows fed from the loose soil, filling their beaks and bellies with an easy breakfast of worms. In the centre of the field was a tall oak. Elsewhere, the ploughed furrows of the field were so uniformly straight, it looked as if a comb had been scraped across the land. But around the tree, the furrows curved in flowing lines to avoid it.

Suze studied the oak. Standing in farmland it seemed out of place. It would be better among a copse of trees, in a wood or a forest, thought Suze. Trees must be happier in such places, standing together, branches touching. This tree was all alone. She felt sorry for it. And life seemed to flow around it, ignoring it, in curving furrows of neglect.

She knew the feeling well.

◄—●—►

'But there's no mention of my father,' said Suze, pointing at the birth certificate. 'Do you know who he was?'

'No,' said Ava. 'Your mother kept that a secret to her death.'

Ava Carfax sat in her cramped office. She'd spent the morning verifying Suze's paperwork. She'd made calls. She'd checked Suze's identity against her driving licence, bank records and National Insurance Number. Even after confirming Suze's story with the Registry of Births, Marriages and Deaths, and records held by the County Council, she still seemed guarded.

'My mother never married?'

'No.'

'Is that why she gave me away?'

'I can't say. Who knows? But a single mum in the early fifties? Almost unheard of in those days.'

Suze considered this. *Had she been an accident? An unwanted embarrassment?*

'And the estate? What did she leave me? You can tell me now, you have to, don't you?'

'She left you nothing,' said Ava.

Suze was shocked.

'She left nothing to anyone because she left *no will*,' Ava explained. She shifted uneasily. 'There are several things that *fall to you*, that's all. You're set to inherit because you're her next of kin, not because she wanted you to have anything. There's a difference.'

Suze sensed a deeper meaning. Was Ava implying that there was a worthier beneficiary, someone more deserving of her mother's estate? 'Okay, so what are they, these several things *that fall to me*?' Suze asked. Her mother's estate didn't feel quite so extensive any longer.

Ava glared. She didn't answer.

Suze was about to repeat her question when something occurred to her. 'Why didn't my mother leave a will?' she asked. 'You're her lawyer, so why was nothing arranged?'

Ava's eyes gleamed briefly. Suze couldn't tell whether from amusement or malice. 'Are you up for a drive?' asked Ava.

'Where to?' asked Suze.

'I think we should go see her.'

8

AN UNSOUND MIND

AVA'S CAR WAS MUCH like her office – small. It was an Austin 1100 with a cramped interior that seemed to accentuate her size. She drove them both back towards Bodmin, hunched over the wheel. Before reaching the town, she turned from the road, steering between granite gateposts and onto a broad gravel drive. From the passenger seat, Suze twisted round to read the painted white signpost standing on the lawn as they passed.

'Bosvenor Sanatorium?' said Suze. 'What is this place?'

'It's where your mother is, where she spent the last twenty years of her life,' explained Ava.

The gravel drive that stretched before them led to an austere Cornish manor house. The house was made of hard granite, box-shaped and devoid of any ornamentation. An incongruous wheelchair ramp sloped up to the front door. The building was well-maintained: gleaming windows, fresh paint, a new roof of Delabole slate. Sprouting from the manor house on either side were newer buildings, one and two-storey, with double-glazed windows and flat roofs. It was a mismatch of architecture, around which spread mowed lawns, winding paths and well-tended gardens.

'Is this an old people's home?' asked Suze.

'No, it's not,' replied Ava. She parked the Austin in the large turning circle at the front of the main building and turned to Suze. 'There's a reason your mother never left a will, why she was *unable* to leave a will,' said Ava.

'Oh?'

'She was not of sound mind, Susanna.'

Suze looked towards the manor house. 'So it's an *asylum*?'

'They don't use that word here. It's a *hospital* – for the mentally ill. You'll see it's actually quite nice inside. Now, we have a little time, so we'll meet Doctor Passmore. He's in charge here, and knew your mother.'

'So, my mother was insane?'

'Mentally ill,' corrected Ava.

'Was she here long?' asked Suze. 'Was she like this *always*?'

'No, not always,' said Ava. 'Although I gather it was a slow slide. Her condition went undiagnosed for many years. She lived independently for as long as she could, then she spent the end of her life here.'

So her mother could have raised her, after all? She could have looked after her? And, in later years Suze could have looked after her mother in return. Suze might even have prevented her from ending up in the Bosvenor Sanatorium. What would have been so bad about that?

That's how it should have gone, how it should have played out.

Us against the world.

Wasn't that what families *did*?

Familiar feelings of despondency and rejection pulled at her.

Lock it away, Suze.

Her mother had been able to raise her, but didn't.

Did she choose not to?

———◄—●—►———

They stood in an upstairs room in the old manor house. The room was bright, cheerful even, with a large, barred window that overlooked the rolling lawns to the rear of the property. There was the usual medical paraphernalia: a commode, a walking frame, triangular grab-handles above the bed. In one corner stood a small sink, in the other a narrow wardrobe. The flocked wallpaper looked fresh: satin-white with a brocade of climbing roses. Yet on the walls around the room, between knee and shoulder height, there appeared patches of grey. Damp? Suze sniffed. The room didn't smell damp.

'She spent a lot of her time here, enjoying the view from this window.' Dr Passmore was a sprightly, bright-eyed man with a dark, closely trimmed beard. 'She liked her room.'

Suze nodded, she hadn't asked for the guided tour.

'Thought you might like to see how she lived,' added Dr Passmore, as if reading Suze's thoughts.

'Do you mind if we move on?' asked Ava.

'Why yes, I know you're short on time,' said Dr Passmore. He turned to Suze, bright eyes now dim with sympathy. 'Would you like to see her?'

Suze felt her heart buckle. She'd always wished that one day she'd meet her mother. Just not like this. 'Did she ever mention me?' she asked.

Dr Passmore and Ava exchanged an unsettled glance. 'Afraid not,' said Dr Passmore.

'She never mentioned having a child?'

'No.'

Ava gave a grim look. 'Let's go say goodbye, shall we?'

As they walked from the room something in the areas of greyed wallpaper caught Suze's eye. She leaned close to inspect one of the dark patches, then caught her breath.

'Of course, the room will be redecorated shortly,' said Dr Passmore, noticing her interest in the wallpaper.

They were not patches of damp, but thousands and thousands of tiny pencil marks – two words, written over and over in the neatest, smallest hand.

'What's this?' asked Suze, pointing.

Dr Passmore's expression seemed weighed with sadness. 'We have no idea. She repeated those words often. They were the last thing I ever heard her say.'

Suze looked back at the two words, written again and again across the wallpaper.

I follow.

◂━●━▸

Suze had never seen a dead human before, so she didn't know what to expect. There was something waxy and artificial about her mother's body. It seemed vacated, a shopfront mannequin with white hair and slack, wrinkled skin. If someone had once lived inside, they were long gone.

'Is she supposed to look like that?' asked Suze, indicating the body on the steel stretcher. Dr Passmore had pulled the stretcher from the wall like a drawer in some giant filing cabinet, then removed the sheet covering the face. The room had a cadaverous, bleached smell to it. It was fearfully cold.

'Like what?' asked Dr Passmore.

'How old was she?' said Suze.

'Your mother was sixty,' replied Dr Passmore.

'Then why does she look so *old*?'

The body on the stretcher certainly did look far older than its sixty years of life. The limbs were thin, as was the white hair. There was a frailty, an exhausted, used-up quality to her mother's remains that looked more suited to a woman of ninety.

'People here don't age well,' said Dr Passmore. 'Medication, lack of mobility, reluctance to exercise and socialise all take their toll. And then, we often don't know what's happening inside, what kind of trauma is being experienced. The body doesn't shape the mind, Miss Newman. In my experience, it's usually the other way round.'

'What did she die from?' asked Suze, her gaze resting on her mother's face.

Dr Passmore hesitated. Suze locked questioning eyes on him.

'She was frail,' he said.

'She died of frailty?' pressed Suze.

'Of exposure, hypothermia, we think. The exact cause isn't certain yet,' admitted Dr Passmore. He drew a long breath. 'She found her way out of Bosvenor during the night. It was cold, wet. We found her on the moors to the north. Being as frail as she was didn't help.'

'She escaped?' asked Suze.

'This isn't a prison Miss Newman,' said Dr Passmore. 'The days of locking our patients up or strapping them to their beds are long gone. She just managed to get past us, somehow.' He looked sheepish, as if expecting Suze to launch into a tirade. Ava's eyes bounced between the two of them as if watching a tennis match.

'To go where?' asked Suze, her eyes on her mother's face once more.

'It looked like she was heading home, to Storm Bay,' said Dr Passmore. He let a pause hang in the room before continuing. 'Her death was – *unusual*, and because she wasn't in our care at the time, a post-mortem is required – to pinpoint the exact cause. In a way it's an opportunity. It may help us learn more about your mother's condition. With your permission I'd like a thorough examination made. It can help us understand more about mental illness, and how best to treat our patients. I'll need you to sign something.'

'Sure,' murmured Suze.

'Good. I'll get the paperwork ready. We'll leave you alone for a moment.' He and Ava left the room, closing the door.

Suze gazed at the body. If her mother had shown any sign of life, she would have dragged her back to the world of the living, screamed in her face, poured out all her hurt and told her mother how cruel, how callous she'd been. But all that remained was a broken, empty shell. No one home. Suze reached for her mother's hand, then recoiled. It was cold, and Suze was ashamed.

'We could've had a different life, you and I,' said Suze.

The aquamarine suitcase strained at the hinges.

'Did you ever love me?'

There was no answer.

And Suze knew she'd never hear one.

———◆———

'It's unfortunate, but this won't happen soon,' explained Dr Passmore, sliding a bundle of papers over his desk towards Suze. He'd placed an "X" in all the locations he needed her signature.

'You mean the post-mortem?' asked Suze.

'Exactly,' said Dr Passmore. 'The Medical Examiner is attending an inquest at the County Courts in Truro. It's a big case, might be lengthy, too. The County Coroner is there as well.'

'How long?'

'A couple of weeks, *maybe.*'

Suze groaned. She thought of the cold caravan. She couldn't afford to stay, even if she wanted to.

'The deceased can remain here until then?' asked Ava.

'Yes, all very normal.'

Ava turned to Suze. 'Will you stay until the funeral?'

'I can't,' muttered Suze, pen in hand, leafing through forms.

'So you'll head back to London?'

'Yes.'

'If the funeral was later, like a month's time, do you think you'd come back then?' asked Ava.

Suze looked up from the paperwork, searching Ava's eyes. *Did she want Suze out of the picture? Was she glad to be rid of her?* Suze looked for motives but the woman was unreadable as a closed book. 'I'd like to,' said Suze.

Dr Passmore patted his desk with both hands. 'Now, your mother's belongings.' He stood and moved to a nearby credenza. Sliding one of its doors open, he lifted out a sizeable cardboard box with a lid. Returning to the table he placed it before Suze. 'This is what your mother was wearing when she was admitted.' He continued, his voice trembling, 'It's also what she was wearing when she passed. It meant a lot to her. We thought it might mean something to you, too.'

Lifting the cardboard lid, Suze peered inside the box. Neatly folded were layers of silk, once white, but now grubby, crumpled and torn. She lifted a corner of the fabric to find a collar embroidered with tiny flowers. 'What is this?' gasped Suze, looking up.

'It's a wedding dress,' said Dr Passmore as if all was normal.

Suze lifted part of the dress from the cardboard box revealing a fitted lace bodice embroidered with intricate flowers and set with pearls. The dress was breathtaking, although it had seen better days.

'Why did she have this?' questioned Suze.

Dr Passmore cocked his head slightly, as if waiting for the rest of the question.

Suze turned to Ava. 'But my mother never married, right?'

'Correct,' said Ava.

Suze looked back at the dress. 'So why would a woman who never married have a wedding dress?'

Dr Passmore opened his hands in absence of an answer. 'We only know it was *very important* to her.'

'In what way?' asked Suze.

Dr Passmore sighed. 'She asked for it constantly, she wanted to wear it. I believe if we'd let her, she'd have worn nothing else.'

'And did you let her?'

'Occasionally. But we didn't want to reinforce any neuroses we didn't understand. So we took a balanced approach. The dress seemed to alternately soothe and agitate her.'

In Suze's hands the dress looked sad, tired, worn-out.

'We don't know what significance this dress held for your mother, but it formed a large part of her *condition*,' said Dr Passmore.

'And now it's *mine*,' said Suze with a touch of resignation. *What would she do with an old wedding dress*? But it had been her mother's, and Suze knew she'd never be able to part with it.

'And now it's yours,' said Ava without sentiment.

Suze turned to her. 'When we spoke earlier, you said she left me *a couple of things*.'

'I said *several things* now fall to you,' corrected Ava.

'So there's something else?' asked Suze, her eyes narrowing.

'There most certainly is.'

9

'THIS FALLS TO YOU'

'THIS FALLS TO ME, TOO?' asked Suze.

'This falls to you,' said Ava.

'It's *mine*?'

'I suppose it is. For now. And everything in it. But you won't be able to keep it, not with the inheritance tax that's due. You'll have to sell the place to cover your debt.'

Suze gazed at the house. It was gloomy, neglected and wore the untouched patina of a bygone age. Weather-damaged chimneys pointed accusations at the sky like broken fingers. Slates had slipped from the roof and lay in pieces below the rotted eaves and hanging gutters. Cracked windows were boarded and ivy seemed to be holding the place together. An army of weeds had invaded the lawn, conquered the flower beds and annexed the ornamental flower pots.

'Does it have a name?' asked Suze.

'Aeolus House,' announced Ava.

'*Aeolus?*'

'From Greek mythology,' explained Ava. 'Aeolus was keeper of the winds.'

This made sense, the house was perched high on an exposed clifftop with a commanding view of Storm Bay to the north. Wind would assault it from every point of the compass and had flattened the landscape all around. A single tree stood some distance from the house, a Scots pine, bent to an impossible angle by the savagery of the Atlantic gales. Apart from this, there were only the short clifftop grasses, clumps of wild campion, tamarisk, and thorny gorse that rolled over the high clifftop towards the sea and gave way to a blur of moorland furze in the east.

'Before the Laceys bought it, it was a hotel, a *boutique* hotel I guess you could've called it. Just twelve rooms, but it had a very specific appeal for a specific clientele,' explained Ava as they walked the overgrown path up to the house.

'What kind of clientele?' asked Suze.

'Stormwatchers.'

Suze's eyebrows gathered in question.

'In the middle of the last century, people travelled from all over in the morbid hope of witnessing a shipwreck.' Ava now produced a heavy set of keys and nodded out to sea. 'It's a treacherous stretch of coastline. A busy one, too. Plenty of shipping moving up and down the Bristol Channel. If a vessel passed too close to land in rough seas, the nor'westers would blow it onto the rocks. There's more than a hundred wrecks at the bottom of the bay. There's a library in the town with accounts of all the wrecks. You should take a visit. Grim reading though.'

Suze looked up at the house, the late afternoon sun was

throwing the giant portico of its entrance into shadow. She saw the house shiver for an instant. *Had she imagined it?* It was the smallest of vibrations, a wink, a welcome.

'Then, in the early nineteen-hundreds the Laceys – your family – bought the place and made it their home,' continued Ava.

'Were they a big family?' asked Suze, taking in the size of the building. From the front door hung a heavy door-knocker: a hoop of cast iron with the head of a curly-haired god. From his lips he blew a cloud of wind. *Aeolus.*

'Quite the opposite. And you're the last.' Ava unlocked the front door and pushed. The hinges ground as it swung open.

From inside came a loud, persistent banging. It sounded like footsteps, a giant loose in the house.

'Damn – the shutters,' said Ava, moving into the house.

Suze followed. The interior was dim, murky. She could make out the dark shapes of furniture and the black openings of doorways. Moving further inside, she saw a repeated flash of daylight that synchronised itself with the incessant banging. Closer still and she saw that Ava was now outside, struggling with a storm shutter. Ava restrained it, latching it open. Then she opened another shutter, and another, until the room in which Suze stood was flooded with light. In front of her lay a large bay window framing the ten-mile curve of Storm Bay – a breathtaking sight. The room was a raised area with chairs and couches, a kind of viewing platform. Suze imagined a gathering of stormwatchers seated here, like ghouls in anticipation of disaster at sea.

A door opened somewhere and Ava reappeared, dusting her hands.

'So this is where people watched the storms at sea?' guessed Suze.

'Actually, no,' said Ava with a wry smile. 'Too dangerous. A good storm would've blown the windows in. Glass all over the place. That's why the shutters are there.'

'So how did they watch them?' asked Suze.

'Quite the thing, actually,' she said, 'Want to take a look?'

'Sure.'

Ava crossed the room to where a large tapestry hung. She took hold of a corner and pulled it away from the wall. Suze could now see that the tapestry was suspended from a hinged iron rod, allowing it to be pulled open like a door. Behind the tapestry lay a narrow opening in the stonework with nothing but impenetrable darkness beyond.

'There's a handrail on either side,' said Ava. 'Come on.' Then she stepped into the dark.

The tapestry swung back into place behind Ava, concealing the opening once more. The hinged rod was weighted to close automatically. Suze approached, pulled back the tapestry, took a breath and stepped through. Holding the handrails on either side, she followed the echoes of Ava's footsteps on the stone flags. She was in a passageway or corridor just wide enough for a single person. It sloped downwards at a gentle gradient. The interior of the passageway felt uncomfortably cold and confined. Every few steps, Suze stopped and raised a hand in front of her to check. Nothing. She slid her feet across the floor in the darkness. 'Are there any steps?' she called out.

'No, it's quite safe,' returned Ava.

Some way ahead, Suze heard the clang of metal and the creak of hinges. 'Inside the door you'll find another handrail,' said Ava, her voice bouncing across the stone. 'Just grab it and wait.'

The passageway was long. To Suze's reckoning, it must have sloped downwards for fifty yards or so. The handrails stopped and she found the door. It was made of steel, heavy and cold, with a massive bolt on the inside. She stepped over the threshold and found another handrail, then heard Ava's voice close beside her. 'Wait here.'

Suze heard the steel door close and the bolt drawn across. The floor was level here and the echoes told Suze they were no longer in a corridor, but a much larger space. 'What is this place?' asked Suze.

'It used to be an old pilchard hut,' explained Ava, moving away. Her voice was strained with effort as if she was struggling with something. 'Fishermen took turns here to watch the ocean for shoals of fish. When the house was built, it was converted.'

'Into what?' said Suze into the darkness. She heard the creak of metal and the winding of gears. Then a spear of daylight pierced the blackness. As the gears wound, the daylight increased until Suze could make out her surroundings. She was inside a large, circular room. One wall was traversed by a long strip filled with metal. In its centre was a massive glass lens that lit the room like a spotlight. In front of this were arranged curving rows of chairs, some now broken, missing legs, or on their sides. They were positioned with their backs to the lens, their fronts following the path of light across the room. It looked like the interior of a theatre, or some ancient cinema.

Ava stood nearby, winding one of two wheels on the wall. She turned, out of breath, and nodded to something behind Suze. 'Take a look.'

Turning around, Suze was dumbstruck. Projected onto the curving wall opposite the lens was a sweeping panorama of Storm Bay. Gulls swirled in the wind, waves in the bay were whipped with white foam and the clifftop grasses bent and swayed. Yet here, behind thick stone walls, the sounds of the wind, the sea, and the shrieking gulls were all but silenced.

'It's a *camera obscura*,' said Ava. 'Like a pinhole camera, only much, much larger. The lens inverts the image so it's the right way up. And it magnifies the light.'

Suze stepped close, throwing her shadow across the scene. Ava wound a handwheel and the scene shifted to one side. 'It can move?' asked Suze, surprised.

'Sure can. That's why the circular shape of the old pilchard hut was ideal, the curved walls make the perfect screen. They just had to make it lightproof.'

'I didn't see it from the house,' said Suze.

'You can't, it's right on the edge of the cliff. The only way to get here is along the passageway cut through the rock. When there was a storm, guests could make their way down here under cover. Then they'd sit in comfort sipping brandy while they watched people drown.'

'That's – *macabre*,' whispered Suze.

'Certainly is.'

From higher up, in the house, Suze had only seen the clifftop rolling out of sight, blue water far below. From here she could now see the towering cliffs themselves: walls of dark granite that rose from a maelstrom of crashing waves. The jagged shoreline of the cliffs gave way to one or two narrow coves of yellow sand. Other than that, it was a murderous coast of black rock and dangerous sea.

Suze lifted a hand, catching the light. On the curved wall, the shadow of her finger pointed to a grassy island below the cliff. 'I didn't see that either,' she said.

Ava wound the handwheels and the projection on the wall centred on the island. It was raised high above the sea with a narrow isthmus of rock leading back towards them and out of sight below the cliff. 'That's Klegger Dhu,' said Ava.

'Is that some kind of *folly*?' asked Suze, pointing to a jumble of granite shapes on the island. They looked like a miniature, tumbled-down castle.

'No, that's the remains of an old chapel.'

'Is that part of the property, too?'

'Yes, everything to the low tide mark is part of Aeolus House, although there's a walking track along the clifftop that belongs to the National Trust. Other than that, it's all part of the estate.'

'Can you get down there from the cliff?' asked Suze.

'You can, but it's a dangerous climb,' replied Ava. 'Best way down is from here.'

'Here?' asked Suze.

'The causeway you can see from Klegger Dhu leads to a cave in the cliff right under our feet. You can climb down into the cave from here.' Ava pointed to a steel hatch in the middle of the floor. 'But I wouldn't trust that old ladder. It's a long way down.' Ava began winding the handles, returning the room to darkness. 'Anyway, grab a handrail and head on out. I need to get going.'

Suze did as she was told and returned to the main hall. As she waited for Ava, she looked over the dreary old paintings on the wall:

horses and gundogs, pastoral scenes and haughty landowners in three-cornered hats holding hunting rifles and dead gamebirds.

Near the bottom of the stairs was an oval patch of bright wallpaper with a picture hook. Around it the paper was aged and faded. 'There must've been something here,' said Suze, running a hand over the oval of bright paper. 'The place hasn't been robbed or anything?'

'Doubt it,' said Ava. 'The town is quiet and this old place has been locked up.

Suze turned from the strange oval and scanned some framed black-and-white photographs hung nearby. She was drawn to a portrait of a young woman. She was slender as a wand and quite lovely in a wistful, old-world way. She was smiling – but only with her mouth. Her gaze seemed fixed elsewhere, a formless expression that seemed to hold a burden of sorrow. She wore an incongruous headscarf tied about her forehead and sat with hands folded across her stomach.

Ava appeared at Suze's side. 'That's your mother as a young woman.'

Suze sighed, leaning close. She was trying to match this young face to the waxy, lifeless one she'd seen at Bosvenor. There was no resemblance.

'Pretty, wasn't she?' said Ava.

Suze searched her mother's face. 'Was this before...?'

'Before she became ill?' said Ava. 'Hard to say. It's likely she struggled with mental illness for most of her life. Like I said, it was a slow slide.'

Suze studied the hands folded across her mother's middle. Were they protecting something? Or was she mourning for something she'd lost? 'And she lived here all alone?' asked Suze.

'For a time, after her father – your grandfather – passed away.'

'What was his name?'

'Henry Lacey.'

Suze searched the photographs on the wall. There were no other portraits. Only the one of her mother. 'Were you my grandfather's solicitor, too?'

'No, I began working for your mother just before she moved to Bosvenor.'

'What was she like?'

'Well, she always seemed very capable. I never knew about her – *episodes*. She seemed very bright. Well read. Well educated. Although, when we spoke, I couldn't help feeling...'

'What?'

'That she was never in the same room,' said Ava.

Suze pulled her attention away from the photographs on the wall. 'And my grandmother, did she live here too?'

'Geraldine. I suppose she must have, but that would have been a very long time ago. She died giving birth to your mother.'

Standing here, in this house, made Suze feel closer to her family than she'd ever been. Now there were names and faces to remember. The dark was rolling back and history was revealing itself.

The two women turned, heading for the door. They stepped onto the weed-strewn pathway outside. Ava locked the front door while Suze watched the landward horizon. Late afternoon shadows swept like a dark horde across the eastern moorland. Ava turned, still clutching the heavy set of keys.

'May I?' asked Suze, holding out a hand to receive them.

Ava remained motionless, unwilling to part with the keys.

'If the house falls to me, then those do, too,' said Suze.

'Like I said, you won't be able to keep the place,' protested Ava.

'We'll see.'

'Best if I keep these while you go back to London.'

'I'm not going back to London,' said Suze. 'At least, not yet.'

With a bewildered look Ava handed over the keys. 'Very well, do you have a place to stay?'

Suze looked back at Aeolus House, shadows now clawing at its walls. 'I do now,' she said.

◄━━━●━━►

Suze remembered the camping shop on the high street and asked Ava for a lift if she was headed back into the village. It turned out she was.

For the duration of the two-mile drive into Storm Bay Ava tried to convince Suze not to stay at Aeolus House. She explained there was no hot water, no electricity, no heating or light of any sort. The place was derelict to the point of being condemned.

The disagreements flowed back and forth until Suze had to come clean. 'I don't have a job,' she admitted, staring gloomily at the passing countryside. 'I don't have any savings.'

Ava leaned back in her seat, drawing a breath.

'I don't have *anything*, really,' continued Suze.

'Even more reason why you can't keep it,' said Ava. 'You could never make it habitable. You can't afford to repair the place.'

'Then I'll find a way. I'll look for work,' said Suze.

'It's a ruin. It's best demolished. The only value is in the land it stands on. And that's not much – it's not exactly good farmland. My advice is to sell the plot. You'll have a lot of expenses soon and the estate will only stretch so far.'

Suze retreated into silence.

'I'm sure someone would be happy to take it off your hands,' suggested Ava. 'For the right price.' She let the idea hang.

Suze fumed. Aeolus House had been her mother's home and now it would be hers. It was the only real thing she'd ever owned.

Like hell she'd give it up.

— ● —

The late October afternoon was fading into evening when Ava parked her Austin on the high street. The camping shop was still open. Light from inside illuminated its window-dressings of camouflaged jackets, trousers, tents and rucksacks. It looked more like an army-surplus outlet but Ava had explained it also sold camping equipment and climbing gear for the regular influx of hikers who flowed into the harbour town from the coast path, and the rock climbers who came here to pit their skills against the granite cliffs.

As Suze opened the passenger door, Ava spoke. 'I'll come to the house tomorrow. I need you to sign some things and, well, I want to discuss your – *situation*.'

'What about it?' asked Suze.

Ava offered a counterfeit smile. 'I'll explain tomorrow.'

'Okay.'

Ava paused, her face now serious. 'I hope you'll be alright up there, on your own.'

'Why wouldn't I be?' asked Suze.

—◆—

She hadn't really thought this through. The whole idea of camping inside a house seemed straightforward, unlike camping outdoors. But she hadn't considered how much equipment she'd still need.

Or how much it would cost.

The balding, walrus-moustached man in the shop – dressed entirely in camouflage like his window display – had badgered Suze into trading up from the inexpensive sleeping bag she had her eye on, to something more substantial. She'd need the extra warmth with winter on the approach, he insisted. She felt cheated out of her dwindling reserves but couldn't find fault with his logic. Better to be too warm than too cold, she admitted to herself. She supplemented the sleeping bag with an airbed, a Calor gas stove, a camping kettle, candles, a plastic torch and batteries. These she bundled into a cheap nylon rucksack. Pots, pans, cutlery and crockery she hoped to find at the house. She also bought a cheap transistor radio, knowing that her Sony Walkman tended to chew through batteries.

She signed a cheque while the camouflaged shopkeeper scrutinised the signature on her guarantee card. The cheque would go through but it'd send Suze into the red. An overdraft. The last thing she needed.

Suze marched into the chilly night as the camouflaged man shut up shop. She entered the Spar mini market and nodded in greeting to the ruddy-faced, middle-aged woman. She bought tinned food, UHT milk, instant coffee, a loaf of Mother's Pride and a copy of *The Western Morning News.*

There was no form of public transport that could take her from Storm Bay up along the coast to Aeolus House. This much she'd learned from the woman in the mini market. The local buses ran a route between Boscastle, Wadebridge and Bodmin, and never at night. Suze marched for as long as she could into the darkness then swung her rucksack off, found the torch and switched it on. All she could see in front of her was a shroud of white, damp mist swirling in the beam of light. She turned the torch off and continued, allowing her night vision to return. It was better this way. She'd find her way home without the torch.

Home.

Was it really *home*?

It had been once. Perhaps very briefly.

Now it was home again. *Her* home.

Suze felt the reassurance of the iron-cold keys in her pocket. She had a door she could lock on the world now. Not a rented door in an attic apartment unlocked with borrowed keys, but her very own door, her very own keys. She'd creep inside that huge house, a field mouse seeking shelter from the cold. She'd find a warm, dry corner and curl up. The house would claim her, embrace her. She'd lock the door and find peace in the one place she'd searched for all her life.

Ava Carfax hadn't understood. It didn't matter that it was a beaten-down ruin of dust and rubble. It didn't matter that the walls were lined with cracks and the roof riddled with holes. It didn't matter that the windows were broken and the woodwork rotten. None of it mattered.

What mattered was that tonight, Suze Newman was coming home.

—◆—

In torchlight, the dusty air inside Aeolus House was hung with shadows. To a visitor, the place might appear ominous, threatening. But Suze told herself it was where she'd always belonged. This house had seen her brought into the world, so what would she ever have to fear from it?

'You'll look after me, won't you?' she asked the darkness.

Her belongings lay just inside the front door where she'd unloaded them from Ava's Austin. She left the holdall in favour of the cardboard box with the wedding dress and, with the rucksack still slung over her shoulders and swinging the torch's beam, she walked past her mother's photograph and climbed the stairs past the strange, oval patch of bright wallpaper.

On the first floor she found a bedroom to her liking and lit a candle. The shadows danced with excitement as she blew up her mattress and unfolded her sleeping bag.

Her eyes moved to the cardboard box.

What did the dress mean?

She stooped and lifted the lid. Then she took the dress by the shoulders and, in one swift movement, pulled it out. The room hissed with the sound of flying silk. She held the dress up. Even in the candlelight she could tell it would have been beautiful once. Laying it across her opened sleeping bag, she pulled the arms wide and the hem straight. Then, with great care, she lowered herself onto it and wrapped the arms around her.

Why had her mother given her away?

Had this act led to her mother's madness?

Or had her mother's madness led to the act?

Now that she lay in her mother's embrace, she hoped the answer might come. She drifted towards sleep and the question glimmered at the edges of her consciousness.

Sleep claimed her, and the question remained unanswered.

10

'DEATH IS EXPENSIVE'

SHE WOKE in the middle of the night, frozen, and in darkness. She'd pushed the wedding dress aside and climbed into the sleeping bag, still fully dressed. Then she'd slept again.

Now she was gazing at an unfamiliar ceiling. Daylight filtered through the grimy window and gathered in pools to expose the damage and neglect. The room was the smallest of all those she'd found on the first floor. For some reason, the closeness of this room felt comforting. The larger rooms were filled with too much junk and seemed as if they'd never been inhabited. Here, an old brass bed stood centrally, its mattress stripped of bedclothes. Suze considered using it but chose a spot on the floor for the airbed instead. There was no telling what lived inside that old mattress.

In a corner was a battered armoire, and a jug and ewer on a stand. Next to it, a narrow, cast-iron fireplace. Evidence of a long-dead fire lay in the firebox. Above the mantel hung childish embroidery and needlework patterns in frames. A dressing table was loaded with crusty, dust-laden bottles and atomisers. This room had been used, lived-in. It was a girl's room. A woman's.

Suze knew whose room this was.

If you were going to live in a draughty old house all by yourself, you'd choose a room like this: close to the stairs, accessible, easy to heat.

She unzipped herself from the sleeping bag and stretched. On the floor beside her lay the wedding dress. She hauled herself to her feet and gathered it up for a closer look.

The skirt was made from layer upon layer of silk tulle, flaring outwards from the waist. She ran her hand through the folds of crumpled, damaged material. The dress had seen use. A lot of use. The silk was torn and dirty in places, with patches of dried mud and ground-in grime. Suze inspected the bodice. It was made of lace, with a high, mandarin collar and long sleeves. The lacework was stunning: swirling floral motifs set with hundreds of pearl-like tambour beads and miniature silk flowers. Many of the beads were missing and loose threads hung from the ragged embroidery. The back of the bodice was fastened with a row of tiny silver buttons, each inlaid with glass enamel the colour of milk. Inside the neck was the dressmaker's label: *Kerenza's*.

She shook out the folds and draped the dress over the brass-framed bed.

Why had this dress been so important to her mother? And why was it '*a large part of her condition*' as Dr Passmore had explained?

She felt sure the answers lay here, somewhere in the house. So today, she'd explore, starting with this room.

The walls around her showed patches of grey, like the ones

she'd seen at Bosvenor. Here they were more likely to be damp or mould. But she inspected them anyway and was surprised to discover the same tiny inscriptions. Unlike the ones at Bosvenor, which were clear to see, these were largely hidden: behind the mirror of the dressing table, on the wall behind the back of an armchair, behind the headboard of the bed. It seemed as though they were placed to avoid discovery by prying eyes. But in a woman's bedroom? Somewhere that was private? What risk was there from unwanted visitors? Perhaps the phrase was hidden because it was a secret – something too precious to share.

I follow.

'But *who* were you following Emma?' asked Suze. '*Or what?*'

<hr>

A house can reflect much of its owner. Just like a mirror. And Aeolus House reflected much of Suze's mother, Emma Lacey.

To start with, Suze could tell that her mother had been a hoarder. Many of the twelve upstairs bedrooms was piled to the windowsill with newspapers, magazines, furniture, boxes, crates and junk stacked under sheets. Decade upon decade of detritus was accumulated inside each one. She tried to walk across several of the rooms to pull back the dusty curtains but gave up on account of the unnavigable piles of rubbish. To Emma Lacey this may not have been junk at all, just a past she couldn't bear to throw away. The house told Suze other stories: that her mother was either without the financial means to keep the place clean and habitable, or else she didn't approve of change. The darkest, and most likely reason for the house's condition was the failing of her mother's mind. As her reason fell apart, so did the house she lived in. Emma Lacey and her house had deteriorated together.

In other ways, the place looked as if it hadn't been touched since well before her mother's time. Everywhere was dark wood, dark fabrics and dark furnishings. There was a pervasive, musty smell of disuse and damp. Then there was the decor. The walls, if painted, were coated with what seemed like centuries of candle soot, lamp oil, tobacco smoke and cooking fat. The rugs were etched in sweeping, threadbare pathways that traced the high-traffic routes between the various rooms. Cobwebs trellised the corners and high places. Wallpaper hung in strips from the walls and everywhere was dust, dust and more dust.

In each wing of the first floor Suze found a communal bathroom. Presumably one was for the ladies, the other for the men. Each contained a row of sinks, toilets in cubicles, and heavy, claw-foot baths behind head-height partitions. She managed to twist one of the taps open and, at once, the house shook with the hammering of the pipes. The water from the tap flowed brown and sludgy for some time, then became clear. Cold water only. Better than nothing. She noted the location of the tap and finished her reconnoitre of the first floor.

Suze stepped down the broad staircase and jumped with shock at a knocking from the front door. The striking of the heavy iron knocker rang through the house like a death knell. She opened the door to find Ava Carfax dressed in a different shade of tweed.

'Morning,' said Ava. From her hand swung a leather briefcase that seemed to bulge with officialdom.

Suze held the door wide and Ava stepped inside.

'Sleep well?' asked Ava while Suze closed the door.

'Yes, okay,' said Suze.

Ava seemed disappointed for a moment, but quickly recovered. 'I brought the documents I mentioned. We'll need a place to go through them. How about the study?'

'Sure,' said Suze, 'if I only knew where that was.'

Ava turned and headed into the house. 'Come with me.'

Suze followed Ava to a hallway on one side of the grand staircase. She'd already explored the hallway on the other side of the stairs and found a colossal dining room with kitchens, pantry and scullery beyond. But this latest direction was unfamiliar territory. At the end of the hallway Ava turned, opened a tall door and disappeared inside.

The room was dim, lit only by slivers of daylight that peered through holes and slits in the heavy curtains. In one corner, Ava wrestled with a decorative rope. She pulled it and the curtains slid open, releasing dust and revealing a magnificent view of the moorland to the east. In the foreground stood the bent and bowed Scots pine. Like many windows in the house, there were no storm shutters here. Suze guessed these were reserved only for the windows overlooking the sea, where the nor'westers did their worst.

'Your grandfather's study,' announced Ava.

'Henry Lacey?' asked Suze.

'The very same.' Ava cast a look of approval around the room. 'Always wanted a study like this myself.'

Suze recalled Ava's cramped office in Storm Bay. Sure, there was more space here, but the study had an oppressive quality. Every available stretch of wall space was lined with shelf upon shelf of dreary-looking books. Some were motheaten and mildewed, their spines and jackets rotted away. A massive desk with a green-glass banker's lamp dominated the room, facing away from the view through the window. It was dismal, dusty and academic – perhaps the perfect place for a tweed-armoured lawyer like Ava Carfax after all.

'Who's this?' asked Suze, inspecting a porcelain bust of a stern, bearded man on a stone pedestal. 'Another of my ancestors?'

'No idea,' came Ava's reply as she began to dust the chairs and wipe down the desk with a handkerchief. 'Best we get started.' She sat behind the desk, back to the window, waving Suze over like some draconian headmistress.

Dutifully, Suze sat, facing her.

The rest of the morning passed in a tedious slew of paperwork. Ava explained the process that would now unfold: the definition of probate and what it meant for Suze, the post-mortem and what its findings might bring. How Suze would need to demonstrate to the satisfaction of the courts that she was heir *in lieu* of a will and any other beneficiary. Ava stabbed her finger at various documents where she required Suze's signature. Suze obliged but felt she was being led blindly.

'So, you're my lawyer now?' asked Suze.

'No.' Ava's response was blunt. 'I only have your mother's interests and the interests of her estate at heart.'

'But my mother's gone. What about me?'

'You don't pay me.'

'And my mother does? How?'

Ava interlaced the fingers of both hands with a sigh. 'I am owed *from the estate.'*

Suze was about to question her further when Ava spoke. 'I'm owed from the time your mother's been in Bosvenor. Until now, I've been working *gratis*. Bosvenor haven't been paid the whole time your mother's been there, either. So, as you can imagine, a lot of people are owed a lot of money. Then there's the inheritance tax you'll have to pay and your mother's funeral costs.' She lifted her palms, indicating the house around them. 'And it's all tied up, *here*.'

Suze felt the house slipping away from her. 'There's nothing else?'

'Not that we know of.'

'How am I going to get by? I'm on the dole, remember? And they'll probably cancel my benefits when they learn I've inherited this place.'

Ava locked eyes with Suze. 'As I mentioned yesterday in the car, I've been thinking about that. The best way I can help is to set up a trust or account against which you can borrow. That way you'll have access to funds, whatever you need. Then, when the sale of the house goes through, you settle the debt and keep any proceeds of the sale that are left.'

Suze's eyes narrowed. It felt like a plan to push her into selling. Perhaps she could get away with claiming the dole until the DHSS found out. 'What if I don't want to sell?' she offered.

'Be reasonable, Susanna. We've all been doing this on the proviso that the house will be sold. This has been going on long before you arrived. I know, a windfall has dropped into your lap, it's like winning the pools or something. Now it seems like everyone's coming to cash in, but this is the way it works Susanna, this is a *transaction*. It's just money, and death is expensive. Whichever way you look at it, you're still far better off than before.'

'It's not just money, though is it?' replied Suze. 'It's where I was born. The home I never had. The home I should've grown up in. And now, it's come to me, the way it always should have. Is it so bad to want to keep it?'

Ava returned a dark look.

Suze sat back in her chair. 'Suppose you *were* my lawyer?' she hypothesised.

Ava inclined her head in question.

'And I asked your advice?' continued Suze. 'Tell me, how can I remain in this house? How can I stay here without selling up?'

'It won't happen Susanna.'

'Tell me, what would you advise?'

Ava glared at Suze. 'The best you could hope for...'

'Yes?'

'Is that there's something of value here...'

'Such as?'

Ava looked around, at a loss. 'I don't know, investments, shares, hidden nest-eggs, deeds to other properties, company titles, details of offshore accounts, uncashed cheques...'

'Buried treasure?' suggested Suze.

Ava searched Suze's humourless face. She relented. 'Buried treasure might do it, yes.'

Suze leaned forward. 'So, if you were to search for buried treasure in a place like this, where would you begin?'

Ava's eyes never wavered from Suze's. 'Here,' she offered. 'It's a study right? Any useful scrap of paperwork will be here somewhere.

The thing is, you have to know what you're looking for.'

'I can make a start, I don't mind,' said Suze, looking at the shelves around her. 'It's not as if I have anything better to do.'

'Everything here has to be catalogued for probate: furniture, ornaments, antiques, bric-a-brac, everything, right down to the last brass candlestick,' said Ava. 'Then it has to be valued. The house too. I was going to send one of my juniors over to start sifting through everything. If there's anything here that could change your situation, they'll find it.'

'Okay, good.'

Ava offered a grim nod. 'Just don't get your hopes up.' She stood, bundled the paperwork back into the leather briefcase and made to leave. As she passed the porcelain bust on the pedestal, she stopped to inspect it. 'Pavlov,' she declared.

'Who?'

Ava pointed to the engraved name at the base of the bust. Something caught her eye. 'Hello, what's this?' She placed her brief-case on the floor then lifted the bust, handing it to Suze. Ava dragged the pedestal clear of the alcove. 'I missed this,' she said.

The pedestal and bust had been positioned in a curved alcove. Timber panelling reached to waist height and above it was a concave of smooth plaster through which ran a thin vertical gap, almost unnoticeable.

'So, what is it?' asked Suze.

Ava pushed the alcove at its centre, there was a soft click and the two sides of the curved alcove opened a fraction, like a pair of doors. Ava grasped both sides and pulled them wide. Beyond lay a small, dark room, bordered by shelves filled with more books. The space was heaped almost to capacity with tall, untidy stacks of paperwork. It looked to Suze as if decades' worth of bills, letters and all manner of correspondence had simply been tossed there, unread.

'Some kind of hidey-hole,' replied Ava. She bent down and retrieved a few scraps of paper.

'Why is it hidden? Is this stuff important?' asked Suze.

'Could just be junk,' said Ava, reading. 'Maybe your mother wanted it out of sight.' She dropped the sheaves of paper back onto a teetering pile and at once caused an avalanche of paperwork that slid through the alcove doors, over their feet. Plumes of dust rose into the air, forcing both women to beat a hasty retreat, forearms over faces, coughing.

Ava nodded toward the dust-clouded alcove. 'Well, if we're digging for treasure, that's where we'll start,' she said.

◄—●—►

Once Ava had left, and to give the dust in the study a chance to settle, Suze began exploring the rest of the house. In the kitchen she found a small gas-fired water heater above the sink. It didn't look too old. She checked the gas was on and tried lighting the pilot but it failed to ignite. Cold water would have to do for now.

Near the front door was an old, wall-mounted, black Bakelite phone with a dial. She held the receiver to her ear. Nothing. Disconnected, just like the gas.

She moved outside, desperate for some fresh air. The wind buffeted her about. She circumnavigated the house, stopping for a time to contemplate the huge Scots pine, bent to an impossible angle by the storms. As her hair lashed her face, she realised she was standing in what would likely be considered a light breeze. Winter here would not be for the faint-hearted.

On one side of the house she found a kind of brick and tile garage without a garage door. Built next to it, in similar materials, looked to be a workshop or shed, a door opened into it from the shelter of the garage. Both the workshop and garage looked like afterthoughts: tacked onto the house at a later date, and hidden from view beneath the windows. Suze unbolted the workshop door and went inside. There was a long wooden bench over which hung some tools, rusted beyond usefulness in the salt sea air. In one corner was a bin or bunker of stone, above it a pair of timber doors that rattled in the wind. Suze moved closer and peered inside. What she saw made her gasp with excitement: coal.

After hunting down a steel bucket and a shovel, she loaded up with coal and headed back into the house. Tonight she'd keep her bedroom warm. She collected a bundle of newspapers from one of the nearby rooms and lit them in the grate. Then she dashed outside to look. A thin plume of smoke trailed horizontally in the wind from one of the chimney pots. She'd feared the flue might be blocked with bird-nests or rubble from the damaged chimneys, but today the hearth-side gods were smiling on her.

She swept the small room, lit a fire and went downstairs to make a start on the paperwork in the study alcove. She needn't have bothered for the dust to settle. As soon as she moved the first few sheets of paper, she felt it in her nostrils and the back of her throat once more. In the kitchen she wet a tea towel and tied it over her nose and mouth like a bandanna. Then she made another foray into the study. She began to sort the various documents into three piles in the centre of the room: the first pile was the outright rubbish, of no value whatsoever, the second pile contained the *maybes*, the *worth-looking-at-more-closely* documents. She'd bring these to the attention of Ava's 'junior'. The third pile was reserved for the documents genuinely worth something: *the treasure*. After a few hours of sorting, the first pile had grown large, the second pile contained only a few sheets of paper while the spot reserved for the third pile showed nothing at all. She groaned at the burgeoning tide of paper in the room inside the alcove. She'd made no impact upon it at all.

The day was growing dark and she'd done all she could. Retiring to the now-warm bedroom, she heated water in a saucepan over her gas stove and washed herself with the help of the jug and ewer. She changed into pyjamas, lay on the airbed and read *The Western Morning News* by candlelight. She scoured the jobs section near the back but found nothing near Storm Bay. Without transport she'd only be able to work locally. Suze decided she'd take Ava's advice and visit the library. She'd become a member, borrow some books to while away the dark evenings at Aeolus House and check the noticeboard there and in the Spar mini market for any jobs in the area. Things weren't looking too hopeful. She'd need some kind of funds soon, but she'd have no part of Ava's bargain.

'Please let there be something here,' she whispered. 'Just something to get me by.'

11

YESTERDAY'S MAN

SUZE WOKE in the pale light of morning. The fire was out, and a chill had crept into the room again.

She jumped up and dressed quickly into her dusty clothes. As she left the room she eyed the wedding dress still draped over the bare mattress of the brass bed. She folded it with care and made to place it back inside the cardboard box. What she saw lying in the bottom of the box made her stop.

A delicate silver crown shaped like an ornate wreath of oak leaves lay on top of more layers of silk. Tiny pearls set in the silver formed buds of mistletoe that grew from the intricate weaving of leaves. Suze pulled it carefully from the box and realised it was connected somehow to the remaining fabric. As she held the crown high, she understood what it was.

It was the wedding veil.

The fabric was of the finest silk tulle: sheer, diaphanous, possessing almost no weight. It looked in better condition than the torn, grubby dress, although there were several scorch-marks, like cigarette burns, at intervals in the material. At first she couldn't figure out how the veil might have been worn. It looked as if the silver wreath-like crown was designed to sit outside the fabric, holding it in place. Suze slipped the fabric over her hair and it fell down to her waist. With care she positioned the crown over her head, the thin, translucent fabric underneath. The tips of the wreathed crown seemed to sit naturally just above her forehead.

As a delusion, it was beautiful. Her mother had never married but she must've dreamed that one day she might. Surely this was the reason for the dress and the veil? Had she planned something? And what had Emma planned for Suze, for the child she would call Celeste? Did *she* feature within her mother's plans, or was she outside them, an accident, an inconvenience to be disposed of?

She flung the veil back over her head, uncovering her face, and stared at her stormy expression in the dressing table mirror. Would she ever learn the truth?

I could've helped you.

We could've helped each other.

She threw back her head and groaned at the ceiling, 'So *why?*'

The room seemed too small to answer such a big question. She flung the bedroom door open and walked along the landing to the top of the grand staircase.

'*Why did you give up on me?*' she shouted into the vastness of the house. Her question clattered through the halls and rooms, reverberated in each cavernous space, rang down each corridor and staircase, into every dark, dusty corner.

No answer came. None ever would.

Suze felt her emotions swell, agonising and destructive. She was struggling now, on top of the aquamarine suitcase of her childhood, reaching to close the rusty silver latches.

Lock it up, Suze.

She brought her hands to her head and sat heavily on the top step of the grand staircase. Then, as if to hide her weakness from the eyes of the house, she pulled the veil over her face.

Everything became shrouded in a white pall, as if she was shining a torch into sea mist. Her eyes adjusted slowly and the hall below her gained focus. Something moved, growing in proportion, gaining mass.

Through the veil, she saw a man standing at the bottom of the staircase.

Suze felt the shock flash through her – an ice-cold current of electricity that paralysed, yet sharpened every sense. The man was about her age, athletic-looking, and tall with slender hands and long fingers. He wore an antiquated, double-breasted suit, buttoned closely. His hair was oiled and raked back from his forehead in a short-back-and-sides. His face looked kindly and clean-shaven save for the thin line of a moustache that ran along his top lip. He was looking straight at her, his eyes brimming with emotion. He lifted his hand, beckoning.

Standing, Suze clawed the veil away from her face and searched the empty space at the bottom of the stairs. She tore the veil free, cursing as it caught in her hair and parted roots from her scalp. Throwing it wide, she ran down towards the great hall, half-expecting to feel the residual presence of the dark stranger as she burst through the spot where he'd stood. Nothing. She continued running, across the hall, through the vestibule. She fought with the bolts of the main door and ran out into the weeds and wind. Falling, her knees weak, her legs shaking, she looked back at the house. Above the keening wind and the shriek of whirling gulls, her heart hammered in her ears. A thin rain, more like a damp mist, wet her face and plastered her hair to her forehead. She had no need to question her own sanity. This was no trick of the light played upon her by the thin translucence of the veil. She was certain of what she'd seen. The house was not empty. There were others who might call it home. The world she thought she knew was altered, something she no longer recognised. Every dark monster that lived under her childhood bed, next to the aquamarine suitcase, had crawled out and into the open.

Anything was possible now, and it petrified her.

What had frightened her most was not just the presence of the dark man in the double-breasted suit.

It was that his feet were on back to front, his toes pointing behind him.

◀ ● ▶

It didn't take long for the rain and wind to drive cold deep into her bones, forcing her back into Aeolus House. She found the veil still lying on the stair and gave it a wide berth. Then she changed into dry clothes, threw on a raincoat and trudged the two miles into Storm Bay in search of a drink.

The pub with the low door near the harbour was named *The Lugger*. Inside, Suze found a corner near the fire and nursed her frazzled nerves with a gin and bitter lemon. The place was quaint –

the perfect spot for summer holidaymakers to grab a ploughman's lunch or a pasty, the ideal haven for local fishermen and farmers to drink their way through the harsh winters.

Best of all, it was reassuringly *ordinary*. Nothing untoward or otherworldly. Just a dartboard, a bar billiards table and a cigarette machine. An RNLI charity box in the shape of a lifeboat sat at anchor on one corner of the bar. Glass fishing floats and crab-pots hung from the walls. An assortment of older men sat among the mismatch of chairs and tables in the lounge. Snippets of their hushed conversation floated towards Suze – trivialities debated with all the earnestness of world events: car trouble, neighbour trouble, the price of a pint. Suze stared at her drink, not wishing to make eye contact. She needed this. She needed to ground herself. She needed *ordinary*.

The vision of the man was burned into her mind. Like the afterglow of sunlight on her retina it remained residual. Everywhere she looked she saw him. He was a thin layer of the impossible, transparent in front of the denser, existent images of the everyday. Suze was trying hard to forget the episode, but how could she? The pub remained quiet, but the thoughts inside her head were screaming.

She couldn't help but think that the man was something from the past. She was guessing as much from his old-fashioned suit, his moustache, and the way he wore his hair. He belonged to the house, but a different version of it, an older version. She couldn't shake the feeling that he might have stood there at some point in time, beckoning with mournful eyes the way she'd seen him. A word surfaced in Suze's mind, a word that might describe him. She clenched her jaw, not letting the word take shape. It was a childish word, a word that floated like a trickster in a white sheet with holes cut for eyes. It was better to think of him as just a memory, an impression left upon the house after his being there, like the smell of cooking that hangs in a kitchen, or the mark left on a cushion where someone once sat.

In the strangest, most insane way, it almost made sense to her. *He'd been there, hadn't he*? He was a *recording* – one that played like a song on a Walkman. The singer was absent but their voice could still be heard.

Yet she'd only seen him through her mother's wedding veil. Not afterwards. Not before.

Perhaps these were the things that needed to be in place for the recording to play itself back? Like fresh batteries, sliding in a cassette and hitting *Play*. Everything needed to be aligned – all the parts in place.

Suze felt another possibility claw at her. *Was this how her mother had once seen him? Through the same veil? Beckoning? What was he trying to show her?*

Yet try as she might to convince herself that this was all plausible, just shadows of the past imprinted on the fabric of the house, her logic was torn apart by a thought that screamed louder than any other: *why were his feet like that?*

Suze felt certain she'd never know the answer until she knew who the man was – or *had been*.

She sighed and finished her drink.

She'd come to this place – Storm Bay, and Aeolus House, too – in search of answers.

But the burden of her questions was growing.

By early afternoon a dense slab of grey cloud was sliding in from the sea, increasing the drizzle and making the sky feel lower than the ceiling of The Lugger. Suze left the pub with a plan. Part of this plan was not to return to Aeolus House, not yet, not until she was calm, her thoughts in order. She walked along the main road to the bus stop outside the chip shop and checked the times for buses into Wadebridge. Another twenty minutes. She ducked into the warmth of the chip shop and ordered a bag of chips – *yes, open please – yes, salt and vinegar, please.* Then she waited for the bus.

The journey into Wadebridge was less than half an hour. This was the closest major town, closer than Bodmin, although it lacked a railway station. Wadebridge was inland too, which gave Suze hope she might escape the dreariness of the coastal weather. But the dense slab of grey seemed to follow, sliding over the entire county.

The town, with its characteristic granite and slate houses, was big enough to accommodate some local government offices, including a branch of the DHSS. Here, Suze stood in more queues and filled out more forms until she'd succeeded in getting her giro cheques forwarded from London to the post office in Storm Bay. Until she found anything of value at Aeolus House, this would be her only financial support. What she was doing wasn't illegal, at least not yet. But once probate was concluded and the deeds were in her name, what then? She'd have to declare the house as an asset and she wouldn't pass the means test. No more dole, no more income. She had until then to find a job, or something of value up at the house, under the dusty sheets in the guest bedrooms or in the alcove filled with paperwork. Suze knew a countdown had begun, one that ended with her finding a way to save the house, or being forced to sell it.

She wandered the main street and crossed the old stone bridge that spanned the River Camel. She gazed into the cold, slow-moving river with nothing particular in mind, then recrossed the bridge into the main part of the town. Clothing shops, bakeries and gift shops lit the damp afternoon gloom with their warm, yellow light. She stepped into a phone box and dialled the number of the Bosvenor Sanatorium. Dr Passmore's assistant assured her that there was no further update. The coroner and medical examiner were still embroiled in their inquest in Truro, and were likely to remain so for at least the next few weeks. Then they'd have a backlog of work to catch up on. There was still no indication when they could turn their attention to Suze's mother. Dr Passmore's assistant apologised but Suze was grateful in a way. This would buy her time; time to search Aeolus House thoroughly; time to find a solution. It was a way to draw out that inevitable countdown. More and more, she considered Aeolus House to be her birthright. If she never learned the answers to the questions that burned inside – why her mother had given up on her, who her father was – then at least Aeolus House could be hers, the way it was supposed to be. The house was a kind of justice for everything she'd suffered. It was the only sure thing she might take away from this strange event.

The afternoon was giving way to evening. Soon the shops would close and the cold night would drift in from the sea, riding the river's tide. Suze slunk towards the bus stop, resigned to a return to Aeolus House and whatever this night might hold. She boarded the bus and climbed to the top deck. It smelled of cigarettes, the windows damp with condensation. She sat and wiped a window with the cuff of her raincoat, then gazed at the frosted points of light that vibrated beyond the wet glass. The bus began to move and the lights revolved, refracted. She pulled her coat closer and fell into a warm doze. The shop signs drifted past at window height: Miller's the Estate Agent, Blewett's the Bakers, Lloyds Bank, the Nationwide Building Society. One of the signs shook her from her dozing as surely as a shake to her shoulder. She fumbled for one of the upright posts and her thumb found the bell. She pressed it once, twice, three times in her urgency. The bus slowed to a halt at the next stop. Stumbling and tripping down the stairs, she stepped into the street. She was now a good few hundred yards away from what she'd seen. Panting, she walked quickly back along the stone flags of the pavement. Her heart was in her mouth. The drizzle now began to fall as a light rain and she lifted her collar. Fractals of light from the shop gathered into focus as she marched towards it. Minutes later, she stood in front of its window, bathed in the gleaming white of its shopfront display: silk, satin, organza, taffeta, ribbons and lace. The shop was still open. She lifted her gaze to the brightly-lit sign that had caught her attention: *Kerenza's Bridal Couture.*

— ◆ ▸ —

'We is closed!' came a woman's voice from the back of the shop as the bell above the door tinkled, signalling Suze's entry.

Suze turned, pointing at the door. 'But the sign says...'

'I know, I know,' came the reply. 'But I can't be taking no measurements nor going through no samples now. You'll have to come back.'

Suze stepped between mannequins bedecked in shining white fabric into the open centre of the shop where a young woman sat on a footstool beside a dressmaker's dummy, pinning the hem of an elegant wedding gown. 'I just have a quick question,' said Suze.

The young woman looked up, her mouth filled with pins. 'Then ask away while I finish up,' she said from the side of her mouth.

'I have one of your dresses.'

'Oh yes?' said the young woman, returning to her work.

'And I wonder if you could tell me anything about it.'

The young woman looked up, puzzled, and pulled the pins from her mouth. 'When was you married?'

'Oh, I'm not married,' explained Suze. 'The dress belonged to my mother.'

'Well, when was *she* married?'

Suze looked to the ceiling, realising how difficult this request was becoming. 'Well, she wasn't married either. That's the mystery. I just wondered if there was anything you could tell me about the dress, why it was made, and – anything really, anything about it at all.'

The young woman's gaze was a distrustful frown. 'Well, I'd have to see it.'

'I can bring it in.'

'Alright.'

'Next week, perhaps?'

'Very good.' The woman's frown melted. 'When do you think it was made? The dress?'

'I'm guessing sometime in the nineteen-fifties. Probably early fifties,' guessed Suze.

The young woman gave a short laugh. 'Before my time, I wouldn't know nothing 'bout it.'

'Is there anyone here who might?' pleaded Suze.

'No,' said the young woman, shaking her head. 'This is a one-woman operation, and you're looking at her.'

'Oh.'

'Sorry.'

Suze turned to leave as the woman resumed her pinning.

'Although...' said the woman without looking up. Suze turned back. 'This shop's been in the same family for generations. I took my apprenticeship here when my Aunt Dolly ran the place. Before that, it were her sister, Kerenza Pengilly herself. That's her name over the door.'

Suze turned back, warmed by this glimmer of hope. 'So, is your aunt still around?' she asked.

'Nope. Moved upcountry.' The woman's reply sounded final, irreversible, like a death in the family. 'But old Kerenza is still with us.'

Suze took a step back into the middle of the shop. 'Then, is there any chance – I can ask *her* about it?'

The woman stood, and cast a critical eye over the pinned dress. 'I wouldn't recommend it. She don't do well with strangers. She's in a nursing home now, up Polzeath way.' The young woman shot Suze a pained look. 'Her thinking's a bit addled these days. 'Tis her age. Outsiders can give her a fright and she clams up. She can't remember her last meal, but she'll remember things from years and years ago, clear as day. I visit her once a month. So, if you bring me that dress,

I'll ask her about it.'

'Thank you,' said Suze, grateful.

The young woman smiled. 'No promises, hear me?'

Suze nodded and left. Outside, the late autumn afternoon seemed less dark, less cold, less hopeless.

12

THE SHOOTING OF
CHARLOTTE BRONTË

THE VEIL LAY in daylight on the broad staircase.

There was nothing frightening, nothing untoward about it now. It looked like a scrap of discarded cloth, a rag or duster dropped by a careless cleaner. Suze felt a pang of remorse for leaving it there and stooped to collect it.

She'd returned from Wadebridge after dark last night, and had felt her way along corridors and up the stairs to the bedroom where her sleeping bag lay. She'd resisted sleep by imagining all kinds of possibilities the women at the bridal shop might uncover about the dress – why her mother had commissioned its creation; that it might lead to a name, a husband, a father. It was her best lead yet.

Now, in the wan light that struggled through the landing window, Suze realised she was holding out far too much hope for any kind of answer. She was pinning everything on an old woman's damaged memories. With pinched fingers she removed a few balls of dust from the delicate voile of the veil and scowled. She pulled out the long strands of her own hair trapped in the wreath-like crown and, holding the veil up, gave it a gentle shake. Then she was struck by a sudden thought: perhaps the bridal shop wasn't the only way to find out more? What if the veil had things to reveal, too?

She shuddered at the thought and walked down the stairs and into the entry hall. Today she'd continue the more worldly task of hunting for treasure in the dust of the study alcove.

Stopping at the study doorway, she surveyed the three unremarkable piles of paper on the floor. She had to make better progress than this. Looking around, she searched for a place to deposit the veil, somewhere free of dust and grime. Stepping inside, she crossed to the pedestal beside the alcove, spread the veil wide, and placed it over the head of the porcelain bust. She stepped back. Pavlov glowered at her through the layers of the veil. With his thick beard and moustache, and brow lowered in studious concentration, he looked like some furious, intellectual cross-dresser.

Suze knew that resuming her search would create a dust-storm, so she struggled with the bolts on the set of French doors framing the view of the Scots pine and the moorland to the east. The bolts gave up their fight and the doors swung open onto a narrow stone balcony. Suze presumed this was above the garage and workshop she'd discovered two days previously. Re-entering the study, she pulled down a large sash window to create some kind of cross-ventilation. It was cold, but it would quell the dust and she welcomed the fresh air. For a moment she sat at the massive hardwood desk, her grandfather's desk, now her base of operations. She ran her palms across its writing surface, over the bottle-green leather inlay that matched the green glass of the banker's lamp. It was a desk for a man of letters, a desk made in a world before typewriters, and she wondered what type of work, what sort of things the old man had written at this desk, and whether her mother had ever used it after his death. The view from the desk faced directly towards the alcove of secrets where Pavlov's bust had stood only days ago. Now the alcove doors hung open, revealing the mountain of work Suze needed to conquer. Next to the alcove was a fireplace of white stone, intricately carved with trees, deer and hunting hounds. On the mantelpiece was an old carriage clock that had given up marking time. Above this, a gilt mirror, spotted where the gilding had failed behind the glass. The effect of the mirror was wonderful: it reflected the light of the eastern windows, bathing the room with a watery incandescence, like the baleful eye of some monster from the deep. The mirror's light ran along the shelves, colouring the spines of the dusty books and casting impish shadows onto walls behind the mounted heads of stuffed animals.

Wrapping the tea towel over her nose and mouth, and with fresh batteries in her Sony Walkman, Suze pulled on her earphones and hit *Play*. Then she ploughed into the pile of paperwork in the alcove. She worked with purpose now, and it helped her to forget the incident with the veil. She stacked the paperwork into its various piles. The pile of worthless paper grew exponentially and Suze considered using it to kindle a fire in the fireplace. The study could certainly do with some heat but, for now, she preferred the fresh air from the open windows. It also encouraged her to keep busy, to work quickly. The first documents that presented themselves were mostly bank statements, power bills, charity appeals, rates demands, a variety of trivial correspondence. The ones nearest the front were the most recent, which seemed to indicate that any document or scrap of paper had simply been tossed here without further thought. Deeper into the pile were double-entry book-keeping records for household staff, letters from companies the Laceys had some kind of interest in. Most dated back to the thirties and forties; companies which, in all likelihood, no longer existed. There were ancient invoices and receipts of sale, contracts for long-dead employees, letters from the Laceys' lawyers and their representatives. Suze was gaining a better idea of how the Laceys lived. Much of the paperwork was signed by or addressed to her grandfather, Dr Henry Lacey. It seemed he was something of a celebrity, although there was no clue as to his field of speciality. Apart from his income as a doctor of who-knows-what, Henry Lacey seemed to be the beneficiary of some kind of research grant. Aside from this, her mother's name appeared in only a few of the documents Suze found.

By mid-morning, Suze had cleared a small path into the room. She could now see that under the layers of loose paper there were several stacks of cardboard filing boxes. She pulled one clear and lifted the lid. It looked to be filled with more documents. Fed up with the constant bending and stooping, she lifted the box and hauled it onto the desk in the study. Sitting down, she began to sort through its contents. Sheet after sheet of paper revealed nothing of interest. Just more junk. She lifted out a folder and was surprised to discover a wooden box beneath it. The box was beautifully made, like an antique jewellery case. She pulled the box free and set it on the desk. It was large and heavy, so much so, that it accounted for the remaining weight of the cardboard box she thought had been filled with paper. Suze threw the empty cardboard box aside and removed her earphones and tea towel bandanna to investigate this new marvel.

The wood of the box was dark and close-grained. Each corner was protected by an ornately engraved silver overlay. The lid was fastened with hinges of the same metal and closed with a small sliding latch. Adorning the lid was an elaborate crest also in the same silver metal. Engraved upon it was the inscription: *Crossley & Son, Sheffield, England. 1840.*

Suze slid the latch and opened the lid. She drew a breath, not believing what she'd found. Her eyes passed quickly over the cleaning rods, the powder flask and the bullet-maker. She wrapped her hand around the stock of the pistol and pulled it from the red velvet in which it lay.

It was heavy. The pistol was over a foot long, with a rounded walnut butt. It was certainly old, a one-shot muzzle loader. The wood of the butt was cross-hatched in a diamond pattern for grip and the hatching felt sharp to the skin of her palm. The dark steel barrel was long, not tubular, but octagonal. She studied the delicate engraving around the trigger-guard and the side-mounted hammer and casings. She didn't much care for guns but this was beautiful. She held the pistol up, looking down the sights, and aimed at one of the heads of the stuffed animals on the wall. *Pschew*! Suze mimicked the recoil of the old pistol, then lifted the muzzle to her lips and blew away imaginary smoke. She trained the pistol on other animals in the room, the carriage clock and the old mirror. Then she pulled the hammer slowly back. It clicked once – *half-cock*. Then it clicked again – *full-cock*. Still looking along the sights, one eye closed, Suze swung her aim to the study doorway. A man stood just inside the room, a look of alarm on his face. Suze recognised the black hair and the kindly, sensitive features. It was *him*: the man at the bottom of the stairs.

Suze started, squeezing the trigger by accident. The percussion cap sparked and sputtered. There was the smell of burning powder and the pistol flared from the opening in the casing beneath the hammer. *It was loaded?*

'Not at me!' shouted the man in the doorway as the pistol continued to flare and sizzle, its barrel pointed directly at him. Suze swung it away, aiming at a stuffed deer head, then at Pavlov, veiled on his pedestal. A bad choice, she now realised.

'Hold tight!' commanded the man in the doorway. 'Don't let go.' Suze closed her grip firmly around the butt.

At the last moment she swung the pistol away from Pavlov and the veil, pointing it at the alcove. It discharged with a thunderclap of fire, sparks and smoke. The recoil was brutal, the pistol nearly jumping from her hands. Suze dropped it on top of the writing desk. The sharp, diamond cross-hatching of the butt had scored tiny abrasions across her palm. She shook her hand in pain.

'You okay?' The man's words were muffled by the whining in Suze's ears. He approached through a pall of blue smoke.

Suze was incapable of any reply. She was shocked to the core, by the explosive discharge of the pistol, and by this apparition – this man from elsewhere.

'Christ, lucky this old thing didn't blow up in your face!' he said, examining the smouldering pistol. He walked to the alcove where the lead ball had split open the timber of the door frame. He whistled, placing a finger in the hole.

Suze's panic began to subside. Her thoughts were recovering, ordering themselves back into some version of awareness. She studied the man. His hair and features were similar, but he was different. *Where was the thin moustache? Where was the double-breasted suit?* This man was suited, yes, but the jacket was modern, single-breasted, with a thin woollen jumper underneath and an overcoat on top.

'Oh, dear me, no,' lamented the man, leaning inside the alcove to retrieve something from a bookshelf at the very back. He turned back to Suze displaying a torn-apart edition of *Jane Eyre*. The ball from the pistol had penetrated the spine and shredded the pages inside. 'You shot Charlotte Brontë,' he exclaimed. Walking back to Suze, he placed the book on the desk and smiled. 'Not to worry. I'm sure she'd find it terribly romantic.'

Suze's head spun.

The man offered a hand in greeting. 'Name's Harlan.'

Nothing Suze wanted to say would make any sense. 'Where did you come from?' was all she could manage.

The man stabbed a thumb over his shoulder. 'I did knock. Perhaps you didn't hear?' He glanced at Suze's Sony Walkman and earphones lying on the desk. The offending articles.

'But where? How are you *here*?'

'I'm from the office,' he explained.

'What office?'

'Didn't Ava explain? She wants me to help out.' He extended his hand again. 'Harlan Grey.'

'You're from the office?'

'Yes.'

'Ava's office?'

'Yes. Carfax and Bell.'

'You're the junior?'

'Well…' he began, head bobbing from side to side, disinclined to agree. 'I'm not a solicitor or anything, *not yet*. But I am *actually* a paralegal. But I guess even a junior partner would be *junior* to Ava.' His brows gathered in question. 'Did she really say that?'

'Yes.'

His brows lifted. 'Oh well.' He extended his hand in a third attempt at introduction. 'Harlan Grey. And you, I assume, are Susanna Newman?'

'Yes,' said Suze, shaking his hand. It was warm, taking her briefly by surprise. Had she expected anything different? 'But *Suze* is fine.'

'Then *Suze* it is,' said Harlan.

They studied each other. Harlan wore a nervous smile. Suze liked that. She preferred nervous people because they didn't intimidate her. Cocksure, arrogant types with fake smiles made her run a mile. Either that, or they quickly realised that she was immune to their charm. Cheerful people, especially confident ones, never stayed cheerful for long in her company.

'Where did it come from?' asked Harlan, nodding at the pistol.

Suze pointed to the alcove. 'I found it there, it was in this box. I had no idea it was loaded.'

Harlan studied the opened gun case. 'I wonder where the other one is?'

'The other what?'

'The other gun. There should be two of them, look.' He pointed to the red velvet of the gun case. Inside were two depressions, created for a pair of guns lying side-by-side, head-to-tail. 'Shame there's only one. A pair of boxed travelling pistols like this might have been worth something.'

'Maybe it's inside somewhere,' said Suze, raising her chin in the direction of the alcove.

'Maybe,' replied Harlan, following her gaze. 'Looks like you've started work without me.'

'I'm trying,' she replied, nodding at the three piles of paperwork on the floor. 'That's everything so far, the junk, the maybes and the treasure.'

Harlan began removing his overcoat and jacket. 'Then why don't I take over? If there's anything here, we'll find it.'

'I'm sure you'll have a better idea than me,' said Suze. The job had become a dull chore anyway and she was glad of the help. Harlan offered another nervous smile. It gave Suze a chance to study his face. He certainly looked similar to the man at the foot of the stairs, but not identical. His dark, thick hair was longer, and instead of being oiled and raked back from his brow, it was tousled in a more careless manner, with loose strands that fell across his eyes. The other man had been athletic, an outdoors type, whereas Harlan appeared more scholarly – an indoor person, an intellectual. Suze's gaze rested on the anxious smile.

'What?' asked Harlan, feeling Suze's scrutiny.

Suze realised she was staring and looked quickly away. 'Oh, I'm sorry,' she said. She stood and made for the door. 'I might leave the document sorting to you while I rummage around upstairs.'

'Sure.' Harlan turned to the alcove, commencing work.

From the corner of her eye, Suze stole one last look, checking his feet. Everything about him was normal. He was a flesh and blood version of the other man. They were different sides of the same coin: one confident, the other less so, one real, the other – something unknown. Suze shivered and walked from the room.

13

THE OVAL PHOTOGRAPH

BY NOW, SUZE WAS FAMILIAR with the layout of the house, but not where anything of value might be stored. She decided on a thorough sweep of the ground floor, checking every cupboard and cabinet. While Harlan busied himself in the study alcove, she stood inside the front door, gazing with determination into the dark maw of the house. Leading off from the entry hall were doors to several large rooms. The first of these was panelled with dark wood. Suze guessed it was some kind of receiving room, a vestibule for guests perhaps? At its heart stood a large round table draped with a tasselled red velvet tablecloth. The fabric was moth-eaten and faded, dull with dust. Eight matching chairs were arranged around the table as if in preparation for a game of cards, or a séance. A mirrored drinks cabinet stood along the farthest wall, now empty of any cheer and the dust-rimed windows were framed with even dustier, dark red curtains.

Next was a door leading into the main lounge. Inside, three

long leather sofas, now split and revealing their stuffing, formed three sides of a square in front of another white stone fireplace, a low table between them. Around the walls were various cabinets which contained nothing in particular. The cabinets were warped and ruined by damp. The walls held several paintings of what looked local scenes: clifftop vistas, stone-fringed beaches and ships foundering in storms at sea. Most of these were mouldy and black from a leak in the corner of the ceiling where the cornice had bowed and split. Long tendrils of black streaked the walls down to the ruined carpet.

Emerging from the lounge, Suze crossed the entry hall. It was strewn with leaves: refugees from the wilderness beyond the front door. She walked through the huge dining room with its long oak table, high-backed chairs and serving benches. A sideboard contained a few tarnished platters and serving dishes that looked as if they could be silver. She pulled these out and placed them on the dining table, making a mental note to inform Harlan. Elsewhere she uncovered an incomplete set of crystal wine glasses, a few tumblers and a decanter. Some of the drawers still housed formal cutlery, piled haphazardly inside. Behind doors at one end of the dining room was the narrow corridor which ran between the entry hall and the kitchen. Turning right, Suze followed the dark, stone-floored corridor to the kitchen. The kitchen was large too, the kind that was run by servants in days gone by. Today, its old-world glory of sweeping timber benchtops, porcelain sinks, coal-fired ovens and copper chimney breasts was interspersed with trespassers from the modern world: an electric kettle, a toaster, and an upright fridge-freezer – all of which were now obsolete due to the lack of power.

Suze sifted through the cupboards of the kitchen and scullery, finding only chipped china and worn utensils. Nothing of any value. The only possibility left on the ground floor was the room with the bay window, its storm shutters and panoramic views of Storm Bay. She made her way to it, finding that it took nothing more than a cursory glance to see it was filled with only broken furniture.

She sighed and lifted her eyes to the bedrooms above. She prayed there might be something up there – something stored under the dust-sheets and layers of rubbish that might prove valuable, that might help her keep this house for herself. Above her, the intricate, now crumbling plaster mouldings of the ceiling shimmered and blurred.

The house was winking again. It knew she cared.

Something was here.

And it wanted to show her.

⊷ ● ⊶

The upstairs rooms were burial grounds where old furniture had crawled away to die. Rusting steel bed frames, mouldering mattresses and splintered, worm-eaten furniture littered their dusty spaces. These must've been the guest rooms where the stormwatchers had resided. They'd left no lasting impression of themselves. The rooms were empty of life now, empty of memories. She started with the most cluttered one, throwing the junk into a pile in the corner of the room. She'd see to the removal of the debris later.

A large tallboy stood against a wall, behind it something was covered with old bedsheets. Suze tried leaning around it to remove the sheets but couldn't reach. So she pulled out a few of the tallboy's empty drawers and, using them as steps, climbed on top. Kneeling, she reached down and pulled back the sheets to discover a row of picture frames stacked on their edges.

Jumping down, Suze manhandled the tallboy away. With just enough room to squeeze behind, she began sorting through her find. It was a collection of photographs: large, black-and-white images taken with old plate cameras. Stiffly posed, void of expression, they were family portraits. The Laceys on display. Many were very old, with blotchy images of forgotten progenitors and unknown branches of the family. She leafed through them until, eyes wide, she discovered a portrait in an oval frame. Wrestling it from the pile, she held it up to the light and drew a breath.

It was a large, formal photograph of her mother as a young woman seated on a chaise. She wore the same incongruous headscarf as the photograph in the entry hall. The scarf covered her forehead and temples. It looked out of place and unsuited to the time, or any time for that matter. Suze put it down to a personal quirk, some ill-conceived attempt at glamour. Heaven knows, Suze had been guilty of worse crimes of fashion in her youth. Beside her on the chaise sat an older, heavyset man with broad shoulders, large hands and greying hair. Suze could tell from his lifted chin and the air of hubris that this was a man who took himself seriously. He seemed a man without mirth or compassion, wrapped in a world of his own importance, a world of his own manufacture. Suze didn't need to look any further. She knew him in an instant. He was Emma's father, Suze's grandfather – Dr Henry Lacey.

Taking the framed photo in two hands, Suze hauled it down to the entry hall. Breathing hard, she lifted it onto the hook at the foot of the stairs. It swung into place, covering the oval of bright wallpaper completely.

Suze stepped back.

Why hide it away, Emma?

And yet, she knew why. The answer lay in the photograph itself. It told her everything she needed to know about her mother's relationship with her father.

Something sharp had been raked across the photograph, over and over, scratching out the eyes of Henry Lacey, right down to the white backing of the photographic paper.

◄ ● ►

The bedroom next to her mother's was the only locked room in the entire house.

Suze tried each of the heavy iron keys one by one until the tumbler turned and the door groaned open.

Suze knew the room was Henry Lacey's. It was the grandest bedroom in the whole house, the only one with double doors, a giant bed and tall casement windows overlooking the front entry. An important room. A room for a man who took himself seriously.

Yet there was something odd about it, something distasteful.

All the bedrooms on the first floor had been used for storage, converted into scrap heaps. The squirrelling away of junk in each one was evidence of some kind of ongoing process. Even her mother's room showed more recent signs of activity. Her armoire and drawers had been emptied and her bed stripped, presumably in preparation for her move to the Bosvenor Sanatorium.

But Henry Lacey's room was a time capsule.

Here, the immense wardrobes were still hung with rotting shreds of shirts, coats, jackets and trousers. Shoes, furry with blue-white mould lay underneath, carefully arranged and undisturbed. Each and every drawer was piled with decomposing clothing that writhed with earwigs, silverfish and woodlice. The bed was still made, its pillows and sheets filthy with years of dust, soot and mouse droppings.

Suze felt the bile rise in her throat. If there was treasure here, the room could keep it.

She thought of the photograph – of Henry Lacey's scratched-out eyes.

Her mother had left his room the way it had always been.

Not in his memory.

But because she could never bear to step inside.

14

'THIS IS ALL A BIT SHADY, ISN'T IT?'

SUZE AND HARLAN fell into a loose working schedule. Every weekday, he arrived early and struck the iron knocker with the curly-headed god firmly against the front door, then waited patiently to be admitted. He waited even if it rained, or the wind made a mess of his hair. He'd surprised Suze once before and nearly got himself shot into the bargain. He wouldn't surprise her again.

Harlan would set to work in the study, reading, sorting and cataloguing for probate. The transistor radio Suze bought from the camping store found a home on her grandfather's desk. They mostly listened to Radio 1 but sometimes switched to Radio 2, Radio 4 or Radio Cornwall. Harlan showed her where the shipping forecast was on the dial and explained the meaning of its strange monologue. Here on her own, it was important she knew what the weather was doing, he had explained. Suze removed the veil from the bust of

Pavlov and stored it in her room. She searched each of the bedrooms thoroughly, finding little but old furniture and a burgeoning pile of dilapidated household effects. If any artefact showed the slightest promise of value, she brought it to Harlan who catalogued it and set it aside in the room with the séance table that served as a vestibule and now, their *treasury*.

Together, they checked the flue to the fireplace in the study then lit homely fires of waste paper, broken furniture and coal.

She began to appreciate his company. He worked quietly. She made tea on the Calor gas stove for the both of them and the day was punctuated with occasional conversations over the rim of chipped mugs from the house's capacious kitchen.

'Aren't you a bit old to be a junior?' Suze asked during one such break from work. They sat at the desk in the study.

Harlan responded with a choked laugh. Suze's directness often caught him by surprise. 'Well, I've led a chequered life,' he responded.

'Doing what?'

He searched the ceiling, gathering the various strands of his past together. 'Well, I started off with a double degree from Exeter.'

Suze gave an impressed look. 'In?'

'History and antiquarianism.'

'Anti-what?'

'Antiquarianism – the study of antiquity, and antiques.'

'Wow,' murmured Suze.

'Wow, indeed,' confessed Harlan. 'I thought I'd land a job at Sotheby's straight away. I had dreams of becoming a valuer.'

'And did you?'

'No such luck.' Harlan sighed. 'It's not an industry that's easy to break into. In the end I returned to Storm Bay with my tail between my legs.' He drained his mug, set it down, then collected his pen and notepad from the desk. 'I took a course in cabinet-making and antique restoration. In the end I got to enter the world of antiques, but from the craftsman's side.' He rose and ambled over to the tall bookshelves, opening his notebook. 'I loved it, working with my hands, fixing stuff, bringing old things back to their former glory. But it doesn't pay very well.' He drew a long breath. 'So I retrained again, for a job with better pay, a job with more – *headroom.*'

'The law?' offered Suze.

Harlan nodded. 'That's why I came to the law later than most. And without a legal degree.'

'And now you're working your way up, to what – a solicitor?'

'That's the plan. Have to study first, get my qualifications and serve my time as the oldest paralegal in the business.' He removed a book and opened it.

'I guess having some knowledge of antiques would help with *all this*.' Her eyes scanned the library.

'It's why Ava gives me the these jobs – going through people's old stuff. I honestly think I'm more valuable to her doing this than being a solicitor.' He flashed her a grin.

Suze watched him work while she finished her tea. Methodically, he removed book after book from the shelves, inspected their inside covers, jotted an entry into the notebook, then replaced them. 'What are you looking for?' she asked.

'I'm cataloguing the library.' His gaze swept the room. 'You never know, there might be a first edition here, or something collectable.'

'That's a lot of books,' said Suze, taking in the packed shelves.

'It's got to be done. Should take me a week or two,' he confirmed. 'Then I'll finish with the rest of the documents in the alcove and you'll have finished going through the rest of the place.'

'And that'll be it?'

'Pretty much,' said Harlan. 'I'll put a rough value on everything and submit my report to Ava. She'll likely get an independent valuer to double-check anything we think is valuable. Then an estate agent will value the property, and we can put a sum total against the entire estate.'

Suze frowned. This had already been explained to her by Ava. The value of the land, the house, and everything inside it would then be declared to Inland Revenue. They'd calculate the Inheritance Tax and Suze would get stung with a bill before anything came to her. It didn't seem fair.

'Do you think,' began Suze, 'there might be enough left over, after the tax I mean, for me to rescue this place, to keep it?'

Harlan offered her a sad look. He made no answer. He didn't need to.

'So, what we've found isn't enough?'

Harlan shook his head. 'Not yet. Just have to keep looking, I guess.'

Suze curled her hand into a fist and gave the desktop a soft thump. 'It'd be nice to find a shoebox filled with cash under one of the beds.'

'It'd need to be *a lot* of cash.'

'Even just enough to get me by,' said Suze.

Harlan tilted his head in sympathy. 'What if I could help with that…?'

'With what?' Suze met his gaze.

'Help you *get by*.'

'Go on.'

'It's a secret though,' said Harlan.

'Okay.'

'You'll have to promise not to tell anyone.'

'Sure – I promise,' said Suze with uncertainty.

Harlan cocked his head towards the door that led into the great hall beyond. It was an invitation. 'C'mon,' he said.

Mystified, Suze rose and followed him into the hall. 'I spotted this the first day I was here,' said Harlan, crossing the space to stand before the wall hung with old paintings. He pointed at one. Suze followed his outstretched finger to a small painting of a horse. The horse's coat shone in the painted sunlight, its detail luminous against the stylised pastoral background. In contrast, the horse's legs looked to be painted by a child: impossibly thin, too short and incorrectly jointed. To Suze the painting looked unremarkable. 'Do you think anyone would miss that?' asked Harlan.

'Not me,' said Suze. 'I hate it.'

'Good,' said Harlan. He reached out and removed the painting from the wall.

'Is it worth something?' asked Suze.

'That's what I plan to find out, if you're okay with that?'

'Sure, go ahead,' she replied.

'It's a Frobisher,' explained Harlan, studying the painting in his hands. 'Not exactly a Stubbs, but it could be worth something, could be worth a lot more if you had time to go to auction. I have a few contacts. I'll ask around. I could get that old pistol valued, too.'

'I'm happy to wait,' said Suze. She wanted to prolong the inevitable countdown. She suspected that as soon as Harlan was gone she'd be pining for company. She loved this house, but it was too big for one person. 'Are any of the others worth anything?' Her gaze ran hopefully over the paintings still hanging on the wall.

'Perhaps, not much though, mostly unknown artists.' He held the Frobisher up to the light. 'But the beauty of *this* is not many people would know its value.'

'So no one would know it's gone?' added Suze.

'Exactly,' said Harlan. 'Hopefully it's even evaded Ava's eagle eye.'

Suze looked from the painting to Harlan's face. 'Why are you doing this?'

A grin of conspiracy lit his features.

'I mean, this is all a bit *shady*, isn't it?' asked Suze.

'Depends how you look at it,' Harlan went on. 'I believe it's *your* painting. If the taxman misses out on a few quid, I won't lose any sleep. I'm happy to be guilty of a small accounting error and forget to catalogue it. As long as this stays between us. I just think you deserve a break.'

'Thanks Harlan,' said Suze. As usual her tone carried no emotion. But she meant it.

Harlan seemed to catch the sincerity in her eyes. 'My pleasure,' he replied.

15

L'Enfant Caché

THE WEEKEND ARRIVED and Saturday morning dappled the treeless landscape with sunshine. The wind flattened the clifftop grasses and shunted clouds across the bay. Suze stood in her grandfather's study, watching the flying patchwork of light and shade race across the eastern moors. The day was cold, but at least it was sunny.

Harlan wouldn't return until Monday and Suze was at a loss. She'd grown used to having him around.

She ate a bowl of cereal, drank instant coffee and imagined Harlan busy on her behalf today, finding a purchaser for the portrait of the horse, or valuing the old pistol. She made a half-hearted attempt at sorting the dwindling heap of paperwork in the alcove. She reminded herself that she still didn't know what she was looking for and that she might even be disturbing Harlan's system.

She looked again through the study window. Rather than waste the day in the house's gloom, she decided to enjoy the day outside.

She made her way to her bedroom and collected the box with the wedding dress inside. She thought about placing the veil inside too, but changed her mind. She'd keep the veil here. She had plans for it.

Throwing on her coat, she scooped up the box and trudged two miles to the bus stop in Storm Bay.

The bell above the door tinkled.

'I'll be with you d'rectly!' came the shout from deep inside Kerenza's Bridal Couture.

Suze moved inside and waited.

'Oh, 'tis you again,' said the same young woman, appearing from the back of the shop.

'I brought my mother's dress,' said Suze.

'Let's 'ave a look then,' said the young woman, leading Suze to a cutting table. She cleared away bolts of white fabric, dressmaking scissors and ring-binder files thick with dress designs. Suze put down the box and opened the lid. The young woman removed the dress, spreading it across the table. In contrast with every shining fold and pleat of material in the shop, the dress looked dirty, damaged and pitiful. The young woman's expression hardened. She tutted quietly a moment, flipped the dress inside out and looked closely at its seams and stitching.

'Looks like Kerenza's work to me,' confirmed the young woman, her attention buried in the dress.

'Great,' sighed Suze.

The young woman looked up, eyes narrowing. 'I normally see her of a Sunday. I can go tomorrow. But it'll break her heart to see one of her old dresses come to this.'

'I'm sorry about that. Can you still ask her about it?'

'I'll try. But not if it upsets her, mind.'

'I understand.'

'What d'you want to know?'

'Anything at all really – who ordered it, when it was made? I'm trying to find out if there was ever a wedding, and who was married.'

The young woman placed a hand on her hip and studied Suze. 'You'd best inquire at the Registry of Births, Marriages and Deaths.'

'I've tried.' Suze sighed.

'Or check the parish records at the church,' continued the young woman.

Suze's mind raced. *If any wedding had been planned it could have been a church wedding. But which church?*

'I'll do what I can,' said the young woman, returning to the dress. 'But if she's not up to it...'

'Of course.'

'Pop in next week sometime. I'll let you know.'

Suze muttered her thanks and turned to leave.

The young woman gave a small cry, half in astonishment, half in laughter. 'Be damned,' she said.

Suze looked round. The young woman was studying the dress. ''Aven't seen nothing like this in years. Clever ol' Kerenza!' She beckoned Suze over. 'Look 'ere, the waist is higher than usual and these diagonal panels, see?' She pointed at the inside front of the dress, where a lattice of broad strips offered support below the waistline. 'Couturiers call this *L'Enfant Caché.*' Her Cornish accent made a rounded parody of the French. '*The Hidden Child,*' she explained with a broad grin. 'Whoever wore this dress was *pregnant*.'

* * *

So her mother had been pregnant at the time – with Suze?

Other possibilities unravelled, like bolts of cloth tumbling from a cutting table.

Whoever the father was may have stood Emma up at the last moment. And the Laceys, haughty with pride, gave Suze to a foster home rather than face the scandal.

Such cowardice where there should have been mercy, love.

Is this what had sent her mother mad? The guilt? Grief for a lost child?

On the other hand, perhaps it was Emma who'd done the standing up. She may have run away from an unsuitable match. Or, at the last minute she decided that her lover, having made her pregnant, was an unsuitable travelling companion for the long, hard road of marriage.

Suze frowned. Was she nothing more than the result of a casual fling, some dirty little tryst?

Injustice and self-doubt strained against the hinges of the aquamarine suitcase.

Lock it away.

The trouble with either line of thinking was that her father was either a runaway groom, or a womaniser. Not someone she'd be proud to know, or want to find. Worse than that, it painted her mother as weak, selfish, and a slave to appearances.

Even if this was true, it still didn't explain her mother's fixation with the wedding dress. Why obsess over a dress she didn't want to wear? There had to be another explanation, a different truth. Had she grieved for a lost love? Had their union been censored?

She thought of the man at the bottom of the stairs. His feet facing backwards.

The bus wove its way along narrow roads that led back to Storm Bay. Through the window of the upper deck she could see above the tall hedges across a winter landscape of bracken the colour of rust and leafless trees that stretched dark branches to the sky. The day was bright and still not spent. The wind had died. She wanted to think of other things.

Stepping down from the bus in Storm Bay, she turned along the main street and passed the signpost for the library.

Ava's words came to mind. *There's a library in the town with accounts of all the wrecks. You should take a visit. Grim reading though.*

Suze mulled this over, her eyes fixed absently on the sign. Libraries were storehouses of local knowledge. This one should be no different. Here she might find the history of Aeolus House, the Laceys, and her mother. Suze checked her wristwatch: *three o'clock.*

She didn't need to think. Her feet began walking in the direction of the sign.

The library was quite different from the older, quainter stone buildings that lined the main street of Storm Bay. Instead, it was modern-ish, squat, box-like and made from nineteen-sixties concrete with a flat roof and white Venetian blinds in the windows. It also stood on a side street, the one which led to the caravan park. It was as if the locals wanted the offensive architecture hidden.

Suze pulled open the heavy entry door and found herself inside an exhibition of polished linoleum, pine furniture and brown carpet. It smelled of old books and floor polish. She crossed the reception area where a small, middle-aged woman sat behind the returns counter sorting books. Her hair was raked into a tight little parcel at the back of her head and she wore reading glasses suspended from a gold chain around her neck. She blinked rapidly over the rims of her glasses, watching Suze pass. Suspicious glances from locals were something Suze was becoming used to. Even though she was born here, she'd always be an outsider.

In the library's main room, she found a section marked 'Local History' and browsed for a while. Above a waist-high bookshelf, an old nautical chart ran across the wall. It marked the sites of all the wrecks in Storm Bay. Below it were books recounting the history of the wrecks, and chronicles of Storm Bay's more infamous forms of commerce: smuggling, piracy and wrecking.

She leaned close, squinting at the chart. She found the island and narrow isthmus of Klegger Dhu in the very centre, but no evidence of the house on the cliff above it. The chart must be older than the house, or concerned itself only with matters of the sea.

'Is there anything I can help you with?' came a voice from behind her.

Suze turned to see the diminutive woman with the tight bun in her hair. Suze read a label pinned to her cardigan: *Nola*.

'Oh, I'm just interested in the history of the place, actually,' said Suze in reply.

'Anything in particular?' Nola smiled.

'Well,' began Suze, turning to the nautical chart. 'What can you tell me about this place?' She stabbed a finger at the island.

The woman lifted the reading glasses suspended from her neck and placed them over the bridge of her nose. She leaned towards the chart, squinting. 'Ah, Klegger Dhu,' she said. Then she stood bolt upright, fixing Suze with widening eyes. 'So you'd be the new owner of Aeolus House!'

Suze felt her eyebrows lift. 'Hadn't realised I was that famous.'

Nola laughed. 'Oh, don't worry none, 'tis a small town, word spreads like jam here.'

'Obviously,' observed Suze.

'Klegger Dhu is an iron-age holy site,' Nola continued.

'Is that why there's an old chapel there?' asked Suze.

'It's no chapel. It's a cell, built by the Irish monks who brought Christianity to Cornwall.'

'A cell? Like a prison?'

'More of a hermitage,' explained Nola. 'It was home to Saint Carras the Anchorite. He was a monk who chose to shut himself away from the world and dedicate his life to prayer. After his death there, he was made a saint.'

'Lonely place to spend your life,' said Suze, her eyes on the chart.

'That was the idea.' Nola smiled. 'That's why it's such a holy place, though many believe it's haunted.'

Suze shot Nola a dark look.

'But that's just local superstition, before Saint Carras it was a *joining place*, a kind of pagan marriage site. Couples were sworn together there, under pain of death.' Nola pointed at the map. 'And there's a cave *here*.'

'I know,' said Suze.

'Oh, have you seen it?'

'No,' said Suze.

'Well, if you choose to take a look, just be careful. The cliffs are deadly. The cave has a reputation, too – was used by local wreckers long ago as a place to hide their spoils. Been a lot of bloodshed on this stretch of coast over the years.'

'And do you know anything of Aeolus House, of the people who lived there?' asked Suze.

'Your family, the Laceys?'

Suze felt her cheeks colour. She didn't think of herself as a Lacey and perhaps never would, but she couldn't deny they were her family. 'Yes,' she said. 'Is there any record of them here?'

'Well, all I know is that old man Lacey was a big-shot doctor of some kind.'

'Henry Lacey?' asked Suze.

'That's him. Something of a local celebrity, he were. Even wrote a few books.'

'Do you keep any here?' asked Suze.

Nola offered an embarrassed smile. 'We like to reserve our shelf space for lighter reading – crime, mystery, romance and such. We've a reference section of course, but it's very general.'

'So you don't keep any of his books?'

'Sorry, no.'

Suze frowned.

'But I can see if we can order copies from the County Library in Truro?'

Suze's expression brightened. 'Really?'

'Let's take a look,' said Nola, heading back to the returns desk.

She cast eyes over an index card cabinet housing a multitude of tiny drawers, then removed one. Turning to Suze, she leafed through the cards, lifted one free and read aloud. 'Well, there's only one publication of his on record.' She pushed her reading glasses to the very top of her nose. '*On the Pavlovian Principle of Behavioural Conditioning and Therapy of Aversion. Author: Doctor Henry Lacey.* Sounds like heavy reading.' Nola's expression fell. 'But it's out of print and the library doesn't keep a copy. Sorry.'

Suze pursed her lips. 'Pity.'

Nola offered a sympathetic smile.

Pavlovian? Suze pictured the bust of Pavlov in her grandfather's study. 'Do you have anything here on Pavlov?' she asked.

Nola considered. 'Well, as I said, we have a general reference section. There's bound to be something in science. But you'll have to become a member.'

'Okay.'

While Suze filled out the short membership application, Nola searched the shelves. She came back with a weighty hard-backed volume. Along its spine ran the title *A History of Twentieth Century Science*. Nola stamped the book and handed it to Suze. 'So, what you going to do with the place?'

Suze handed her the completed form. She knew that any admission to Nola would be as confidential as an advert in the Western Morning News. 'Don't know yet,' she lied.

Nola's eyes narrowed as she handed Suze a temporary membership card. 'Well, you just be careful near them cliffs.'

16

'WHAT DO YOU WANT ME TO SEE?'

OF ALL the questions Suze had asked Harlan, one remained.

It had nothing to do with probate, antiques, his past, or why he was the oldest junior in the legal profession.

It was why he looked so similar to the man at the bottom of the stairs.

She could never ask him such a question. She'd sound crazy.

Yet the two men were connected to each other somehow, to this house, to her mother's story and her own.

And she had no way of understanding how or why.

Sunday morning found her alone in Aeolus House. She was in her room, the room that was once her mother's. A new question began to drag at her like gravity. *Did she trust Harlan*? She thought she did. The fact he'd offered to help her by valuing the Frobisher painting and not involve Ava demonstrated his kindness. Suze would have sniffed out any deceit in him, any darker motive. She felt sure. *But was he hiding anything from her?*

What she'd seen through the veil wasn't random. The veil was trying to show her something. Like the house, it wanted to *help*. It wanted her to see what her mother had seen.

Was it an answer? Or was it a warning?

Suze's stomach felt like a bottomless pit. She was plummeting headlong into it, that horrible, falling sensation of *fear* – fear of what she needed to do; fear of the only thing she *could* do under the circumstances. She needed answers. *Who was the stranger? Who was her father? Most of all, why had her mother given up on her?*

Suze told herself that what she was about to do was no different from reading a horoscope or placing a silver coin in the palm of a fairground fortune teller. It was just a way to understand the world by otherworldly means. The visions would be harmless, nothing more than recordings.

Crossing the room, she lifted the veil from the open cardboard box. She studied it for a moment, summoning courage, then flung the bedroom door wide and marched to the top of the stairs.

Trying not to think, to worry, to examine the consequences, she threw the transparent cloud of silk over her head and positioned the silver crown on top. She closed her eyes, steeling herself, then opened them on a pale, misted perspective of the hall below.

Nothing.

She waited.

Still nothing.

She let out a long breath. In a way, it was a relief. Minutes passed and there was no sign of the man at the foot of the stairs. She hadn't even considered what she'd do if she saw him. *Would she question him, follow his beckoning finger? What?*

The dark stranger's backward-facing feet she supposed could be a product of her mother's damaged mind. As a recording, it may not be accurate, not representative of anything real at all, just how her mother had perceived things, felt things.

For a good part of the morning, she stood at the top of the stairs with the veil drawn over her face. The house was hers and she wanted to experiment alone. She tried standing on the same step, in the same place, then other steps, other places. Nothing.

She called the same question into the vastness of the house, trying to summon the same feelings she'd felt on the day the vision appeared.

Still nothing.

Aimlessly, she wandered the ground floor with the veil in her hand. She moved through the entry hall to the north-facing viewing room with its dais, bay window and expansive view. She turned on the spot, her gaze sweeping the room. It came to rest on the wall-hung tapestry. She hadn't noticed its painstakingly embroidered design before. It was old and very discoloured, but wonderful.

On the tapestry was a scene of Klegger Dhu. The crested waves around the island and causeway may once have been stitched in sapphire blue, tipped with white silk. Now they clutched at the black cliffs in dull tones of navy and grey. The top of the island was a field of dusty green, at its centre an ostentatious and oversized representation of the monk's cell. It rose like a tower, disproportionately large, dwarfing the island on which it stood. At its foundations slept a unicorn with a golden crown. Through an arched window Suze could see a tonsured monk, kneeling in prayer. Above his elongated head was a halo ringed with light, and the words

Sanctus Carras Monachus Anachoreseos. St Carras, the Hermit of The Rock.

The tapestry was more than just a secret door that hid the way to the island beyond. It was a passage to the sacred. To Suze, the monk didn't seem lonely. It'd be easy for her to read this into the imagery, to see herself as the lone figure captive behind stone walls, isolated by rough seas. Instead, she saw sacrifice as a way to something greater.

That's what the tapestry meant. It was a sign. On the other side lay a pilgrim's path. A path to understanding through devotion.

Suze pulled back the heavy tapestry on its hinged rod and gazed into the cramped darkness beyond the open doorway. Something lay within, she felt sure of it. Holding the veil, she moved inside, letting the tapestry close behind her. On her own, the coal-black dark was more unnerving than before. She trusted in her knowledge of the gentle slope downwards, the smooth stone floor and the handrails on either side. She arrived at the heavy steel door and swung it open on its complaining hinges. Stepping through, she felt her way along the curve of the room to the handwheels on the wall. She turned the uppermost wheel and daylight reached into the room, casting a sharp image across the opposite wall of the bright day outside. Suze marvelled, lost in the splendour of the image for a while. She pulled the veil down over her face and waited. Whatever lay here would reveal itself soon, if she was patient.

For almost an hour she waited in different spots, gazed at the projection of the day outside and hoped. She closed the steel door, stood in the room's centre, on top of the hatch to the cave below.

Come on, what do you want me to see?

Whatever hid in this room was unwilling to reveal itself. Not today. Not like this.

Giving up, she shouted a curse at the ceiling and turned for the handwheels on the wall. She wound the wheel which covered the lens, protecting it from the elements outside, and the light in the room shrunk to darkness. Frustrated, and still wearing the veil across her face, she felt her way along the handrail to the door. As she reached it, a breath of air, soft as a whisper, moved across her face. From somewhere in the dark room came the quiet sounds of movement. 'Hello? Is someone there?' said Suze, instantly regretting her violation of the silence. Something moved towards her and her skin shrunk across her bones, chill with fear. Beyond the thin white mist of the veil she saw only blackness. Her breath came rapidly. She remained perfectly still, trying to calm herself. Then, as if blown upwards, the veil was lifted from her face, the mist of white giving way to an abyss of darkest black. There was no current of air, no draught that she could feel. The air in the room was perfectly still, yet the veil remained lifted from her face and hung there, motionless. She parted dry lips, her breathing now deathly shallow. Something was here.

Then she felt it.

Suze had been kissed before, but not like this. This was no act of possession, of claiming. There was no embrace of ownership, no arms around her, binding her. There was no hormonal clumsiness, no lust. No urgent, primal need. She only felt two slender hands cup her cheeks, lifting her face. The kiss was warm and she closed her eyes, leaning into it. It was a kiss of respect, of adoration.

A soulmate's kiss.

Too soon, the warm lips withdrew, then the slender hands, back into the darkness. Suze remained motionless, not wishing to break the enchantment. Then the veil floated down, back over her face.

Minutes passed but the lover in the shadows had gone. She pulled open the steel door with trembling hands and made her way back out into the light. Her heart hammered like bad plumbing.

— ● —

Suze stood in the viewing room, beside the tapestry, trying to reassemble her emotions. She felt broken and somehow remade at the same time. Everything she had pushed away or hidden from, everything that scared her, that she believed would end in pain now seemed trivial. The reward, however impermanent, was far greater than the risk. For rapture like this, any pain would be worth it. All she believed she ever knew about intimacy had been dismantled, picked apart, then pieced together into something new. Nothing inside the aquamarine suitcase compared to this. She had no means by which to measure it. This feeling, this sensation, glowed inside her with a brute naturalness that was old, raw, and so very *right*. Yet it shocked her how unknown, how distant from her it felt. It put the dark feelings to flight, absorbing and filling the space they left behind with light and warmth.

But this wasn't *her* feeling.

It was her mother's.

And her mother had been totally, desperately head-over-heels in love.

She knew this now.

But it wasn't the house that told her this.

After all these years, Emma Lacey was trying to explain.

Dazed, Suze walked through the house, the veil pulled back over her head. She left the viewing room with the storm shutters and meandered through the entry hall. At the bottom of the stairs she stopped and looked up towards the landing. This would have been the spot he stood in. Emma would've stood up there, wearing the veil and the dress, looking down.

She dropped the veil over her face in experiment. Would she now be standing right beside him? If so, would he kiss her again?

The veil revealed nothing. Suze sighed and turned for the study. She'd embarrass Pavlov by dressing him in the veil once more. Just for today. In a cruel way she found it amusing.

She walked mechanically, her mind elsewhere. Her downcast eyes saw only the toes of her shoes and the worn, threadbare carpet of the study.

A wave of something approaching nausea moved over her.

She halted, looking up. Something was here, too. But nothing like the presence she'd felt in the darkness of the camera obscura. Nothing about this feeling was good. It was malign, perverse, threatening rage and brutality.

Her eyes flew to the alcove in fear. Through the veil she saw it was closed now, the pedestal and bust standing centrally in front, the way her mother had seen it.

Something rumbled towards her, ominous and terrifying: the sound of engines of torture at work behind walls. The presence came at her slowly, as if from a long way off, yet its source seemed to emanate from a point behind the bust of Pavlov, behind the alcove.

She was standing in the path of something terrible, a leviathan bent on cruelty and torment. It thundered closer, unstoppable, and a sickening paralysis seized her.

She knew its name now.

Dread.

Dread gripped her throat and crushed the air from her chest. Dread screamed in her ears and racked her body. It shook her senses and flooded every corner of her mind with the most uncontrollable terror. The alcove, the pedestal and the bust warped and contorted through the veil as dread roared through her, around her.

She turned away, seeking refuge in the view through the study window.

The room stretched into a confusion of unnatural angles. It grew gigantic, dwarfing her. A mad, hissing sound filled her ears. Outside the window the bright day was gone. The sky swirled, a bloodshot maelstrom of purple, black and red, veined with lightning. The Scots pine, twisted and bent, now hung, uprooted in the menacing sky. It revolved slowly, a silhouette, trailing dark roots in dark air. The scene was that of another world, a ghastly, storm-lashed landscape, a place fixed in nightmare.

Suze tore the veil from her face and fell to her knees. Dread released its grip on her throat and she drew in lungfuls of air. It seemed to pull back, to retreat to its place within the alcove. She cast a frightened look after it. If the tapestry of St Carras stood at the doorway of all that was sacred, then the alcove stood at the gates to perdition. No longer wearing the veil, she saw the alcove was open and strewn with papers, just as she'd left it. She looked in the other direction, towards the window facing the eastern moors. Through it, the day was bright with sunshine again.

What she had just seen was a window of a very different kind.

A window that framed her mother's worst fears.

A window through which she could now see her mother's madness.

17

'IS THIS GOING TO BE DANGEROUS?'

SUZE'S SPIRITS LIFTED at the sound of the curly-headed god hammering on the front door. Monday morning ushered in a return to routine, and Harlan was back at Aeolus House.

The events of the weekend had left Suze with more questions. Unnoticed by Harlan, she studied his face as he pulled off his overcoat. She tried to picture the man at the foot of the stairs. She'd only seen him for a moment. Had she imagined the similarity between he and Harlan? The resemblance had struck her with so much force, but now she doubted herself. The man's face was beginning to fade in her memory and she was no longer sure. In the darkness of the camera obscura she'd seen nothing to convince her otherwise.

Harlan was quieter than usual. He resumed the work of cataloguing the books in the study with such fixed concentration that Suze felt he was avoiding her. Something was bothering him.

'You okay?' she asked.

Harlan turned to her with an apologetic smile. 'Suze, there's something we need to discuss...'

Intrigue sparked inside her.

'I spoke with Ava this morning,' said Harlan. He took a deep breath. 'Bosvenor have started thinking about the arrangements for your mother, once they've finished their – *examination.*'

Suze knew that *examination* was code for *post-mortem.* He was being delicate. He was trying to save her pain.

'They've recommended a funeral director and wanted to know if you'd any requirements?'

'Requirements?'

'Anyone you'd like to invite, order of service, hymns, that sort of thing.'

Suze shook her head.

'What kind of service, then? Religious, non-religious?'

Religion? Belief, the Afterlife? These were things Suze never found room to fit inside her head. She'd always been consumed by the questions she needed answers to in *this life, this world.* The larger questions of life and death had been elsewhere. Now she was facing them, for her mother, for herself, and she had no idea what she believed. She thought of the visions she'd seen through the veil, images see couldn't explain. The world had flipped like a pancake and the universe was now more vast and more complicated than she'd ever known. These visions – they were just recordings. This is what made most sense to her. This is what she wanted to believe. The alternative made her feel small. And scared.

'Suze?'

Her attention returned to him. 'Sorry?'

'What kind of *service*?'

'I've no idea.'

Harlan's unease hung in the library. 'Bosvenor have suggested a cremation at Bodmin. Then a non-denominational service and interment at the church here in Storm Bay.'

'A cremation?' asked Suze.

'All the Laceys are cremated. It's been a family tradition,' explained Harlan. 'And their ashes are all here at St Carras.'

'St Carras?'

'The local church.' Harlan let the information sink in. 'You may want to talk this through with Reverend Tonkin. He's the vicar there.'

Suze flinched from a memory. *Or check the parish records at the church* – the words of the young couturier at Kerenza's. Would this be the place her mother had intended to marry? Would this vicar, this *Reverend Tonkin* know anything?

'It'll be a respectful service, but economical,' Harlan continued. 'And don't worry. Ava said she'll cover the costs for now.'

Suze blew out a sigh. She felt the burden of her debt grow heavier.

'I know this is a lot to take in. Perhaps you'd like to think it over?'

Suze looked up. 'I need air. Walk with me?'

———◄•►———

They walked from the lee of the house towards the cliff, in long grass between clumps of campion flower and tamarisk.

Being outdoors helped. The bright, blustery day blew away thoughts of cremations and church services. Suze lifted her eyes to the wide seascape rising in front of her from the top of the cliff. Her foot struck something solid in the long grass and she pitched forward, almost falling. She turned, searching for an offending rock or tree root. 'What the hell is this?' she asked, bending down and removing a short stake embedded in the ground. The wood of the stake was new, unweathered, and was painted bright blue.

'No idea,' said Harlan. He swept the fringe from his face as if about to look at the stake more closely. His eyes never rested on it. He glanced away, towards the sea.

Suze studied him, then tossed the stake into the long grass and dusted her hands. 'How odd,' she said.

Harlan hummed an agreement.

Near the cliff edge they found the coastal path with its broad track of ruts and furrows worn by the boots of campers and hikers. From here, the view over the wide bay was spectacular. The wind whipped the sea into a frenzy of whitecaps and catapulted shrieking, stiff-winged gulls across the sky. Beyond the path the cliff plummeted to the sea. Suze wanted to take a closer look and led Harlan to the edge. Even on a calm day it would be putting your life at risk, but today the wind felt like murderous hands, jostling, shoving you along, pushing you over.

'Be careful!' shouted Harlan, above the wind.

'Look,' shouted Suze in return. She pointed below them to the squat, pillbox-shaped structure of stone, painted in flaking white. The seaward corner of the building was visible, crouching for shelter against the shoulder of the cliff.

'Yes, that's the old pilchard hut,' said Harlan, standing closer.

'It's a room for a camera obscura now,' said Suze. 'Have you seen inside?'

'No, but I heard about it.'

'I can show you.'

'Great. I should check it for the record,' said Harlan.

Suze studied the old stone hut. 'How the hell did the fishermen ever get to it?'

Harlan pointed. 'There's a path, further along.'

They climbed back up to the coast path through billowing grass and into the full fury of the wind. A hundred yards along the path was a junction. Here, a narrower path of loose rocks and rutted soil led down to the rolling edge of the cliff. 'It goes all the way down to Klegger Dhu,' shouted Harlan.

Suze turned, taking this new direction down to the hut. Her heels skidded over the loose stones in the centre of the path. She quickly adjusted her technique, walking along the edges of the path, using larger stones and tufts of grass to slow her descent. Harlan called something she couldn't hear, then shook his head and followed her. Below the clifftop the path turned back along a more gentle gradient towards the hut. Suze followed it and arrived at the hut minutes later. Waiting for Harlan, she studied the external workings of the camera obscura. A large disc of pitted black steel now covered the recess that hid the lens, no doubt operated by one of the handwheels inside. Harlan caught up and Suze pointed downwards along a steeper, narrower path that disappeared from view below them. 'Is that the way down to Klegger Dhu?' she asked.

Harlan nodded. He looked scared by what Suze might do next.

'The fishermen had it easy,' said Suze, still looking at the path leading down. 'I take my hat off to that old monk. He must've been a mountain goat.' She turned to Harlan. 'I want to see it. I want to go down there.'

Before Harlan could protest, Suze began the descent. Maintaining balance with outstretched hands, she slid more than walked down the precipitous trail. The island of Klegger Dhu came into view, its causeway still obscured below the cliff. Suze stopped to marvel at it, taking in a long breath. The island was a natural wonder. Dark rock towering above the boiling sea. Suze tried to imagine what it would have been like to live there, in the constant violence of the wind and the thunder of the ocean. She pictured the stone cell, small and crudely built, not like the one embroidered on the tapestry. She imagined it in the tumult of a storm, huge waves arching over the isle, over the roof of the monk's cell. She shuddered at the thought.

Harlan skidded to a halt beside her. 'Suze, we should turn back.' His voice was edged with alarm.

She looked towards the isthmus and the island. Harlan had started this. He was the one who'd raised today's questions of burial and belief, religion and the afterlife. She wanted to follow in the footsteps of the saint. She wanted to explore this sacred site that now belonged to her. She threw Harlan a reproachful look and continued down the path.

Her descent became faster now. It was almost impossible to check her speed. The safest way seemed to be hopping from side to side, not to resist the slip and slide upon the stones of the path. She took her eyes off her feet, off the path for a moment to see a looming bend, a sudden right-angle. The lapse in concentration cost her. Her heels flew out from under her on the loose stones and she went down hard, hands behind her to break the fall.

When Harlan caught up to her, she'd rolled to one side, examining her bleeding palms. He knelt beside her, his face dark with concern. 'You okay?'

'I think so, just winded,' said Suze, her palms burning.

Harlan helped her to her feet and dusted her off. Then, supporting her, his arm under hers, he led her back to the top of the cliff. The climb back was far harder than she'd anticipated. She should have realised. Every two steps forward meant a slide back. They walked along the verges of the path as much as they could, hauling themselves upwards by handfuls of cliff grass.

At the top Suze turned, panting, to gaze back at the island. 'I really wanted to get down there,' she said.

'Why?'

She turned to him. 'I don't really know. Just a feeling. It's part of the estate, right? It's such a special place. There might even be something down there. Don't you want to take a look?'

Harlan shrugged.

'It'd be an adventure,' Suze suggested.

'You're out of your mind,' said Harlan. A fleeting smile lifted the corner of his mouth.

The white signage of Bosvenor Sanatorium flashed in her memory. *Perhaps it runs in the family*, thought Suze.

— ◆ —

Her palms stung in the bowl of warm water and antiseptic. She drew

153

in a sharp breath. Harlan lifted her hands from the water, turned them over, and gently dabbed away spots of dirt and clotted blood with cotton wool.

His own hands were slender, with long fingers. Like the man at the foot of the stairs, like the hands that cupped her face in the darkness of the camera obscura. She watched him while his attention was focused on her injuries. Unlike Suze, he didn't hide his sensitivity. She liked that about him. It was commendable in a man. Her own feelings scared her. That's why she'd locked them away so long ago, safe inside an aquamarine suitcase where they'd never make her vulnerable. But the events of the last few days had changed her. Something had shifted inside. She'd denied herself so much just to be free of the pain others might inflict. Yet her denial was buried so deep it seemed ingrained and unchangeable.

His long fringe fell over his eyes as he tended her. She considered brushing it back. It was the merest instinct, unbidden, and the thought surprised her.

Who are you Harlan Grey?

Until she knew, knew for certain, she'd need to keep her distance. She was drawn to him in a way she couldn't fathom. Whether it was just the normal forces of attraction at work or whether their bond was more familial, she couldn't tell. Did the blood that coursed inside them come from a common ancestor? Was their history shared? All Suze knew was that she liked having him around. And she wanted things to stay that way.

'There might be another way to get down there,' said Harlan, drying her hands in a soft towel.

'I'm sorry?' said Suze, her train of thought derailed.

He looked up. 'There might be another way to get to Klegger Dhu. If that's what you really want.'

'I do,' said Suze in earnest.

'Then I need to pick up some things from the camping shop – before it closes,' he said, checking his wristwatch.

'Okay,' said Suze, unsure. Whatever his plan, it sounded outdoorsy, adventurous. 'Is this going to be dangerous?'

'Almost certainly.' He smirked.

'Good,' replied Suze.

18

THE PIRATE'S CATHEDRAL

SUZE WAS INTRIGUED by the previous day's announcement that Harlan had a plan to get them down to Klegger Dhu, but she hadn't pushed him for an explanation.

She imagined him at the camping shop, locked in discussion with the walrus-moustached, camouflage-wearing owner. Harlan would be convinced to trade up, the way she had. She pictured him returning with military-grade grappling irons, bridge-building equipment, cables, ziplines and rope ladders.

The reality was only a little less extraordinary.

Today Harlan appeared with a lengthy coil of white rope over his shoulder, in his hand were a few items of climbing gear. 'It's on loan,' he explained. He wore a light rain jacket with a hood.

'Are we going climbing?' asked Suze.

'More like pot-holing,' said Harlan with a nervous smile.

She followed him from the front door into the stormwatchers' viewing room. He stood near the tapestry of St Carras on the rock of

Klegger Dhu. 'Ava said there's a kind of secret passage or something?' He gazed in wonder at the tapestry.

'We'll need a torch,' said Suze, heading from the room to go look.

'And throw on a pair of jeans and some track shoes!' shouted Harlan, after her.

———◆———

Suze studied Harlan's open-mouthed amazement at the image projected inside the camera obscura. She recalled her own reaction the first time she'd seen it.

'That's incredible,' he murmured. Then he turned to her, his face lit with boyish wonder. 'It's even better than looking at the real thing.'

He was right, something about the projection was magical. They were standing in a darkened room, yet by way of enchantment the bright day had been brought inside. The scenery cast against the wall was a copy, yet it seemed more vibrant, more captivating than the original.

'I don't think there's anything of value here – for probate,' said Suze, looking around at the broken chairs and side tables.

'No, suppose not,' offered Harlan, eyes still on the colourful image of the bay beyond the walls of the circular stone room.

'So what's the rope for?'

Her question jolted Harlan back to the present. He looked round, his eyes finding the hatch in the centre of the room. 'So this is the way down, right?'

'Uh-huh.'

Harlan swung the rope from his shoulder and deposited the climbing gear. 'We'll drop the climbing rope into the cave. Help me open this.'

Together, they strained against the handles of the steel hatch. The rust that sealed it gave way and it opened with a groan of stiff hinges. A sudden blast of cold sea air hit them. It smelled of salt and rotting seaweed from the cave. Harlan knelt, shining a torch into the darkness below. A short flight of steps led down to a landing of metal grating. From it, a steel ladder attached to the wall of the cave dropped out of sight.

'We'll secure the rope to something up here,' he said, looking around the room. His eyes rested on the metal door to the camera room. He tied one end of the rope to its heavy steel handle and threw the rest into the cave. It uncoiled into the blackness. 'Now, the plan is, we go down the ladder. The rope is just for safety.' He buckled a climber's belt around Suze's waist and clipped a long nylon sling into its carabiner. At the end of the sling was a strange clamp with a handle. 'This is a *jumar clamp*. It clips onto the rope like this.' He demonstrated. 'As you move down, pull in the handle and it'll slide down the rope. Release the handle and it'll lock in place. If you slip, it'll hold you. I'll go first.'

Securing his own belt and fitting a jumar clamp to the rope, Harlan stepped down through the hatch and stood on the steel platform below. He gave a few tentative jumps then grinned upwards. 'It's fine, come on down.' He moved to the ladder, making way for her. As she stepped down onto the platform, he tugged at the ladder. 'Seems okay,' he said, swinging himself onto the topmost rungs.

It was far colder in the cave than Suze had anticipated. It was like being locked inside a vast, echoing refrigerator. The wind funnelled through the cave from the sea, moaning as it slid over dripping rock. It blew upwards, against them, as if in opposition to their descent. The metal rungs of the ladder were cold against Suze's hands and she wished she'd thought of wearing gloves. She also reproached herself for not thinking to wear a rain jacket like Harlan. Step by step, rung by rung, she became used to the rhythm of the jumar clamp and the downward motion of her own body. *Release. Step. Clamp. Release. Step. Clamp.* Below, she could hear Harlan's breathing. He called up to her from time to time, offering encouragement, or assuring her that the ladder was sound. Pitted flakes of rust from the rungs dug into the wounds on her hands. She could hear the pounding of the waves against the cliffs now. Shards of daylight skipped off wet rock. Her arms began to ache but the ladder stretched downwards without end. The cave would be hundreds of feet deep. Harlan gave a sudden whoop of triumph and she looked down to see the beam of his torch flash over rock beneath his feet.

'I can see the entrance!' he shouted.

Twenty or thirty rungs later, Suze stood on the cave floor beside him. Ahead, she could see a narrow fissure of daylight slanting upwards across the darkness. It framed the wave-lashed causeway and Klegger Dhu beyond. Despite her chattering teeth, Suze felt a surge of joy.

Harlan flashed his torch around their feet, guiding them over rocks and wet sand. Suze ran her own torch across the stone walls and into corners, partly out of intrigue but mostly from fear of what the dark might be hiding. No passages appeared to lead away from the main cave. As the light grew, the immensity of the cave revealed itself. It was a vast, ringing cavern of vaulted stone – a ship's graveyard, a wrecker's treasury, a pirate's cathedral.

They emerged into the shade of the towering cliff. Even without direct sunlight, even with the wind now whipping about them, Suze felt warmer. Below the face of the cliff the causeway was a wide shelf of rock that narrowed along its path towards Klegger Dhu. They walked quickly at first, keen to make it out of the shadow into sunlight. As they did, the wind increased and the causeway became a narrow, rounded ridgeline of slippery rock. Suze had always thought the metal ladder and the descent into the dark, wet cave would be the greater danger. From the cliff above, the causeway looked passable, safe. Now that she was standing on it, she realised that a trip or stumble could send her rolling over the edge with nothing to cling to, into the violence of waves crashing against rocks below.

'You okay about this?' asked Harlan.

'Sure,' she said, hoping to appear unconcerned.

'I'll go first,' he said. 'Just look straight ahead and follow me. Don't stop.' He walked across the narrow strip of rock to the foot of a natural staircase and turned. He beckoned her.

She stepped along the narrow ridge to join Harlan. It wasn't that difficult, just a simple walk in a straight line, the kind a person would make a thousand times a day. It was only the prospect of the deadly plunge to either side that made it such a challenge.

Harlan smiled and turned for the stone steps. A short climb later they were standing on a level expanse of clifftop grass. Harlan wheeled in the wind, arms outstretched, then turned to face her. The wind ballooned his rain jacket and thrashed his hood from side to side. 'Welcome to Klegger Dhu!' he announced.

Suze couldn't deny the sense of achievement she felt in reaching the place. 'I wonder how many people have ever been here, apart from us?' she shouted.

'Well, *one* at least,' replied Harlan, nodding towards the jumble of stone in the centre of the island. The rudimentary foundations of the monk's cell could be seen in the grass. The building that stood there would have been no more than three or four paces wide in either direction.

'Cosy,' observed Harlan.

'Do you think this was his altar?' said Suze, running her hand across a flat table of stone.

'Maybe his bed?' mused Harlan.

Suze brooded on the raised plinth of stone. 'No, I like to think this was his altar.' She looked up at Harlan. 'The woman in the library said this was a holy place even before St Carras.'

Harlan flashed an impressed smile.

'She said it was a pagan marriage site. *A joining place.*'

It took only a few minutes to comb the rest of the tiny isthmus of Klegger Dhu. There was nothing but grass, stone, and the feeling of something long gone. Suze imagined that, if the ghost of the old monk had ever lingered here, it would have been briefly. The wind would have soon blown him away.

Harlan gave Suze his jacket and they headed back across the causeway. At the mouth of the cave, Suze glanced back at Klegger Dhu.

She might never see it again from this close.

She was glad she'd been here, just this once.

She thought of the altar on the island. The joining place. The pirate's cathedral. The church of St Carras.

They were all holy places, churches in their own way.

So many places two people could be married.

The engine of Harlan's Land Rover clattered to life, the gearbox clunked into first and he steered through the weeds down to the road. He sounded a *beep-beep* on the horn. A minute later, Suze heard the whine of tyres on asphalt.

She watched him from the front door but her mind was elsewhere. She was lost in the shadowy cave of her mind, swinging a torch around in search of answers. She shook her head and closed the door. Theories and suspicions would get her nowhere. She was writing a story on the wind. Who she was, who Harlan was, who her own father was and why her mother had given her away were all questions with very real answers. Not guesswork or speculation. She needed to see the truth with her own eyes.

Or perhaps – *through her mother's*.

Her attention lifted to the ceiling and the small bedroom above where the veil lay.

The veil had shown her things she could never have guessed at. It might show her a great deal more if she was open to it. She'd already met her mother's lover in the darkness of the camera obscura, but what about in the cave below it, or on Klegger Dhu? Something there still called to her, something hidden.

She climbed the stairs. There were so many places she hadn't tried, so many places her mother could have stood while wearing the veil. Running its gauzy silk between finger and thumb, other possibilities whispered to her. *Was a wedding planned but stopped or foiled in some way? Was her mother attempting to elope?* She was theorising again. She groaned and, with the veil in her hand, left the room.

She wouldn't try the landing at the top of the stairs again. The vision she'd seen there had appeared once and seemed disinclined to offer a repeat performance. She stepped down towards the entry hall. At the bottom of the stairs her gaze fell upon the oval black and white photograph of her mother and grandfather. It set her nerves on edge, like fingernails drawn over a blackboard. She leaned closer, inspecting the deep gouges where Henry Lacey's eyes would have been. In the portrait her mother looked as incidental as a piece of furniture. She was a prop. Henry Lacey was the real subject, dominating the image both physically and perceptually. The pair seemed to pose upon the chaise as subject and object, as owner and property, master and servant. While they sat closely together, their expressions spoke of distance. In her mother's eyes she could read odium, fear. There was something else, something that reminded her of the stranger at the bottom of the stairs. It was a look of entreaty, of pleading.

Suze took a step back and pulled the veil over her head, settling the silver wreathed crown over her brow.

Her eyes adjusted to the mist of the veil, softening her vision like the white of a cataract. The entry hall swam into focus and she became aware that the day was suddenly darker. She looked to the arched window above the staircase landing and saw the sky outside roil in vortexes of mauve and black. The perspective of the staircase skewed violently away from her. It looked impossible to climb now – too high, too steep. Runnels of black shadow flowed down the walls and over everything like spilled ink. The hissing returned, like the curses of lost souls trapped in the panelling, plaster and woodwork. Looking down, she saw the familiar layers of silk spread, bell-like from her waist. She was wearing the wedding dress.

Then she turned to the photograph on the wall.

And saw the figures move.

Her mother began to shrink, falling into herself, an implosion in slow motion. The smaller she became, the more terrified her expression. Her eyes widened with the most abject fear. She became a child, small and desperate, pleading for mercy, for salvation. Inversely, seated next to her on the chaise, Henry Lacey appeared to grow. The scratches on his eyes were drawn over and over, scored deep by a hateful hand. The broad, thickset features grew and expanded. His heavy shoulders filled the portrait's frame from edge to edge. Everything about him now was hulking, monstrous. He seemed to brim with vehemence and the presage of brutality. His hand was clamped about her mother's tiny arm, holding her, restraining her. *From what*? In her mother's eyes Suze could read pain and panic.

Appalled, Suze stepped back from the image as it continued its distortions. It was unbearable to look at. She turned away and heard footsteps, heavy and hard, marching at speed towards her. A figure loomed into view, blocking the staircase and the window above it. Horrified, Suze now saw it was the man from the portrait, her grandfather. His face was inhuman, like the image in the photograph. The scratches across his eyes were drawn and redrawn, exposing white beneath, like bone, like paper. Towering above her, Suze felt his enmity drip like poison. He raised one massive hand, as if about to take an oath, then brought it down across her face. There was a flash of white lightning as the blow landed and Suze's ears rang like a bell. She felt the joints in her neck give, as if from whiplash, and pain cut its way through her head. Her vision grew dim. She reeled, then her knees buckled.

She went down hard on the floorboards of the great hall.

And the world went dark.

19

'PEOPLE GIVE UP TOO EASILY ON THE THINGS THEY SHOULD LOVE'

SUZE WOKE on the filthy floorboards. The various draughts that blew about inside the house had deposited leaves in her hair.

'Bastard,' she groaned, hauling herself to a sitting position.

She pulled the veil back from her face and tested the movement of her jaw. Nothing was broken, but her ears still rang and pain striated across the side of her face, the afterglow of violence.

She couldn't have been out for long. Late afternoon light still struggled through the arched window above the staircase landing. She climbed unsteadily to her feet and pulled the veil free.

Glaring at the portrait, she saw that everything had returned to normal. The figures had resumed their natural poses but the photograph still set her nerves on edge.

She was shaken. This was a frightening revelation, with even more frightening consequences. The visions the veil had shown her were not merely recordings left on the fabric of the house as she'd first supposed. They weren't there simply to be looked at, they weren't passive. She knew now they had dimension, force, and mass. They could reach out, touch, be felt. They could *hurt*.

Limping into the study, she straightened her back and placed the veil over Pavlov's stony expression. She wouldn't allow it in the bedroom tonight, not after this.

Later, zipped into her sleeping bag, she scowled at the ceiling.

He'd hit her.

Somehow, Henry Lacey had come across her mother in the wedding dress and knocked her to the floor.

He'd hit her mother. Hard.

Was this in retribution for the dress? For a wedding without his sanction?

An ember glowed deep inside the aquamarine suitcase. A forgotten emotion: rage. She hadn't felt it since wiping the smile from Raif's face with the tenderising mallet. She'd hidden it because it was dangerous. Now it directed itself at her grandfather, and the sadness she felt for her mother wouldn't smother it, couldn't put it out.

He'd struck her, his own daughter.

Bastard.

Her limbs ached from the long climb down the ladder to Klegger Dhu and the even longer climb back up. Her injured hands throbbed and now her jaw ached.

Exhaustion crawled over her, pawing at her, ravenous.

The fight left her.

And sleep swallowed her whole.

In her dream a colossal, curly-headed god was pounding the front door with his fist. Suze struggled from sleep, recognising the sound of the door knocker. Bleary-eyed, she stumbled downstairs in pyjamas and untied track shoes. She flung the front door open to reveal an excited Harlan. He glanced at her pyjamas without comment. Morning sunshine hammered into her retina from the world outside. She rubbed her eyes.

'Good morning,' offered Harlan.

'Depends how you look at it,' returned Suze.

'Want to hear some good news?' He held the ornate pistol box.

Suze hadn't even had the time to rake a comb through her hair before answering the door. In all likelihood it resembled a haystack. Or a bird's nest. She felt like a mess. Harlan hurried past her, signalling her to follow in wide-eyed invitation. He led her into the study and placed the box on the desk. Then he opened the lid and pointed to the single, long-barrelled pistol inside.

'Turns out this wasn't what I thought,' he said.

Suze yawned, rubbing her neck.

'Not travelling pistols – *duelling* pistols!'

She raised her eyebrows in mild surprise.

'I spoke with a valuer in London who specialises in rare weapons. Seems these are late-model, percussion-cap duelling pistols. Mid-nineteenth century. Highly illegal, because they were manufactured long after duelling was outlawed.' Harlan's excitement was palpable. He was back in his old job, dealing in antiques and Suze saw something of the joy it once brought him. 'That's what makes them so collectable. Crossley only produced a few sets like these. Highly *hush-hush*. The two guns would've been the same in every respect, to keep the duel fair. They were often named,' said Harlan, tracing a finger across the case.

'Named?'

Harlan lifted the pistol from the red velvet of the box and held it aloft. 'Yeah, this pair was called *The Twins*.' He turned to her with a grin. 'Cool, huh?'

Suze had to admit that the idea of duelling pistols was filled with melodrama. She wondered if they'd ever been used in a duel – to repay an insult or avenge a lover. The possibilities seemed violently romantic.

Harlan replaced the pistol in the case, his boyish enthusiasm turning gloomy. 'Shame there's only one. The pair would be worth a fair bit.' Looking up, he flashed her a bright smile. 'But, want to hear the *really* good news?'

'Sure.'

'Remember the Frobisher?' he asked her.

'The tatty little horse painting?'

'Yes, yes. Well, it sold.'

Suze was paying attention now. 'Really?'

'At auction.' Harlan smiled broadly.

'How much?'

Harlan raised his fists in excitement. 'Four hundred and eighty-two quid.'

'Four hundred pounds?' Suze was astonished.

'Well, closer to five hundred, actually.'

'Holy shit.'

Harlan was studying her face closely now, expectant. His cheery mood seemed to waver, then disappear. 'You really don't smile at *anything*, do you?'

'Sorry.' Suze shrugged. 'But I'm turning cartwheels on the inside.'

'Guess I'll have to take your word for it.'

Inside the aquamarine suitcase she found something. It was old and practically forgotten. A smile she hadn't worn since childhood. She considered wearing it for him then, but the thought frightened her. It might not fit her any longer, might not suit her. Like an old dress it might simply make her look stupid. Besides, she had no idea what else she'd open up, where it might lead. 'Thanks Harlan,' she said. It was all she could offer him.

'What d'you think you'll do with the money?' he asked.

Suze drew a long breath. 'Don't know.' She scanned the room as if looking for a place to begin. 'I guess the first thing is to get the electricity connected.' The idea of light and heat made her suddenly optimistic. 'And the gas.' She dreamed then of hot water. 'Perhaps the phone?' She gazed about. These ideas suddenly made Aeolus House seem far more liveable, more homely.

'Okay,' said Harlan. 'Why don't you leave that with me? I'll see what I can do.'

'You don't mind?'

Harlan shook his head. Suze fired a searching look in his direction. 'You know what I *really* want?'

His expression was a question mark.

'A bike,' announced Suze.

'A bicycle?'

'Yeah. So I won't have to walk all the way into the village. Something I can do the shopping with.'

Harlan nodded in thought.

'But first,' said Suze, her mind now buzzing from all the possibilities this windfall might deliver. 'First I want to buy a bottle of wine, and cook you a meal.' She felt suddenly clumsy. This wasn't the kind of thing she normally *did*. 'To say thanks,' she confirmed. In the absence of her ability to smile, it was the least she could do.

Harlan mused. 'What can I look forward to, Lobster Thermidor? Chateaubriand for two?'

'How about macaroni cheese?'

Harlan smirked. 'My favourite.'

◄ ● ►

The morning flew past like the sunbeams that raced across the eastern moor. Suze retreated upstairs to wash, dress, and comb the tangles from her hair. When she reappeared downstairs, Harlan was wiping his hands on a duster. He told her he'd finished the cataloguing of her grandfather's study. The only valuable books he'd found were boxed and now waited in the vestibule, their *treasury* near the front door.

She followed him to gaze at the odd assortment of old, damaged trinkets and labelled cardboard boxes.

'So that's it?' Suze asked.

Harlan nodded, his dismay evident.

'How much do you reckon it's worth?'

'Maybe a thousand, tops.'

'No more Frobishers?'

'No more Frobishers or Crossley pistols,' he admitted.

'And the filing room in the study alcove?'

'I've finished there, too.'

'And?'

'Nothing.'

'No uncashed cheques, no shares or premium bonds?'

Harlan shook his head.

Suze sighed, running her eyes over the pile. This was it – the sum worth of all the treasure in Aeolus House. It didn't amount to much.

'Will this pay for the sanatorium? For the funeral? Will it cover what I owe Ava, what I owe you?'

'Not even close,' said Harlan with a sombre look. 'Sorry Suze.'

'So I'll have to sell, and Ava will get her way?'

Harlan pulled a resigned smile. 'It's not about what Ava wants though, is it? It's about what makes sense.'

'And I'm not making sense?'

'I didn't say that.' Harlan was quick to defend himself. He scanned the broken furniture, the peeling walls and threadbare carpet. 'Look at the place Suze, it's a wreck. Why ever would you want to keep it?'

Now it was Suze's turn to cast her eyes in inventory over their surroundings. Where Harlan saw ruin, she saw something that connected her to the past and to the people who once lived here. It was her home, and yet it was something even more. It was *who she was,* her place in the world. To lose it meant to lose a sense of herself. She turned to him. 'I just think people give up too easily on the things they should love.'

She was right of course, and the sympathy in Harlan's smile confirmed it.

Disconsolate, Suze walked Harlan from the vestibule towards the front door. The day had started hopefully: the cash that was promised from the sale of the Frobisher portrait, the doubtful history of the Crossley duelling pistol. Now it was all being dragged into a miasma of failure and gloom.

Harlan gathered his coat and opened the door. 'I'll try to have that cash ready for you tomorrow, from the auction.' He tapped the side of his nose. Their little secret.

He looked around the house as if viewing it for the last time. Then he left, closing the door behind him.

◄━●━►

Suze turned a circle inside the narrow, cramped space behind the study alcove and the bust of Pavlov. Harlan had cleared it of what was once a waist-high pile of discarded paperwork. Apart from the Crossley pistol, there had been nothing here of any worth. It was a dead-end, hidden away in a house filled with dead-ends, and Emma Lacey had treated this tiny room as nothing more than a giant wastepaper bin.

Yet something dark lived here. Wearing the veil she'd felt its presence: sinister and frightening. With her own eyes she'd seen nothing, felt nothing. But something here had scared her mother almost to death. Suze remembered the weight of dread that had fallen, paralysing, crushing her. This was the one place she'd never wear the veil again. Yet she knew, to uncover the truth, to understand her mother's story, she may have to forego her own safety and face the source of her mother's fear.

This was the way the veil worked. It wasn't just a window through which she could see her mother's past. It also allowed her to step into her mother's experience, feeling what she'd felt, both physical and emotional. Her fear, her madness.

She stared at the walls surrounding her. Rows of worthless books stood on shelves of bare planks supported by steel angle-brackets. Behind the shelves ran the same grotesque, mismatched wallpaper that defiled other parts of the house. Suze considered the makeshift appearance of the place in contrast to the grandiose orderliness of the main study. The two were entirely different. One was opulent, showy, the other was crude and utilitarian – a make-do.

Her eyes rested for a moment on the shattered door frame, a casualty of the Crossley duelling pistol. She traced the would-be trajectory of the musket ball across the space to the bookshelf where the ruined copy of Jane Eyre lay. She took it down and one of the hard covers fell loose. The ball had destroyed the spine and ripped through the heart of the book, rendering it to nothing more than shredded paper. If it had ever been worth anything, it was junk now.

She sighed, about to lift the book back into place. What she saw in the space it came from made her jump with shock – like the sudden feeling of a splinter under her skin.

In the wallpaper was a hole left by the musket ball.

Through it gleamed daylight. Faint but visible.

She stood motionless, ruined book in hand, trying to understand.

Behind this alcove was the great hall and the stormwatchers' gallery, surely? She found herself looking down on the house from above, studying its plan, trying to make sense of the layout. It didn't.

She cast the book into an empty space on a lower shelf and raced out of the study, around the foot of the grand staircase and into the great hall. For almost a quarter-hour she pored over the surface of the adjoining wall, removing old paintings and photographs in haste, stacking, piling and dropping them.

There were no holes. The wall was solid, made of thick stone like the rest of the place. No musket ball could penetrate such a structure.

She ran back into the study and the alcove. There it was, through the hole in the wallpaper – *daylight*.

In a frenzy, Suze began removing the books and transferring them to the main study. She stacked them against the bookcases until the wall inside the alcove was bare. The shelves were loose, just simple, unvarnished planks of pine. She threw them onto the floor and wrestled with the angle brackets. They held fast, secured to the wall behind. She stopped and tried to reassess, to think. *Was there a screwdriver somewhere? Had she seen one in the workshop beside the house?*

Did she even need to remove them?

The hole in the wallpaper sat in a space between the brackets. Right in the middle. She rapped her knuckles on the wall around the brackets, finding it solid. Then she tested the space near the hole. Her hand went straight through the old wallpaper.

What the hell?

The wallpaper came away in strips and handfuls. Behind it seemed to be a recess, an opening. Feverishly, she pulled away as much of the rotten paper as she could, then stood back, dumbfounded by what lay before her.

It was a door. A simple, wooden, four-panelled door recessed within a frame. The musket ball had smashed through one of the upper panels leaving a jagged opening. Through this, dim daylight flickered.

She realised that the door and surrounding wall had been papered over, then shelves placed across to conceal its presence. Books had been stacked on the shelves to complete the deception. Suze frowned. Was this, or what lay inside, the source of her mother's dread? Is this why it was hidden? To keep something safely locked away? Or was it to prevent something from getting out? This door didn't open into the great hall or the stormwatchers' gallery. *So where did it lead?*

She tried the handle. It moved but the door held fast. She rattled the handle back and forth, then leaned against it. *Locked.*

Thwarted, she took a step back and seethed for a while, then marched from the alcove into the study to retrieve the set of heavy iron keys. They'd opened every door in Aeolus House, surely this door would be no different?

Key after key, the hidden door remained locked.

Was it not meant to be opened?

Thoughts of locksmiths spun in her head. *How could she open this?* She calmed herself, breathing deeply, and the answer came.

My house. My door. Fuck it.

She raised a leg and landed the sole of her foot hard on the door near the lock. Like much of Aeolus House, the door was sturdily made and didn't give easily. She tried again. It gave way on the third go, the deadbolt tearing the striker plate from the timber frame. The door flew inward and creaked to a stop, revealing a murky interior.

It was a narrow room layered with dust. To her right shone a slit of daylight between heavy curtains. She stepped carefully inside, nagged by an irrational fear of the door closing behind her, locking her in. Shapes loomed inside the room, strange and unknown. She realised now that the room ran parallel with the study, its curtained window facing the north. She hadn't noticed this from the outside during any of her walks.

Halfway across the space she came across a high-backed chair. Nothing sinister. Making her way around it, she headed towards the small gap of daylight between the curtains. There was a stale smell here, something that caused her imagination to churn. She felt some of Emma's dread creep back. Shadows flew around her, black wings. She wanted to thrash at them, tear at them like birds tangled in her hair. She wanted to get out.

Finally reaching the window, she covered her nose and mouth with one hand and carefully drew back one of the long, heavy curtains. Dust fell around her like thin rain and the larger motes floated in the diagonal shafts of dirty light that now filled the room. Suze looked about, but the sight that greeted her made no sense.

The room itself was almost bare. There were no wall coverings, no carpet and no furniture except for the high-backed chair which stood centrally. Facing the chair, against one wall was a collapsible stand with a screen. The kind used with movie projectors. A movie hall designed for a single person?

Beside the chair was a bench supporting two curious objects. These must have been electrically operated because their cables trailed towards an outlet in the wall. Both were still plugged in. Suze moved closer and recognised one of them immediately. It was an old slide projector for 35mm slides. Unlike the newer, carousel-type projectors that Suze was familiar with, this had a manually-operated push and pull slide carrier that only held several slides at a time. The carrier was empty. The lens of the projector faced towards the collapsible screen at the other side of the room.

The second object was far more obscure. It looked like a complex battery charger or a device used in hospitals. It had knobs, dials and switches which seemed to control a variety of settings and two long cables which ended in button-like, steel terminals. The whole device sat in a kind of portable flight-case. It was baffling.

On the top of the bench Suze found a plastic container. Inside was a long row of photographic slides. Perhaps fifty in total. Pulling one out, she walked to the dirty window and held it to the light. The image was of a man stripped to the waist, a woodsman's axe in hand. He stood next to a felled tree, posing for the camera. Suze looked through more of the slides and the theme seemed to continue: a male high-diving team in bathing suits demonstrating their musculature for the viewer; two men wrestling, smiling towards the camera mid-grapple. Then Suze found the image of a woman. Although naked, she protected her modesty with crossed legs. The woman held a flower to her nose and eyed the camera provocatively.

Although the images were innocent by today's standards, Suze still found their subliminal sexuality disquieting. What disturbed her more was that a secret room had been created for their viewing.

Her lip curled in distaste. She dropped the slides haphazardly onto the benchtop and turned away. Now she saw the high-backed chair clearly and was gripped by a sudden palsy of alarm. On the arms of the chair were leather straps with heavy buckles. There were similar straps on the chair's front legs at ankle height and, hanging from the back where the sitter's head would have rested was a strap with a gag. It looked like a homemade version of the electric chair.

Suze felt ill and was about to scurry from the room when she noticed a book lying on the seat of the chair. Picking it up, she blew dust from its cover and read.

On the Pavlovian Principle of Behavioural Conditioning and Therapy of Aversion.

The author was her grandfather – Dr Henry Lacey.

20

'THE THING WITH THE DOGS'

SUZE POURED HARLAN another glass of Frascati. The wine hadn't been expensive. It caught her eye because it looked lonely on the shelf in the village Spar, a bottle of cheer looking for company.

This was the first time she'd ever sat in the huge, formal dining room. Before Harlan's arrival she'd dusted the table and the chairs, lit the fire and 'borrowed' some of the silver candlesticks from the treasury in the vestibule. Then she'd set the long table with two settings side by side: chipped Wedgewood, tarnished silverware, mismatched tumblers, a carafe of water and crystal wine glasses from the incomplete set. She tried to imagine the dinner parties that may have taken place here – overdressed guests flushed with wine, a table groaning with food, the scurrying about of the household staff. What would they think of this humble little celebration? Macaroni cheese for two, cooked on a Calor gas stove. It was a mockery of the opulence that had preceded it and, for this reason, Suze felt it appropriate. She was taking a well-aimed kick at the pretentious indulgence of her forebears. If the ghosts of the Laceys looked down tonight, she wanted them to see how far their line had fallen.

Harlan smiled in thanks at his refreshed glass, his face lit by firelight. He'd put on a jacket and tie for the occasion and Suze was delighted that he'd joined in the fun. It was a celebration, after all.

'I like this restaurant,' said Harlan. 'I might come again.'

'Well, there's always room,' said Suze. 'No need to book.' The smile she'd hidden in the aquamarine suitcase wasn't buried like before. It lay close to the top now, easier to find. She was holding the suitcase lid open, examining it, considering, feeling it play at the edge of her lips. It frightened her. *Not yet.*

She closed the lid and fastened the catches.

Harlan was studying her, his smile still in place. She knew what he was trying to do, to lure her own smile out into the open. He'd never have a better chance than this.

Suze drew circles on the table with a forefinger, searching for a path back to safety. 'I've been reading about Pavlov,' she announced.

It worked. Harlan's smile fell away. 'Pavlov?'

'You know, the bust in the study?'

'Oh, sure.'

'I've been trying to figure out the connection to my grandfather. I think Henry Lacey must've been involved in the same work – digestion or something.'

'Pavlov studied digestion?'

'Yes. Even won a Nobel Prize for it.'

'Fascinating.' Harlan's face was beginning to glow from the wine and the warmth of the fire. 'All I remember was the thing with the dogs.'

'That was a fluke, a kind of scientific detour that took him away from his main work.'

'S'funny, I always thought he was a psychologist,' said Harlan.

'Nope. A *physiologist,*' corrected Suze. '*The thing with the dogs was an experiment in digestion. Pavlov was trying to measure how much saliva was produced by dogs depending on the kind of food they were given. Legend has it that a bell was rung to signal when the food was ready. Pavlov saw that the dogs began to salivate before the food even arrived. They were reacting to the sound of the bell.'

'And that's how classical conditioning was born,' concluded Harlan.

Suze was upright now. She thought of the hidden room: the high-backed chair and its restraints, the apparatus and the slides. Nothing she'd seen there had anything to do with digestion. She thought of her grandfather's book lying in the hidden room. In her mind she re-read its title. 'Is that the same as *behavioural conditioning*?' she asked.

Harlan reached for his wineglass. 'Yep, same thing. Sorta.'

'And do you know anything about *aversion therapy*?'

'Only a little,' said Harlan, sipping wine.

'Which is?'

'A way to get you to do something you don't want to. Or, to *not* get you to do something you *do* want to.'

Suze shook her head. 'You've lost me.'

Harlan looked about for inspiration. 'Well, let's say you have an addiction. Like alcoholism.' He poured Suze a fresh glass of wine, then filled a tumbler with water from the carafe. He then placed the wineglass and tumbler within her reach. 'Now, give me your hand.'

'What?'

'Trust me.'

Suze obliged.

Harlan held her hand between his own. 'Now, choose,' he said, nodding to the glasses on the table.

Suze reached out her free hand. 'I'm an alcoholic, right?' she asked.

'Desperately so,' he confirmed.

Suze placed fingers around the wineglass. Before she could lift it, Harlan slapped the back of her other hand between his.

'Ow!' she complained.

'Try again,' he said.

Suze shot him a quizzical frown and reached again for the wineglass. Harlan slapped her hand again, harder this time.

'Ow, that hurt!'

'Again,' urged Harlan with a grin.

Moving her hand away from the wineglass, Suze picked up the tumbler of water. From the corner of her eye, she checked Harlan's reaction and lifted the glass to drink. He made no movement. She closed her eyes and drank, then felt him raise her other hand, open it, and place his lips softly in her palm. He kissed her once, twice, on the wounds in her hand. Her reward.

Suze kept her eyes closed. She didn't withdraw her hand. Her breath came unsteadily. Some part of her was melting; butter in a saucepan; snow in sunshine. Inside the aquamarine suitcase something stirred, something powerful and ungovernable that strained at the rusty silver hinges and latches. She returned the tumbler heavily to the table, hand shaking.

She didn't know if Harlan leaned towards her or if she leaned towards Harlan. Their closing was involuntary, reciprocal. Across her consciousness the warnings flashed: Harlan's lookalike at the foot of the stairs, eyes pleading. *Whoever wore this dress was pregnant* – the woman in the bridal shop.

She placed a hand against his chest, pushing him away. She'd acted on an impulse she couldn't comprehend. She needed him, but in what way?

'We can't,' she whispered.

His expression cycled from hurt, to embarrassment, to apology.

'Yes, yes, quite right,' he agreed. 'You're a client. Well, you're practically a client...'

She reacted with a withering look. That wasn't what she meant, but she couldn't tell him.

There was a long, uncomfortable pause. Harlan broke the silence, standing. 'I should go.'

Suze nodded in hasty agreement. She rose and together they walked from the dining room. Flustered, Harlan took a while to find his coat. She opened the front door and he stood for a moment against the backdrop of the windy night. He turned back with a lost look and opened his mouth to say something. Whether it might have been an apology, or to thank her for a delightful evening, Suze couldn't tell. 'I know,' she said, saving him the difficulty.

He drove away and Suze closed the door. She placed her head against its flaking paint and groaned. She thought of her mother, the dress, the kiss, and the dark stranger who looked like Harlan. This house may have been home to forbidden things before.

Would it be again?

21

'WE SHALL BE APART NO MORE'

THE VISIONS the veil chose to show were fleeting and fragile.

It was like tuning the aerial on a TV set. If she stood in a place her mother had never stood, moved in a way she'd never moved, or looked in a direction she'd never looked, then it was enough to end the transmission. Signal lost.

Suze was certain these images were what her mother had seen, thirty years before, here in this house. The visions were as much a part of Suze's past as her mother's. She was being carried through the same events, only this time not inside her mother's womb but outside it, living her mother's experience. A parallel narrative. Another side of the story.

The warped perspective of the house, the dark stranger's backward-facing feet, she supposed could all be products of her mother's damaged mind. As recordings, they might not be accurate, not representative of real events at all, but how her mother had perceived them, felt them.

Were these visions of a single day? *A wedding day?* The idea seemed to fit. In which case, why not wind this memory right back to the start, and begin that day at its beginning?

Suze stood in the small bedroom. It was early morning and she'd lit a fire to fend off the dawn's lingering chill. Surely this room was where the story started, where that day had begun? She swept up the veil from the bare mattress, placed it over her head then let it fall across her face. She stilled her mind, letting it become receptive, and waited for the pictures to play. Minutes later she was struck by a thought: was everything the same as it had been on that day? Was anything different here? She glanced to the open bedroom door. Emma wouldn't have opened it until she'd left. Tutting, Suze crossed the room and closed it. Then she turned and froze. Filaments of ice shot through her, up her spine, crisscrossing her skin.

The room had changed.

Her breathing came in rapid, shallow breaths. She remained motionless.

The fire was out. In the grate was an arrangement of pine cones and driftwood. The dressing table was lit with a shining brass oil lamp. Upon it was a vase filled with wild summer blooms: corn-flower, campion and long-stemmed ox-eye daisies. The bottles and phials of perfume and cosmetics sparkled. The gleaming mirror framed her reflection. She caught her breath.

She was wearing the wedding dress again.

Looking down, she saw, through the veil, the layers of white silk cascading from her waist to her feet. Floral swirls of lace sleeved her arms. The fabric was undamaged, pristine, new.

She waited, not wishing to disturb the image in the mirror. In height and build it appeared to be her own reflection. Suze moved her arm experimentally and the reflection made an exact replica. Moving closer to the mirror she leaned forward. The face of the reflection rose to meet hers. The two studied each other, the tips of their noses just inches apart. Through the real and reflected layers of silk, the face behind the veil was indiscernible save for two dark, inquisitive eyes. Emma Lacey's, or Suze Newman's?

Standing straight now, she took in the room. The sleeping bag and airbed were gone. Instead, there were clean sheets on the bed; starched, ironed and folded neatly back over a fringed, cream bedspread. The brass of the bedframe glittered. A bright rug covered the polished floorboards at the foot of the bed.

Yet the shape of the room wasn't right. It had grown large, overbearing, making her feel small and insignificant. Its perspective was warped, bent into strange angles, as if seen through the distortions of a lens, during a dream, or fever. The ceiling stretched high above. The floor seemed to slope away from her at a rakish angle and the doorframe canted sideways. Every upright, every horizontal and right angle appeared off-kilter like some architectural *trompe-l'œil*. As she moved, the image swam, evoking nausea.

An all-pervasive sibilance had also filled her ears. *The wind?* It whispered against the windows and blew, flute-like across the chimney pots above. She turned back towards the mirror and noticed, beside the dressing table, that a short length of floorboard had been removed to reveal a compartment under the floor. Something gleamed inside.

She gasped, lifted the veil and the vision disappeared. It resolved into the grimy, careworn room she knew. The fire glowed and crackled in the fireplace. The dressing table was in a different position now. It lay over the hole in the floor she'd seen through the veil.

Removing the veil, she folded it and left it on top of the bare mattress. Then she placed her weight against one end of the dressing table and shoved. It scraped across the floor, revealing a clean patch, and the short length of floorboard she'd seen through the veil. It was back in place, concealing the hidden compartment beneath.

Breathless with anticipation, Suze knelt and ran her fingers over the floorboard, seeking some kind of purchase along its edges but finding nothing. She pressed one end of the board and the other lifted. Pulling it away, she peered into the dark recess. Then she reached inside and felt her fingers close around paper. She lifted the contents out. It was an envelope addressed to *Miss Emma Lacey, Aeolus House, Storm Bay*. The envelope was already open and showed signs of extensive handling. She pulled a single, worn page from inside and ran her eyes over the neat, copperplate handwriting.

> *My Only One,*
> *Our day approaches and it fills me in equal measure with both joy and fear.*
> *I rejoice that soon we will stand before He who cannot deny us, the God of love Himself.*
> *He will join us. And we shall be apart no more.*
> *Until that day, and evermore.*
> *All my love,*
> *Sam.*

Suze let out a long, low whistle. She knew the name of her mother's lover now. This thin scrap of paper rewrote the Laceys' family history. It was incendiary, a revelation of scandal, and would have burned them down if discovered.

She re-read.

...soon we will stand before He who cannot deny us, the God of love Himself.

He will join us. And we shall be apart no more.

A marriage had clearly been planned. A religious wedding, perhaps in a church as she'd first suspected.

Suze's eye drifted from the letter back to the hidden compartment. Something more lay inside: something that shone, metallic in the firelight.

Kneeling once more, she reached inside and withdrew a silver photo frame.

It was a formal, black and white portrait of three young people. Seated at its centre was the dark athletic man she recognised from the foot of the stairs; the one with the backward-facing feet. The memory of his face swam back to her. Apart from the raked-back hair and thin moustache, he could have been Harlan's twin brother. The wounded look of longing was absent, replaced by a smile that lingered in his eyes. He sat between two women, holding the hands of each upon his knees. One of the women was Suze's mother, Emma. She wore the strange headscarf across her forehead and temples as before, but her sadness was absent, replaced now by a sunlit smile. The woman to the man's other side was a stranger. Her striking features seemed to express a deep, almost dangerous intellect. Like the man, she was darkly good-looking, black hair falling across her shoulders. The three figures seemed arranged in a pose of unanimity, of harmonic agreement, a triptych of togetherness. Even hand in hand, they seemed joined in something more than physical.

In the photograph, her mother's smile was genuine, unbridled. It was the only image in which Suze had seen her happy. She looked from her mother to the dark man with kind eyes, her hand in his.

Now she had something to show Harlan, something with which to confront him. Now she'd demand an answer to the question that burned inside.

22

A WIND OF CHANGE

THE FOLLOWING MORNING Aeolus House lived up to its name by becoming the centre of a whirlwind.

Workmen in boiler suits and dungarees blew in, as if from nowhere, and a storm of activity prevailed.

Men from British Telecom pulled cables from the walls and complained about the connection to the exchange. They showed Suze coloured wires as if she would understand the impossibility of their task. Elsewhere plumbers swore at the pipework and twisted their spanners against deadlocked joints. They grumbled about the gas appliances, specifically the water heater in the kitchen and urged her to replace it with something less explosive. At her insistence, they agreed to do what they could for the ageing equipment, but only after issuing prophecies of impending fireballs. Electricians fiddled with fuse boxes, scratched their heads and muttered to themselves while their mop-headed apprentices stood idly by. Lights turned on. Lights turned off. The fridge hummed, the fridge fell silent.

Harlan, good to his word, had arranged the whole thing.

This was the wind of change that now blew through Aeolus House.

Suze was grateful, but the place had never been this noisy, this crowded. It felt unnatural, like a party in a library.

While the workmen worked, she was held in a state of inertia. She was purposeless. More than anything, she desired peace and shelter from the storm.

She couldn't help out in any way and there was no reason for her staying in house. So she pulled on her coat and stepped outside.

———•———

Suze walked along the cliff path with a westerly at her back. She made it as far as the rust-coloured downs that she'd only ever seen from her grandfather's study. The bleakness of the place was meditative. There was no interruption of trees, buildings or landmarks of any kind, just a wide blue sky that stretched overhead and gave her space in which to lose herself.

An hour or two later she turned into the eye of the wind to head home. From the edge of the moorland she watched a Telecom van, a tiny dot of yellow in the landscape, bump and lurch its way from Aeolus House towards the road. The workmen were finishing up for the day and the house would be hers once more.

She could see two men at work in the stretch of land between the house and the road. One looked through a theodolite while the other held a marker pole. They wouldn't be there to help with the phone connection, so the plumbing perhaps? She changed direction towards them. One of the men knelt and, with a heavy mallet, hammered a blue stake into the soil.

'What are you doing?' asked Suze, reaching them.

The kneeling man stood. He was young, perhaps an apprentice. 'A site survey,' he muttered, as if it was obvious.

'Why?' she asked.

The young man looked over his shoulder towards his companion operating the theodolite. The other, an older man, seemed to understand this as a request for his assistance. He shrugged, frustrated by this interruption to his work and trudged towards them. In the long grass Suze could now see rows of blue stakes leading in the direction of the house. The same blue stakes as the one she'd tripped on near the clifftop.

'Can I help you?' asked the older man, reaching them.

'What are these?' asked Suze, pointing to the line of blue stakes.

'They're survey pegs,' the older man explained.

'But what are you surveying *for*?' asked Suze.

'That's confidential,' he replied. 'You'd have to contact my client.'

Suze fixed him with a dark look. 'And who is your client?'

The older man's eyes narrowed in suspicion.

'Well, it's certainly not me,' said Suze, 'and this is my land.'

The older man blinked. His mouth opened. 'You're the landowner?'

Suze gave a grim nod.

The man began to stammer. 'The survey was, *is* approved by Miss Carfax. She's at Carfax and Bell.'

'Ava Carfax?'

'Yes. You'd best talk to her. Look, we were told she managed the site and had authority to approve access. We were told the owner had passed away.'

Suze frowned. Her gaze moved across the blue survey pegs once more. 'So what are these pegs for?'

'They mark where the road will be.'

'What road?'

'The new road leading into the estate.'

'What estate?'

'The new housing estate.' He spoke as if reminding her. 'Twenty-six luxury houses.'

'A *housing estate*?' Suze was incredulous. 'But this is my home.' She pointed at Aeolus House.

The man hesitated. 'We're told that old place is being pulled down.'

23

'FAMILIES ALWAYS HIDE
THE THINGS THAT HURT'

HARLAN RETURNED to Aeolus House the next morning. The day was like the ones before: cold and gusty with bright, squint-inducing sunshine. Harlan rapped out a tattoo on the iron door-knocker. Suze opened it to his familiar, nervous smile. His hands rested on the handlebars of a woman's bicycle. It was mauve and maroon, with a wicker basket over the front wheel.

'This is to say sorry for the other night. I remembered you wanted a bike.'

Suze ignored the bike and locked eyes on his.

'It's not new I'm afraid. But it's in quite good condition.' Harlan shrank from the intensity of her gaze and wheeled the bike through the door. 'Best keep it inside. It'll rust in the salt air.'

Suze closed the door and turned to him without welcome.

Harlan sighed. 'Still angry? I get it. Sorry for being such a dick.'

197

'This isn't about the other night,' she said.

He frowned in question. 'It's not?'

She shook her head and turned, heading back into the house. He followed her.

In the study she swept up the silver-framed photo of her mother seated with Harlan's doppelgänger, then handed it to him.

Harlan whispered a single, elongated syllable. 'Oh.'

Suze pointed to the man between the two women. 'He's a dead ringer for you.'

Harlan looked up, forcing a pained expression. 'I'm sorry.'

Her eyes searched his. 'Is he *related* to you?'

'I should have told you...'

'Is he?'

'Yes.'

'Who is he?'

Harlan took a long breath, his eyes sought refuge in the bright day outside. 'My father,' he admitted.

'You're right, you should have told me,' she said.

'Please don't read anything sinister into this, Suze. They were friends. I've been in this house before. A long time ago. I even met your mother. Ava thought my knowledge might help, that's all.'

Suze levelled dark eyes at him. 'Help with what?'

He looked around the room, lost for an answer.

'With *what*, Harlan?'

He drew a breath. 'To help find anything important, anything *valuable*.'

'And did you, did you find anything valuable here?'

Harlan's eyes rested on her. He shook his head.

'And if you had? What then?'

'She wanted me to keep it from you, not to let you know.'

Suze marched towards him, thrusting her face at his. She was struggling with the latches of the aquamarine suitcase.

'She doesn't want you to find anything you could use to save this place,' he said. 'But Suze, if I'd found anything I would've told you. Honest.'

'But you haven't been honest, have you?' She pointed at the silver frame in his hands. 'You haven't been honest about this.'

Harlan's eyes slid to meet hers. 'Fair enough. What do you want to know?'

'Everything.'

◄—•—►

'I never knew she'd had a child, that she'd had *you*,' said Harlan. He sat behind the desk in the study while Suze paced. 'No one explained that to me. I guess they wanted to keep it quiet. When I first met your mother, you'd have been in foster care. So I never knew.'

'That was the only time you met her?'

'Only once or twice. Her father – your grandfather – didn't like us visiting. He became cantankerous, turned my father away in the end. And me. It's funny, but even though I was very young, I could tell she was sad.'

'But in the photo, with your father, she looked happy.'

'They were great friends,' said Harlan.

She faced him. 'Were they ever *more* than just friends?' she asked.

Harlan looked about. He blew out a sigh. 'Anything's *possible*, but I don't think so.'

'Are you certain?'

'He'd never have cheated on my mother.'

'Oh. So he was married at the time?'

'Sure, my parents would've been married shortly after that photograph was taken.' He attempted a reassuring smile.

'Is there any chance I could talk to him sometime, about my mother?'

'Afraid not,' replied Harlan. 'He passed a few years ago. Stroke. All quite sudden. I think he missed my mother. He was pretty useless on his own.'

'She's gone too?'

Harlan nodded.

'Is this her, the woman with the penetrating eyes?' asked Suze, pointing at the dark haired woman in the photograph.

'No, that was my aunt. My father's sister.'

Suze caught Harlan's meaning – *was*. 'She's gone too?'

'Yes, although I never knew her. She died quite young. Much younger than my mum and dad. Took her own life.'

Sympathy fluttered inside the aquamarine suitcase. Suze had some idea of the pain it took to drive a person to such an end. She'd been close herself.

'I don't really know what happened either. No one ever wanted to talk about it.' He offered her a brave smile. 'Families always hide the things that hurt.'

Suze reflected. *Wasn't that the truth?*

'The only thing I got out of my dad was that he, your mum and my aunt were thick as thieves when they were young. Kindred spirits.' He cast a mournful look at the silver-framed photograph on the desk. 'My dad and aunt are buried here in Storm Bay. Along with my mother.'

'At St Carras?' she asked.

He nodded. 'It's good in a way, that your mother's ashes will be there too. Then they'll all be together again. They'd have liked that.'

'Harlan, what was your father's name?'

He took a deep, shaky breath. 'Samuel,' he said.

◄—●—►

Suze opened the front door for Harlan. Her gaze swept the scene outside: long grass flattened by the wind and the occasional glimpse of a blue stake. She thought back to her walk with him along the clifftop, when she'd tripped and nearly fell over one of the surveyor's pegs. She remembered his reaction. He hadn't looked at the stake she'd shown him. He'd turned away, avoiding her eyes.

'You knew Ava was having the place surveyed, didn't you?' she asked him.

He slunk outside and turned to her from the doorstep. He didn't need to say anything, his guilty expression spoke for him.

She lifted her chin to the world beyond the door. 'Did you know she wants to build a housing estate here? Did you know she wants to tear this place down, to demolish my home?'

He seemed lost. 'Suze, there might be a way to save this house. I've been thinking. Let me help…'

'I don't want your help,' she said. 'Not yours, not Ava's. I'll save this place myself.'

At that moment, Suze saw his resemblance to his father, the

man in the silver-framed photograph, the dark stranger at the bottom of the stairs who faced in one direction and moved in another. The whole time Harlan had stood in front of her he'd been heading somewhere else, walking away from her. With backward-facing feet.

24

HOT WATER AND COLD BLOOD

THE LONG, CAST IRON bathtub did a great job at keeping the water piping hot. If it cooled, Suze drained the bath a little, lifting the plug with her toe, then topped it up with steaming hot water.

There were no windows in the bathroom, but high above was a domed cupola of glass that framed a circle of the day's fading light.

She had hot water now. She had a bath. In fact, she had *eight* of them. Four bathtubs behind partitions, here in this room. Four more in the bathroom in the other wing. If she got the taps fixed in all of them, she could bathe in a different bath every day for over a week.

She also had gas, electricity and a shiny new phone fixed to the wall in the great hall. With comforts such as these she could live here forever. She could grow old here. She could become her mother. She imagined herself then, a white-haired woman in a nightgown, moving through rooms by candlelight, decaying like the ancient house around her.

The place could do without a coat of paint, without a tended garden, without new furniture or carpets. She wouldn't *need* to spend any money. It was fine the way it was. In a way she'd grown used to the desolation and the haunted, Faustian gloom. She only needed hot water, light and heat to call the place home.

A thought surfaced, bringing a frown. Harlan had done this. He'd made all these modern-day comforts possible. How could he be so damn helpful, so gracious on the one hand – selling paintings, connecting phones, giving her bicycles – yet on the other, he'd been working behind her back? How could he be so deceitful? Hadn't he guessed that the two of them might share a bond of blood? Shouldn't that have counted for something?

She ground her teeth. Of course she knew where the deceit really lay.

It was wrapped in layers of thick tweed, hiding behind the respectability of the law.

Suze remembered Ava's command to Harlan in the event he'd found anything of value: *She wanted me to keep it from you, not to let you know.*

So Ava wanted to keep Suze poor, to take her house and land away, then develop it?

I am owed from the estate. A lot of people are owed a lot of money, Susanna.

The conspiracy felt malignant, like the spread of rot.

It was time for Suze to cut this rot out.

Unbidden, thoughts of Harlan floated up through her anger and her heart bent a little. She missed him. *Why had he helped her?* Had he suspected they were family, or was he drawn to her in the same way he was drawn to his precious old sticks of furniture, as something in need of fixing, something he'd like to mend? It'd been painful to push him away – yet another hurt to lock inside the aquamarine suitcase. He'd been a friend, perhaps something more. But Suze wouldn't forgive his duplicity easily. Whether Ava was adept at playing him, whether she'd pressured him or whether he'd just been weak, Suze couldn't tell.

She groaned and slid deeper into the tub. She'd hoped that a long soak might calm her. It hadn't. She wished she had a good book, something to take her mind off things. Then she remembered, and pulled the plug.

Downstairs was a book she'd been meaning to read.

◄—•—►

During the house's more recent pre-electric phase, Suze had retired to bed when darkness fell. Now she didn't have to.

She could wander the galleries and halls, turning on lights, then turning them off behind her. Some worked, some didn't.

She lit a fire in the study and flicked the switch to the green-glass banker's lamp. It illuminated the photograph of Emma Lacey with the Grey siblings – her mother and her kindred spirits. Her mother had been close to Samuel Grey once. Then why did she picture him with backward-facing feet? What had he done? Had he deceived her mother just as Harlan had deceived Suze?

Like father, like son.

Her eyes moved to her grandfather's book.

On the Pavlovian Principle of Behavioural Conditioning and Therapy of Aversion.

She cast a glance around the study. There might be more

entertaining books to read here, but this one had been written by a relative. It was her obligation to read it. She also sensed secrecy: the way it was hidden in the room with the chair and projector. Like the many other secrets this old house contained, it pulled at her.

The book contained no dedication. No names of dear ones. She recalled the hubris of his expression from the photograph in the hall, the aura of self-importance. No, he needed no support, he had no one to thank or congratulate but himself.

Suze flipped through pages detailing Henry Lacey's methods of examination. They were couched in medical terms that meant nothing to her. His writing style seemed purposely complicated, as if to demonstrate his erudition. If there was a simple way to communicate a thought, Henry Lacey would choose a more complex one in keeping with his own soaring intellect.

She turned to the opening chapter and read.

> *This work forms a series of extracts from a wider study of 62 patients over a period of 19 months; the purpose of this study to record and evaluate the results and effectiveness of reverse Pavlovian conditional reflex methodology across a wide range of disorders. In particular, to prove conclusively the benefits of negative stimulus association and reinforcement of positive stimuli in order to treat addiction to unresolved negative emotions, maladaptive tendencies and residual developmental disorders.*

Squinting, she read the introduction again, digging through layers of grandiloquence to get to the meaning.

Aversion therapy. A way to condition someone's response, to cure addiction or adjust a person's impulses by means of negative and positive stimuli. Punishment and reward. Pain and pleasure.

She looked up from the book with a sigh. She thought of Harlan smacking her hand. Then she thought of his lips in her palm. For a moment she was lost in the past and regret.

Giving herself a mental shake she returned to the book. Each chapter that followed concerned itself with an individual patient. It detailed their background, education, employment, social class, blood type, build, height, weight and more complicated measurements of their heads, necks and facial features. The handwriting, gait and speech of each subject was analysed and their personal preferences in colour, literature and art recorded. Each patient was classified as either *sanguine, choleric, melancholic* or *phlegmatic*. Their 'addictions' and disorders were listed: *morbid alcoholic, compulsive gambler, pathological liar, agoraphobic, sado-masochist (punishes ego for perceived self-inadequacy), frigidity, transvestism, hysteria, kleptomania.*

The treatment for each patient was then detailed and a kind of diary followed. These listed the various 'stimuli' and how the aversion therapy was administered. Suze found regular references to a *Farral* device. She guessed this was some kind of medical instrument. There were often lengthy descriptions of settings and adjustments made on this device and their effect on each patient.

A dull, numbing ache crept into her head. The book was heavy reading and still didn't reveal much of anything.

She flicked the pages between finger and thumb like a deck of cards. Just more tedious descriptions of patients and their maladies.

The whole moribund volume was just one massive research document.

Bound into the middle of the book were old black and white photographs printed on glossy paper. She thumbed through them – then stopped. Her hand flew to her mouth. Her blood ran cold as seawater.

In the book was an image of a man strapped to a chair. Beside him was a machine similar to the one in the hidden room behind the alcove. The two terminals that led from the machine were taped to his temples and a gag had been placed in his mouth to prevent him biting his tongue. Underneath the image was the subtitle: *Plate I. Subject 9*.

The image had been captured mid-convulsion. The man's arms and legs contorted into impossible shapes. His eyes were wide, filled with helplessness, fear and agony. Beside the chair stood Henry Lacey, his hands upon dials and switches, the instrument of the man's suffering.

Suze stood, letting the book close. The picture disgusted her. It was brutal, sadistic, but it explained everything in a way the lengthy, written chapters of the book could not. This was the kind of sickening work her grandfather specialised in. A perversion of Pavlov's discovery.

She looked in the direction of the hidden room where the chair and device lay waiting in darkness.

Her mother had done the right thing to hide this room, this book, and their poisoned history from the world.

And she'd done the right thing in making old Pavlov stand guard outside.

25

'WHO WILL BIND YOU?
WHO WILL SET YOU FREE?'

TODAY WAS A FINE DAY for battle.

All night she'd rehearsed the blistering reprimands she would let fly at Ava Carfax. Like flaming arrows. Like rocks and spears.

The exercise had sharpened her resolve and lit a flame deep inside the aquamarine suitcase.

Her bicycle leaned against the wall in the great hall. Suze collected it, then opened her front door to a cold, bright day. She was unprepared for what she saw.

A tall, reedy man in a green Barbour jacket and flat cap stood centrally in the expanse of weeds and long grass between the house and the road. He was turning a slow circle, arms slack at his sides, scanning the landscape around him. His head dropped on more than one occasion to a blue stake hammered into the ground.

Perhaps he was from the same survey company, a town planner

perhaps? An architect? He looked like an architect.

The aquamarine suitcase bulged and warped. Suze growled and dropped the bicycle on the threshold. She disappeared into the darkness of the house and reappeared with the Crossley pistol in her hand. Marching towards him, she raised the pistol and cocked the hammer. At seeing her, the man's eyebrows elevated with alarm. He paled and raised his hands.

'Get off my property *now*!' screamed Suze, advancing on him. '*Now!*'

The man muttered an incoherence, an excuse perhaps. Then he turned and fled in the direction of the road.

Suze lowered the pistol.

A fine day for battle indeed.

—◂—•—▸—

'I'm sorry but she's in Truro this morning,' said the chirpy young female assistant. Suze recognised her voice as the one that had answered the phone when she'd first called from London.

Suze stood in the reception of Carfax and Bell, leaking bravado like a deflating balloon. Her enemy was a no-show. She chastised herself for not calling ahead. She had a phone now, so why hadn't she used it? She'd been so determined to meet Ava face to face. She still was. 'When will she be back?' she asked.

'This afternoon I suppose.' The girl didn't seem certain.

Suze chewed her lip. 'Then I'll drop by later'.

There was a bike rack outside the library where she'd chained her bike. She left the offices of Carfax and Bell and made her way in that direction. She stopped at the bus stop and checked her watch.

Her first thought was to cycle back to Aeolus House and then return in the afternoon. *But perhaps she could put her time to a better use?*

Her eyes ran down the bus stop timetable.

The next bus for Wadebridge was only ten minutes away.

———◆———

There was a frenzy of activity inside Kerenza's Bridal Couture.

The sole dressmaker bustled about, tending to the capricious needs of a group of young women, a bridal party no doubt. They filled the small shop with high-pitched laughter. An open bottle of *Lanson* stood on the cutting table.

Suze singled out the bride-to-be with ease: a pimpled, round-faced girl enjoying her moment in the sunshine of attention. This looked like her first fitting. The loosely-tacked sections of white silk and organza were draped over her. The dress would be wonderful. The dress of love. The dress that would bind her, or set her free.

The dressmaker offered Suze a nod of acknowledgement. *I'll be with you soon*, it said. *Be patient.* Then she set about her adjustments to the dress, her mouth filled with pins.

With time on her hands, Suze absently thumbed through the books of dress designs. The champagne-fuelled shrieking of the bridesmaids ground at her nerves. She gazed at the day outside and wondered about taking a walk. A little window-shopping on the high street might help pass the time. A chorused gasp went up and Suze turned in the direction of the sound. The girl was wearing the veil now. *Her* veil. She beamed with joy as her friends looked on with admiration.

It was an odd tradition, Suze thought, the hiding of a woman's face. More than the dress, more than any other outward aspect of marriage, it was a concealing, the parcelling up of a gift from one man to another, a father to a son-in-law. It was the handing over of a possession. *You may gaze upon her beauty, but others may not. She is yours alone now.*

It seemed ironic to Suze that something designed to hide her mother from the world was now trying to reveal her.

The young girl glowed with vanity behind the folds of silk. Suze hoped that whoever she looked upon through that veil would make her happy.

But who had her mother seen? Who was it she had wished to be bound to, or hoped would set her free?

That truth was still hidden. Only the veil could show her.

The young bride retired to a changing room and shed the dress, reappearing in a travesty of stone-washed denim with red shoes. She led her merry band of followers from the shop and Suze felt her nerves unfrazzle.

The dressmaker blew a long breath from puffed cheeks and held the champagne bottle up to the light. She shook it. Empty. She shot Suze a look. 'Cup of tea then?' she asked.

Suze nodded.

Several minutes later, Suze sat at one end of the cutting table, her hands around a mug of hot tea. From somewhere in the back, the dressmaker reappeared with the familiar cardboard box and Suze was suddenly alert with expectation. 'Did Kerenza remember the dress?' she asked.

'Oh yes,' was the woman's short reply. 'But not much else.' She sighed.

'Did she remember who she'd made it for?'

The dressmaker shook her head. 'She took a close look at the stitching, recognised her own work and seemed to remember. Even remembers it was some time in fifty-two or fifty-three.' She looked away. 'It's hard to keep her on track sometimes, she wanders.'

Suze stared into her mug of tea, despondent.

'She remembers making *The Hidden Child*, though. That part was very clear in her memory. I guess that kind of thing didn't happen much back then.' She took a sip from her own mug of tea, thoughtful. 'Damnedest thing though,' she offered.

'What?'

'Well, I don't know whether to place any stock in it, or no,' continued the dressmaker. 'As I said, her mind is addled these days.'

'Yes,' said Suze, 'please go on.'

'She said this was one of *two* dresses. That there was another.'

'Two dresses?'

'Yes, Kerenza said she made two dresses for the same customer. Sister dresses. Apart from *The Hidden Child*, they were identical.'

◄━━●━►

Suze gazed at the blurring scenery from the upstairs window of the bus as it travelled back to Storm Bay. Her mind was also blurred with thoughts, none of them grounded in fact, just conjecture and theories. She glanced at the cardboard box on the seat beside her.

Two dresses?

A double wedding perhaps?

Suze thought of the silver-framed picture on her grandfather's desk. It made no sense. *Where was the second couple?* There was only

213

one man: Harlan's father, Samuel Grey. So there had to be someone else. Someone was missing. Or, as the dressmaker had supposed, had old Kerenza's memory failed her? *I don't know whether to place any stock in it, or no. Her mind is addled these days.*

She stepped from the bus, her thoughts tangling – a cat's cradle of speculation. She set her jaw and, carrying the wedding dress in its box, walked to the offices of Carfax and Bell.

'Sorry but she's still not back,' said the young female assistant.

Suze gave a sigh of frustration and checked her watch. 4.30pm. 'Do you think she'll back today?'

'Not sure,' came the reply. 'We close at five.'

Suze turned for the door. 'Then I'll be back before you close.'

◂—●—▸

The low, cramped bar of The Lugger was busy with patrons. There was a mingled burr of local accents punctuated by the occasional rasp of laughter.

Suze sat at a table by herself, gazing into space over the rim of her gin and bitter lemon, seeing nothing in particular. She was still meditating on the mystery of the sister dresses. Her mother's lay in its box on the chair beside her.

People passed her, on the way in, on the way out, or to the toilets, or the cigarette machine. She paid them no heed. She became dimly aware of someone standing nearby, on the other side of the table.

'You know it's illegal to threaten someone with a gun?' came a voice. 'Even if they *are* on your property.'

Suze looked up. The man in the green Barbour jacket and flat cap stood opposite, a pint of ale in his hand. His expression wasn't reproachful, the comment not an accusation. It seemed nothing more than an observation.

'It wasn't loaded,' replied Suze.

'How was I to know?'

Some of Suze's aggression was creeping back. She still wanted to pick a fight with someone. She looked around. Here was not the place. Not now.

'I just wanted to talk with you...' explained the man.

'Do you work for Ava Carfax too?'

The man shook his head.

'Then what are you?'

He faltered at Suze's directness. 'I'm a board member of a not-for-profit organisation.'

'What has that got to do with me?'

'Because I have a proposition for you...'

Suze gathered up the box and her drink, about to escape.

The man held out his hands in appeal. 'Don't you want to hear?'

'Not really,' said Suze, passing him.

'There's a way to avoid inheritance tax,' he said, 'and restore the house.'

Suze stopped, turning. 'Is this some kind of scam? I've had it to the eyeballs with dodgy lawyers and cowboy developers...'

'I know,' he confided.

Suze's eyes narrowed. 'You *know*?'

'Harlan Grey told me. He's the one who suggested we talk...'

Suze groaned and turned away once more.

'He wants to help, Miss Newman. Believe me, I do too.'

Suze flashed him a look of distrust.

'I'll only take a few minutes of your time. Then I'll leave you to think about it. I'm staying here at the pub for a few days. If you'd like to talk further, I'll be here.'

Suze stared at him, looking for a darker motive. She saw none. 'Very well,' she found herself saying.

The man bought her a fresh glass of gin and slid it across the table, along with his business card. He removed his cap and sat. 'Name's Hislop. I work for a children's charity.'

Suze read the organisation's name on the card: *The Haven Trust*.

'We take on suitable residences, large houses mostly, like yours. And we convert them into safe communities for disadvantaged children.'

Suze looked up. She leaned across the table. 'Like orphans?'

'Orphans are among them, yes.'

'And foster children?'

'And foster children too, as well as children in danger of violence, mistreatment, poverty or abuse. We take in as many as we can, as many as we can afford to.'

Suze found herself nodding in agreement. Hislop's eyes were kind, now that she noticed.

'If you were to donate Aeolus House to our charity, you'd escape inheritance tax. We'd return the house to its former glory and you can sell the surrounding land for a profit. Harlan has already spoken to a few interested parties: dairy farmers and the like.'

She was glad now she hadn't shot Hislop with one of the

Crossley Twins. 'How do you know I want the house preserved?'

'Oh, Harlan explained all that, he knew you'd insist on it. And it's very much in line with our philosophy, too.' He sipped at his ale. 'It was a beautiful old place once, it can be again. And with all its space, the countryside and the beaches, it'll make a marvellous home for our children.'

Suze sat back, thoughtful. She was grateful she hadn't shot Harlan, too, when they'd first met. 'You know, if I agree to all this, I'd do it on one condition...'

Hislop smiled. 'I'm all ears,' he said.

26

SUBJECT 53

SUZE WOKE TO THE SOUND of hammering on the front door. She checked her wristwatch. 9.20am.

Shit.

Now that she had electricity she was staying up later at night. She was getting up later in the mornings, too.

Rolling from her sleeping bag she threw a coat over her pyjamas and traipsed downstairs.

The hammering continued.

'I'm coming!'

She flung the door open to a vision of tweed, worsted, and unruly eyebrows.

'Ava?'

'The inquest in Truro is over. Your mother's post-mortem is done.'

Suze felt her mouth open and close. She hadn't returned to Carfax and Bell in time to confront Ava yesterday. She'd been with

Hislop at The Lugger. Now that the object of her hostility was standing on her doorstep, she was off-guard, unprepared. The rage of yesterday had evaporated.

'The medical examiner wants to present his findings to you at Bosvenor,' Ava looked at her watch. 'In thirty minutes.'

'In person?' Suze was perplexed.

'This happens sometimes, when they find something – something they weren't expecting.'

'Such as?'

'I really couldn't say. The M.E. just thinks it best to report his findings to you directly.'

Suze drew her fingers across her brow. 'Okay.'

'So why don't you go make yourself presentable,' commanded Ava, taking in the pyjamas, unlaced track shoes and uncombed hair. 'I'll drive you.'

◄—●—►

The journey to Bosvenor Sanatorium in Ava's Austin was brisk and businesslike. Ava gave Suze a rundown of what she could expect from the County Medical Examiner: a brief summary of his findings, any questions, then some form-signing. Her mother's remains would then be transferred to Bodmin to await cremation. Suze remained quiet throughout the journey. In her mind she was rummaging through the aquamarine suitcase, trying to find the rage of yesterday. She'd lost it and feared she wouldn't find it again. Besides, *was this the right time*? She needed to know the reasons for her mother's death. Her showdown with Ava could wait.

At the sanatorium, they were ushered into Dr Passmore's

office. The good doctor himself sat at a distance, his own desk now occupied by an older man with reading glasses: the medical examiner. This man's skin seemed to exhibit the same pale, greasy translucence as the subjects of his many examinations. Suze guessed he hadn't seem much in the way of sunlight recently – just the inside of courtrooms and mortuaries. He also appeared exhausted. Clearly, the backlog of work caused by his court attendance was taking its toll.

The examiner offered a difficult smile and invited Suze to sit.

'I assume you know the circumstances of your mother's death, if not the actual cause?' he began.

'Yes,' answered Ava on Suze's behalf. Dr Passmore directed a sheepish glance at his own shoes.

'She was found on the moor north of here, at night I believe?' said Suze, daring Ava to speak for her again with a stony look.

The examiner removed his reading glasses. He took a shallow breath before continuing. His exhaustion seemed to make everything a labour. 'That's right, an unfortunate *accident*,' he confirmed. The emphasis on his final word suggested he wanted no further accusation. Case closed. He returned his spectacles to the bridge of his nose and read from an open manila folder. 'Now, while the extant cause of death was hypothermia, brought about by exposure to cold weather at the time, we must also understand that the deceased's state of mind was a contributing factor.'

'She died of madness, is that what you're saying?' asked Suze.

Ava shot Suze a frown of warning.

'No,' was the examiner's laborious reply. 'It was a *contributing factor*. If she possessed the faculty to understand what kind of danger she was in, she may not have ventured onto the moor in the first place. My findings indicate she may have been driven to this by a combination of neuroses and, more importantly, *neurotrauma*.' He fixed Suze with a weighty stare.

'What's neurotrauma?' she asked.

'Brain damage – *physical* damage to the brain.'

'So, on the moor, she hit her head on something?' Suze was struggling to understand.

'No,' replied the examiner. 'The damage was old, and – *unusual*.'

Suze's eyes bored into him. 'What kind of damage?'

'Perhaps it's best if I show you.'

◂—•—▸

The press of warm bodies in the small room did nothing to banish the freezing cold.

Suze pulled her coat more tightly about her.

Dr Passmore tugged at the steel stretcher on which Suze's mother lay. It rattled out of its recess and into the room on noisy runners.

Everyone gave the medical examiner space. He approached, lifting the sheet from the face of the late Emma Lacey. Suze had expected to see some kind of decomposition after the three weeks her mother had lain here. Nothing appeared to have changed. Just a more pronounced waxiness to the skin, a more rictus-like expression to her face.

The examiner pointed to a spot on the deceased's temple. 'During my external examination, I noticed this.'

The assembly in the small room leaned close.

'It's scarring from an old burn,' he explained. 'The odd thing is, there's an identical scar on the other side.' He pointed to the deceased's other temple.

Suze gasped in the frosty air. She was looking at her mother's image in the photographs at Aeolus House: seated next to her father; between her friends, the Greys. In both pictures, her mother wore that strange scarf around her head like a dopey turban or a frilly headband. She wasn't putting on airs and graces, wasn't trying to be fashionable. She was hiding something – burn marks, scars, the badges of pain.

The medical examiner continued. 'But it was only during my internal examination, when I opened the cranium, that I found the full extent of the problem. The frontal lobe of the brain showed lateral scarring between these two locations.'

'So the inside of her brain was burned too?' asked Suze.

The examiner gave a grim nod. 'Something passed between these two locations, causing the damage. Most likely an electrical current of some kind. And it doesn't look like a single instance. The scarring is accumulative. This happened over a period of time.'

'This can't be what I think it is – I mean, not here – *electroshock therapy*?' said Ava.

'Well, my findings are consistent with that,' continued the medical examiner, 'but the scarring is quite old. This would have happened long before the deceased's admission to this institution.'

'This did not happen here I can assure you,' said Dr Passmore, reinforcing the point. 'Electroshock therapy is a thing of the past.'

Suze's mind was racing. Photographs from her grandfather's book flipped over in her mind: the man convulsing in agony, electrodes at his temples.

The examiner continued. 'Damage to this part of the brain can result in many cognitive problems: attention deficit, memory loss, but also increased impulsivity and tendency to greater risk taking. It's this part of the brain that helps self-correct us, it helps us make better choices.'

'So, what you're saying is – if her brain hadn't been damaged, she might never have walked out onto the moors at night, in a wedding dress?' pressed Suze.

'Just so,' said the examiner. 'As I explained, the cause of death was hypothermia, but neurotrauma played a part in that.'

Possibilities continued bouncing around in Suze's head. 'If this damage is old, as you say, could it have been the cause of her illness in the first place? Without it, she might never have been admitted here. Maybe she would've been normal? Led a normal, happy life at home on her own?'

'I don't entertain *maybes*, Miss Newman,' offered the examiner without emotion. 'My job here is to investigate cause of death.'

'Okay, but my mother may have been completely sane if it wasn't for this damage to her mind.'

The examiner glowered, offering no answer.

'It's possible, isn't it?' asked Suze.

The examiner sighed, relenting. 'Yes, yes, it's possible. But that's not proven.'

'Not yet,' offered Suze.

The examiner eyed her warily.

'One last thing.' Suze directed the question at no one in particular. 'What does "*I follow*" mean?'

The examiner cocked his head in question.

'My mother wrote these words across the walls in her room, here...' Suze glanced upstairs. 'I found the same words written on the walls in the house where she'd lived. Do you know what they mean?'

Dr Passmore let out a long sigh. 'As I mentioned, those were her last words,' he said.

'So what do they mean?'

Dr Passmore shook his head. 'I have no idea.'

The medical examiner was eyeing the door. 'Well, I've left my examination report with Dr Passmore in case you have any more questions. A copy will be filed at the coroner's office.'

The party turned for the door as Dr Passmore made to slide the steel stretcher away.

Suze stopped him, placing a hand on his arm. 'If you don't mind,' she said. 'I'd like a moment.'

He gave a weak smile and left the room, closing the door.

Suze stood beside the steel stretcher, waiting for the footsteps beyond the door to fade into silence. Then she gazed at her mother's face. Tentatively, she lifted a finger, placing it on her mother's scarred temple. The spot of skin there was cold, rough and calloused.

'What did they do to you Mum?' whispered Suze, surprising herself at her utterance of a word she'd never used before. 'I want you to show me.'

— ● —

'Now that's over, the service and cremation will take place over the next few days,' said Ava, hunched over the steering wheel of her Austin. She was driving Suze and herself back to Storm Bay. 'Will you be staying, or will you return to London?'

You really don't want me here, do you? Thought Suze. *And now I know why.*

Ava flashed her a sidelong look, then returned eyes to the road.

That old companion, anger, glowed like a coal inside the aqua-marine suitcase. There, locked away in the dark, Suze recognised another feeling: sorrow. A sadness for the mother she never knew.

'I'll be here,' said Suze.

Ava shot another questioning look from the corner of her eye. 'Then give some thought to the cremation and the memorial service at St Carras. If there's any arrangements you want made, you need to talk to Reverend Tonkin. You'll need to do it quickly.'

Suze watched the landscape blur through the passenger window. 'I know what you're up to,' she said.

Inside the cramped car the silence grew heavy.

Ava gripped the wheel a little more tightly. 'Whatever do you mean?'

'Your plans for Aeolus House.'

'What plans?'

'Twenty-six luxury houses for a start. I know you're scheming to take the house away from me, to tear it down and develop.'

'Who told you this?'

'I guess you'll sell off each plot for a profit?'

Ava turned to her, eyes fearful. She licked her lips.

'So who else is in on this? Someone at Bosvenor? Passmore? And did you cut Harlan in on the deal, to keep him in line?'

'Harlan no longer works for me.'

'You fired him?'

'He resigned.'

Suze sighed. 'Well, at least someone has scruples.'

'How dare you,' said Ava, under her breath.

'How dare *I*?' returned Suze. 'I know you've been trying to keep me poor, so you can buy the place for a song and cash in. I've seen surveyors crawling all over the property, hammering in pegs, marking out roads. I know you sent them. No, how very *dare you*, Ava!'

'I don't have to justify myself to you.' Ava's tone was edged with spite.

'Well I think you do, because what you're doing is against the law.'

Ava pulled sharply to the side of the road at the outskirts of Storm Bay. She tugged at the handbrake but left the motor running. Then she turned to Suze and spoke through clenched teeth. 'What do you know about the law?' she hissed. 'What gives you any kind of right to question me?'

'Last I looked, the place is *legally* mine. And yet you've sent surveyors out there to carve the place up right under my nose. How is that not illegal?'

Ava's ire cooled. Her seat creaked as she leaned back. She was searching for her next argument, as lawyers often did. 'Do you know how long people have been out of pocket, tending to your mother, looking after her affairs, her needs? No you don't, because you *weren't here*. This has been going on a long, long time Susanna, and people are *owed*. This plan was the best way forward, the only way to repay the debts and square the books. But then *you* arrived, didn't you? And suddenly it's all about what *you* want, what *you're* owed.'

'Well, you made a mistake,' replied Suze. 'You assumed there wouldn't be anyone else, an heir, someone like me. You thought no one else would ever know what you were up to. So you and your friends cooked up a little get-rich-quick scheme and waited for my mother's death.'

Ava seethed.

'So here's what's going to happen: I'm the one who'll decide whether the place gets sold and who it gets sold to.' She unbuckled her seat belt and opened the door. 'And I guarantee I won't be selling to you.'

Ava leaned across as Suze stepped from the car. 'People are owed!' she shouted.

Suze followed the road towards Storm Bay. 'Then send me a bill,' she said.

———◆———

Suze found the iron keys in her pocket and slammed the largest into the lock of the front door. Hurrying inside, she made her way to the study, seething with suspicion, angry with purpose.

The book lay closed on the desk where she'd left it. She snatched it up and opened it to the table of contents, then ran her finger over the list of chapters – just numbers allocated to each patient. That's all they'd been to him: test subjects, experiments, numbers, never people.

Opening the book to its centre, she licked a forefinger and flipped through the glossy pages. One after another, the scenes of cruelty revealed themselves. The images were harrowing, inhumane; torture enough just to look upon. Mouths foaming at the gag, eyes distended in agony, twisted joints, ligaments and tendons stretched to tearing from bolts of searing electricity. Men slumped unconscious, post-treatment, pools of excrement at their feet. Women hung from the chair straps, heads bowed like broken dolls. Desolate children stared towards the camera, not understanding what crime deserved such brutality. She turned a leaf by its corner and her finger fell from the page. Her heart shuddered to a halt. She stared, transfixed by one of the photographs.

Plate IX. Subject 53. In front of the chair, taking notes with cold-eyed indifference, stood Henry Lacey. Strapped to the chair was a young woman, electrodes at her temples. She was convulsing in pain, elbows bent backwards to the point of dislocation. Suze recognised the room and the woman's terrified eyes.

She hurled the book across the study. It struck one of the bookcases and landed, spine broken, pages flapping like a dying bird.

She placed hands on the desk and stared into the silver-framed photograph of her mother.

Into those very same eyes.

27

'WHAT DID HE DO TO YOU?'

SLEEP EVADED HER that night. She chewed her fingernails, struggling to contain her fury and spat curses into the dark air above her sleeping bag.

Henry Lacey – she didn't know much about him, didn't have much to go on, but now she had his measure. She knew his guilt. In her mind he already dangled, blindfolded and kicking, from the gallows of her judgement.

Among the evidence that convicted him was the oval photograph – his eyes scratched out by a daughter who despised him. A daughter he'd tortured, a daughter so sickened by the image of them together that she'd banished it to an upstairs room and hidden it behind a chest of drawers, covered by a sheet. The photograph had troubled Suze from the start and now she understood why. It was a lie, a mockery of family life – tormentor and victim captured in a heartbreaking parody of togetherness. Yet there was something else still buried deep within the image, a perversity she couldn't fathom but only sense.

She thought of him as she saw him through the veil, his hand landing across her face, sending her to the floor. How many times did that hand land upon her mother?

The most damning evidence of all was the photographs in his book – the muscle-tearing, brain-cauterising electrocutions he'd inflicted in pursuit of what – *science*? The room. The chair. They'd all been hidden away by her mother, in shame, in fear.

How could he do that to his own daughter?

Why couldn't he have loved her the way a father should?

The thoughts thrashed around in her brain until dawn. In the weak light that leaked through dirty windows, she rose, made her way downstairs and met the day, numbed and wrung out. She drank a cup of instant coffee.

Her mind cleared a little, forming plans, seeing new ways to proceed.

She knew now that the visions she'd glimpsed though the veil formed fragments of a story. The story of a single day. Whether any wedding took place was another matter. That day had belonged to her mother, *should have* belonged to her mother.

Her eyes lifted in the direction of her mother's bedroom.

She'd already traced that day back to its beginning. She'd wound that day back like a clock, to a morning thirty years before when her mother had slipped from her bed and dressed herself in white.

Begin at the beginning.

And see where it takes you.

Suze dropped the mug on the kitchen table, spilling coffee.

Wide awake at last, she hurried back upstairs.

The late autumn sunshine worked its way through the grime-covered windows of her mother's bedroom.

She left the wedding dress in its cardboard box on the bare mattress and picked up the veil lying beside it. Running the silk between finger and thumb it felt non-existent, just a thin, delicate curtain separating yesterday from today.

Show me, Mum.

What did he do to you?

Suze had nowhere to be today, nothing to do. She wouldn't be disturbed. She could devote this day to the veil and what it cared to show her. She lifted the transparent material over her head and it floated into place, down to her waist. Then she placed the wreathed crown with its silver oak leaves and pearl mistletoe on her brow.

She waited, unsure which way to summon the visions. Should she should concentrate hard, willing the apparitions into existence? Should she become an empty vessel, or let her mother do the work?

The sunlight from the window dimmed.

Dark clouds swept the sky like a storm front.

In the room, the dimming light cast a freshness over the wallpaper. It shone brightly, as if freshly printed. The grey patches, the words her mother had scribbled there, faded and disappeared. The dust lifted. The bed became made. The brass bedstead shone. The dressing table was moved aside, revealing the hiding place beneath the floorboards. On top of the dressing table stood a shining brass oil lamp among vases filled with summer flowers. Beside these lay an opened letter. Suze knew the words it contained.

...Only One...

Our day... joy and fear.

I rejoice... the God of love...

He will join us...

...evermore.

Sam.

The dressing table mirror was polished now. It returned the gleaming vision of a young woman in a new wedding dress. Suze knew where she was. When she was. *Who* she was.

Looking down, she saw the dress as her mother had once seen it: the folds of cloth unworn and uncreased. The material felt stiff with newness, fresh yards of fabric stitched together with Kerenza's clever needle.

Turning from the reflection, she saw the room. It distorted, grew larger, making her feel small, weak. The door retreated into the distance as if standing at the end of a long hallway. The perspective of uprights and horizontals began to twist and contort. The geometry of the walls and ceiling slid into impossible angles. Outside, the sky boiled, purple and black. Sheets of lightning lit the clouds.

Is this how you saw the world?

Did it frighten you so?

Sounds came to her ears, unnatural, otherworldly. Suze guessed these were just distortions of the wind against the windows and down the chimney flues. They became a crescendo of whistling, whispering.

She moved towards the door and the room swam in her vision.

She felt her nausea rise and swallowed hard, quelling it.

These visions were fragile, she knew that. If she moved of her own volition, in a way her mother never had, then the images would vanish. She had to be guided by her mother, *become* her mother. It was Emma's past she was witnessing, not her own. She had to let it play out without resisting.

She felt herself melt into her mother's form, her mother's dress, feeling through her mother's senses, becoming her wholly. She floated along, a soul in her mother's pocket, a passenger on her shoulder. She wasn't Suze Newman any longer, and she wasn't quite Emma Lacey, either. She was both of them and something in between. *Susanna-Emma? Suzemma?*

She was moving towards the door now, and the perspective of the room shifted, a world seen through bottle-glass, turning, warping, making her dizzy. Fear clutched at her. Is this what her mother endured? Is this how her broken mind had seen the world?

Placing an ear against the door, Suzemma listened. There was no other noise in the house except the sibilance of the wind. Inside Emma's mind, Suze listened. It was a hissing that ran into itself, over and over, layer upon layer. Not the wind in the chimney or against the windows. Not the wind at all. *Words.*

Words that whispered in the corners of her mind, words that repeated themselves, insistent, maddening.

Uselessuselessuselessuselessuselessuselessworthlessworthlessworthless worthless...

Suze shivered, cold and afraid.

The door opened and the two women stepped through.

Before them the landing spiralled towards the top of the stairs.

Together, they moved towards it. It was like walking without a sense of balance, dazed and drunk. The arched window above the landing framed the diabolic landscape, the sky churned black, purple and crimson. The bowed Scots pine hung suspended above dark earth, revolving, roots in air.

Suzemma turned at the head of the stairs, a hand upon the banister. One step down towards the great hall. Then another. Another.

And there he was.

Samuel Grey stepped from the darkness in a double-breasted suit, his feet facing backwards. Suze held her breath, taking in his features. He was so like Harlan, although she could see now that his chin was more square, his face rounder. He had the same, slender fingers, and long, dark eyelashes. His hair, unlike Harlan's untidy tangle of a fringe, was oiled and combed neatly back from his forehead. A thin moustache lined his top lip, and where Harlan's eyes danced with nervous humour, these eyes seemed to brim with a sad languor, as if he had been crying.

He held out his hand to her in petition, not a gesture of invitation, but one of pleading. His eyes fell to the dress.

'It's beautiful,' he said. His words echoed down the years. 'But is this the day for such a dress?'

Together, mother and daughter took another step down the stairs, towards him.

He shook his head. 'I beg you – don't do this.'

Suze felt like gasping but resisted. She was frightened she'd ruin the vision. This wasn't the meeting of a couple about to marry, to elope. It was something different.

Emma shot a quick glance upwards, then to the side, across the banister. Suze let her own gaze follow, realising that her mother had looked up to the landing, to the double doors of her father's bedroom, then down to the door of his study. The uppermost corner of the door was visible above the staircase. She felt her mother's chest tighten. *What frightens you Emma?*

'Don't leave me alone,' continued Samuel.

Suze's breathing stilled. *There was someone else?*

He clasped both hands together. '*Please* understand what you are doing – to yourself, to all of us. I can't allow it...' He stepped backwards then, away from her, the hindward-facing feet retreating, disowning her. Samuel Grey lifted his eyes towards the landing and shouted. 'Doctor! Doctor Lacey, come quick, please!' He turned to Suzemma then with burning eyes and shouted again. 'Henry, here! Come quickly!'

Suze felt herself catapulted past Samuel Grey as he shouted the alarm. She felt her mother running, as if for her life, the long skirt of the dress hitched up in her hands. She ran across the great hall, past paintings and photographs, towards the stormwatchers' gallery. Somewhere a door opened and thunderous footsteps rang against floorboards. Voices were raised in panic. Two voices – men's voices. Then the thunder of the footsteps quickened, turning in her direction, clattering down stairs and into the hall. She was being pursued, her mother was being chased. And Suze felt the same fear.

The hall convulsed in shape, becoming more vast and monstrous as Suze was carried along. She felt her mother's fear twist and bend the house into new and more terrifying shapes. The shutters in the stormwatchers' gallery stood open, revealing a doomsday of sea and sky. The infernal panorama boiled in shades of purple and black, a bruise that shrouded the land and hid the sun.

Stumbling sideways, Suze felt her hand reach out and find something to steady her. Under the palm of her hand was fabric, coarse with thick threads. Her mother's head turned then, and Suze saw the tapestry. Her fingers lay close to the saint's elongated head, his hands raised in orison to the storm. She struggled, fought, and pulled it from the wall on its heavy hinges. Before her lay the dark opening in the stonework that led to freedom, to salvation. Her ears rang with the clamour of approaching footsteps and the hissing of whispered curses.

Uselessuselessuselessuselessworthlessworthlessworthless...

Suze felt the paralysis of fear in her mother's body. Emma was too frightened to continue, too frightened to stay, caught between flight and surrender. Another sound rang in her ears, becoming louder, more insistent. It drowned the whispers and silenced the thunder of the footsteps. It was a ringing that filled the house, louder and louder, amplified and electrical. Suze felt herself detach, drift away from her mother, hands slipping from each other's grasp. The sky through the gallery windows cleared, the boiling purple clouds folded in on themselves, became small, and were pulled from the air. The sea calmed, and became the reflected blue of the sky. The ringing sound buzzed and rattled, buzzed and rattled. It had broken the veil's spell – a sound from the real world, from the present, from *today*. Coming round, Suze tried to place it.

The phone.

Throwing the veil back over her head, she ran into the great hall. The twisted perspectives had gone, replaced by the more usual decay of the house. Suze reached for the plastic handset of the new phone. She pulled it to her ear, panting. 'Hello?'

'Miss Newman?'

'Who is this?'

'Hislop. You gave me your number, remember?'

Suze herded her thoughts into some kind of order. 'Yes. Of course.'

'You okay? You sound out of breath.'

'It's just a long way to the phone,' explained Suze.

There was a faint chuckle from the other end of the line. 'I've no doubt it is. Look, just wanted you to know I talked with our partners and a few of the other board members. Good news is, we're happy to agree to your *condition*.'

She was alert now. 'Oh, you are? Great.'

'Is there anything else I can help with? Any further information you need?'

'No, no. Thank you.'

'Because, if you like, I could drive over and discuss...'

'I've made up my mind,' Suze interrupted.

Hislop drew a long breath that crackled down the line. 'You've reached a decision?'

Suze took in the shambolic expanse of the house, the dirt and ruin. 'I have,' she said.

28

'IS THIS WHERE YOU WANT TO SPEND ETERNITY?'

THE CHURCH OF ST CARRAS THE ANCHORITE was a plain, unadorned building of Cornish granite that looked more like a fortification than a place of worship. It huddled low to the landscape, as if in fear of the nor'westers that swept in from the belly of the Atlantic. There was no spire, just a crown of simple crenellations and a roof of black Delabole slate. Suze guessed it was Norman, built long after the exploits and passing of the saint whose name it bore.

She propped her bike against the low granite wall that circled the church and cemetery then walked between the parades of centuries-old headstones, the names and dedications on them worn away by the weather of countless winters. On their southern sides, warmed by the sun, the stones were crusted with dull moss and sage-green lichen. Their northern sides revealed only featureless stone.

Reverend Tonkin was a stocky, red-haired man no older than

241

Suze. His smiling face shone with a ruddy outdoorsiness that made him look more like a jovial wrestler or rugby player than a man of the cloth. He welcomed Suze into a vestry that smelled of candle wax and old flowers, then collected a weighty set of keys and threw a coat over his black clerical shirt. 'Let's take a walk,' he suggested.

Outside, they walked the white gravel to the side of the church where the path became a patchwork of damp grass and uneven stone.

'I was going to suggest a simple order of service,' said Reverend Tonkin, looking at Suze in search of approval.

'Fine by me,' she said.

'What do you think about the Eucharist?'

It seemed like a knotty, theological question. Suze halted, not knowing how to answer.

'Did you plan on Holy Communion? As part of the service?' continued the vicar.

'No, not really,' she replied.

'Very well, it's not entirely necessary and it'll speed things up if we drop it.' They continued walking. 'I'd suggest a psalm, some readings, and no more than three hymns. The locals here like the Wesleyan ones best, and anything about the sea – *Eternal Father, Strong To Save* always raises the roof.' He smiled.

'Whatever you think best,' said Suze with a small frown. If the vicar believed the church would be packed with mourners, then he was going to be disappointed. Anyone attending her mother's funeral would only do so to stick their noses in, or gloat.

'Will you be reading a eulogy?'

'I, I hadn't really thought about it...' she stammered.

'Well, if you want to, there's time. The service will be short.'

Suze nodded gravely, not sure what she could really say about a woman she'd never known.

'And the cremation will be in Bodmin?' asked the vicar.

'Yes, the day after tomorrow. I'm told the ashes will arrive here the following morning,' said Suze.

'Ah, here we are,' he said, stopping in front of one of the monuments. It rose higher than the surrounding headstones, the size of a telephone box, carved from granite and glossy black marble. Above a narrow set of wrought iron gates ran a lintel bearing the name 'Lacey'.

'The family columbarium,' explained the vicar. He fished the keys from his pocket and thrust one into the lock. The iron gates squealed open and Suze peered inside. The interior of the structure was lined with niches, like letter boxes behind a hotel reception desk.

'The Laceys preferred to be cremated,' mused the Reverend. 'That's why your grandfather commissioned this, when your grandmother died.'

'How many are here?' asked Suze.

'Laceys?' He nodded towards two niches sealed with black marble. 'Only your grandparents for now.'

Her eyes ran over the remaining stone compartments, there were dozens. All empty – the way they'd remain. This is where the Lacey family ended. She wasn't one of them. If one of these niches was meant for her, she didn't want it. She glanced up, at the family name, carved in marble and highlighted in gold leaf. The pride of it all, the arrogance. It was just a waste of good stone.

'Your mother will soon be reunited with her parents,' said the vicar, pointing to a vacant niche. It sat beside another bearing the name *Dr Henry Lacey*.

Suze scowled.

Is this where you want to spend eternity?

Beside the man who tortured you?

———◆———

The good Reverend locked the columbarium and hurried away. Suze assumed this was to begin the important preparations for her mother's funeral, although it could equally have been to coach the local rugby team. She threaded her way back through the headstones towards the lychgate. Halfway, she stopped. A familiar figure stooped over one of the graves, a loose bunch of autumn asters in his hand. She approached, her footfall silent on damp grass.

'Hi,' she said.

Harlan looked up. An assortment of emotions seemed to pass across his features. Clouds across the sun. It took him a moment to compose himself. 'Hi,' he replied.

Suze looked down to where his gaze had been fixed. A double grave. *Loving husband. Loving wife.* 'Your parents?' she asked.

'Yes,' he murmured without taking his eyes from her.

Below her feet lay the man she'd seen at the foot of the stairs. The physical remains of a vision from the past. She took in the matched headstones, the grave no bigger than a double bed, and she knew that Harlan's father had never been her mother's lover.

There was someone else.

'I heard you'd quit your job,' she offered.

Harlan cleared his throat. 'Uh, yes. No longer the oldest trainee in the business.' There was the nervous smile.

'Why'd you do that?' she asked, searching his face.

His smile faded. 'I realised it wasn't for me – the law, the subterfuge. I didn't like who I was becoming.'

She nodded. 'So what now? What will you do?'

He drew in a breath of cold autumn air. 'I'll probably go back to restoration work. There's an old workshop down near the harbour I've got my eye on. The rent's cheap.'

'It's honest work,' she said.

'It is,' he replied, 'I just wish honest work paid a little better.'

'It does – in its own way.'

The nervous smile put in another appearance.

'And thanks by the way, for putting Hislop in touch.'

Harlan's mouth formed a circle. 'Oh, you're welcome. Will you take him up on his offer?'

'Perhaps,' she said. She'd already given Hislop her answer but Harlan didn't need to know. Not yet.

'Well, either way, I'm sorry you have to lose the place. I know how much it means to you.'

'It's just a house.' Her eyes fell back to the double grave. She realised now that she'd been looking for answers in all the wrong places. A house wouldn't mend her. A house wouldn't bring back all she'd lost. She thought of the couple deep below the wet earth at their feet, folded in eternal sleep. Home lay in the hearts of others. Not in houses.

'Good to see you, Harlan,' she said.

'Good to see you, too,' he replied. '*Although* – strange place to meet.'

She lifted her chin in the direction of the Lacey columbarium.

'I came to see family.'

'Same,' he said, separating the blue flowers in his hands. Then he crouched and laid half the flowers in the centre of the double grave.

His hand rested a moment on the damp ground. It was a gesture of longing, of loss. Suze guessed Harlan and his parents had been close.

It's us against the world.

Family first, everyone else comes second.

She thought of the stone columbarium nearby, raised in vanity to the memory of her own damaged family. Suze and Harlan's people shared the same resting place, but they'd lived worlds apart. When Harlan stood, half the blue flowers remained in his hand.

Suze eyed the asters. 'Are they for someone else?'

Harlan nodded. 'My aunt. You remember, she was in the photograph with my father and your mother?'

Suze pictured the penetrating eyes. The fierce, dark beauty of Harlan's aunt. Samuel Grey's sister.

'Come with me?' asked Harlan.

'Sure.'

He turned and led her through the churchyard, to a break in the stone wall. There was a stile there, slabs of granite laid upright with others balanced across to create steps. Harlan climbed over and held out a hand for Suze. 'Where are we going?' she asked, placing her hand in his. On the other side of the stile was a well-worn hiking path. 'For a walk?'

'Just a short one, I promise,' he replied.

She followed him to a corner outside the church wall that

formed part of a field. Here, beneath a stunted crab-apple tree, Harlan began pulling away handfuls of bracken and meadow grass. Puzzled, Suze stepped close to see that he'd uncovered a mound of soil. On top of this mound rested a jam jar filled with dead flowers.

Suze looked in the direction of the church, to the other side of the wall, where the rest of Harlan's family lay. 'Why is she *here*?' she asked.

Harlan gave a pained look. 'Like I said, she took her own life.' He looked down at the pitiful mound of soil hidden away in the corner of the field. 'So she had to rest here, on unhallowed ground.'

Suze felt a sudden kinship with this woman. She'd been rejected too, from family, from the society of a world that judged too cruelly, too quickly. Suze wanted to crawl under this apple tree and curl up on the mound with her, to tell her she wasn't alone, she wasn't the only one.

Harlan placed the jam jar upright and dropped the remaining asters inside. He tutted and reached for something in the bracken, it was a small wooden cross, painted white with blue lettering. He forced it into the soil at the head of his aunt's grave. Then he stood and flashed his nervous smile at Suze. 'Always felt sorry for her, here on her own.'

Her own, long-forgotten smile was still locked away in the aquamarine suitcase. But now it shimmered with hope, like a coin in a wishing well. She could wear it now, she felt, and the thought made her heart pound. Then it faltered and stopped as she was struck with a sudden, icy realisation.

On the little white cross at the head of the makeshift grave was a name written in blue letters.

Samantha Grey 1919 – 1952.
Samantha Grey.
Samantha.
Sam?

29

'HERE ARE THE INSTRUMENTS OF OUR UNION'

SITTING AT HER GRANDFATHER'S DESK Suze held the silver-framed photograph in both hands. Her mother. Samuel Grey. Samantha Grey. She studied the language of their poses. Samuel's hands held the two women's. He was looking straight at the camera, as was her mother, that rare smile on her face. Yet Samantha's eyes were elsewhere. They gleamed, and were fixed upon her mother.

Now that Suze was taking notice, there was something else. It was plain, although she hadn't spotted it before.

While each woman placed one hand in Samuel's, the other was at his back, visible just above his shoulder. Here, the two women's hands were in each other's, entwined tightly, fingers interlocked. Their own secret joining.

Suze looked to the torn and broken book that lay on the floor at the far end of the study. She glared at it as if, by the force of her will alone, she could make it burst into flames.

If she picked it up and read, she knew what she'd find inside. She'd learn that the agonies inflicted on her mother by her grandfather were necessary, a cure for her disease, her addiction. Until yesterday, Suze hadn't really considered what this addiction might be. She'd supposed it could have been anything: alcoholism, kleptomania or gambling. But now Suze was circling the truth, she could see it, smell it. Instinctively, she knew the nature of her mother's addiction.

Her mother had been addicted to other women.

Suze could pick up the book and check. She'd find all the evidence inside. There would be notes, there would be detailed, clinical, scientific records of her perversion, her disease. She'd read of the methods used to purge this evil. Of its success. She knew that the arrogance of Dr Lacey would never allow him to admit defeat. All his subjects would be cured, including his wayward daughter.

Was it pride that wouldn't allow him to accept his daughter as she was?

Was he frightened by her addiction?

Did he see the same tendencies in himself and seek to annihilate them through his ministry of pain, torment and electricity?

She could always pick the book up and read. But she didn't want to. It revolted her, made her skin prickle, turned her mouth into a sneer. The thing could rot where it lay. And she had other ways to get to the truth.

Pavlov was wearing the veil this morning. She'd draped it over his stern countenance after Hislop's phone call the previous day, after seeing the visions that led her from her mother's bedroom all the way to the tapestry of the saint. She lifted the veil from the bust, thanking Pavlov for his stewardship, and walked from the room to the stormwatchers' gallery.

Placing the coronet of silver leaves on her head, she dropped the veil over her face. As yesterday, she stood with her fingers pressed to the coarse weavings of the tapestry. She stared into the worshipful eyes of the saint and made her own little prayer for help.

It wasn't answered. She stood for minutes. She concentrated, focused herself on her question, then relaxed, became a vessel and offered her emptiness to the visions. Still nothing.

Perhaps this part of the vision had played itself out here? She remembered pulling back the tapestry just as the phone rang, and so she repeated the action. She stared into the dark opening in the stone. The visions weren't being cooperative today.

Stepping into the darkness, she let the tapestry swing closed behind her. Then she walked a slow walk, her senses alive, listening, probing for the first signs of a return to the past. Her hands ran along the smooth handrails to either side. She followed the gentle gradient downwards. The quiet shuffle of her track shoes rose from the stone flags.

With each step the sound changed, grew louder. Her shoes rang against stone. She was wearing heels now, low heels she could feel. The hiss of silk filled the narrow space, blending with the sibilance of the whispers that taunted and vilified her.

Uselessuselessuselessworthlessworthlessworthless...

Fear clutched at her heart with cold fingers. She was feeling her mother's fear, the fear of capture. Suze hurried through the darkness, heels echoing, the wedding dress brushing against stonework on either side. She was in her mother's form now, she was back, she could feel her mother inside her, or was *she inside her mother*?

She found the steel door and stepped through. Turning, she forced it closed on groaning hinges and slid the heavy bolt across. The sound of grating iron was the sound of safety.

Darkness and silence swept over her.

Then, from the centre of the room she heard the sound of footsteps, soft and slow.

The sound of breathing, close now. Closer still.

As before, she felt the veil lift in the still air, the white mist before her eyes giving way to impenetrable black.

She felt those slender fingers once again, cupping her face, lifting her chin, drawing her near.

Her mother's reaction to the kiss was also her own. A surrender.

Soft lips, warm lips, pressed against hers.

Her heart opened.

The soulmate's kiss.

Once more, those lips withdrew too soon, the slender fingers retreated into darkness. The veil floated back across her face and she waited, breathless, for what came next.

There was a faint whisper of silk in the room – but not the silk of her own dress. She strained her ears into the darkness, listening. Then jumped as words broke the silence.

'Emma, bring light!' It was an invocation, an appeal made in joy.

Suze felt her mother move along the circumference of the room, feeling her way to the handwheels on the wall. She found them and began to turn. A crack of light split the darkness, widening as the wheels turned. The light was corrupt, tainted. It boiled and churned in purples, bible-blacks and bloodied reds. The hissing curses seemed to follow the intrusion of unnatural light and grew to a deafening crescendo.

Suze turned, Emma turned, to see the cliffs and shores of Judgement Day projected, violent and terrifying, across the curvature of the opposite wall.

'You came.'

The words were gentle, affectionate.

At once the hissing of the curses became silent, as if a succession of doors had been slammed against their hatred.

A woman stepped into the light of the nightmarish projection. Behind her the baleful sky ceased its churning, the darkness receded, running to the edges of the projection as if in fear of her. Sunshine replaced the dark, and clouds of unblemished white now stood in the blue vault of a summer sky.

The woman smiled, stepping through the projected image of green clifftop grass and bright flowers of campion and tamarisk. Where her feet fell, the remaining darkness was banished. She wore a wedding dress of white silk, identical to her mother's, the sister-dress Kerenza had fashioned. The woman's veil was drawn back from her face and Suze recognised the dark, intelligent eyes that pulled at her like magnets: black lodestones dropped in snow. She was more striking than any photograph could do justice.

This was her mother's lover in the shadows.

The only person who knew who her mother truly was.

The only person who could drive away the madness.

The only one who could heal her.

Samantha Grey.

Samantha.

Sam.

She held out her hands now to Suze, to Emma and a solemn look drifted across her features. 'Will you be brave now?' she asked.

Suze felt her mother nod, although she seemed to hold on to something. A secret buried too deep, beyond divulging.

Samantha glanced towards the bolted door. 'We must hurry. Will you help me?' She swept across the room, to its centre, above the steel hatch. Crouching together, Suze could see the projection of sunlight-tipped waves dance across Samantha's pale skin and dark hair. The lodestones drew her. 'Ready?' asked Samantha, clutching the handles of the hatch. Together they lifted and a blast of cold sea air blew up and into the room. Samantha hurried away and returned with a wicker basket. Inside lay something hidden in folds of cloth. She tied a length of rope to the basket's handle and lowered it through the trapdoor. The basket swung, heavy with its contents. 'Help me, we must be careful,' Samantha implored. She took hold of the rope, feeding it gently through her hands. The basket slid down into the darkness, out of sight, until the rope went slack. Samantha climbed through the hatch opening and tied the rope off. 'I'll go first, you follow. Be careful, the ladder is wet.'

Suze could feel her mother draw courage from Samantha. Yet behind her mother's racing emotions, Suze's own mind was spinning like a counter-balance, thinking other thoughts, in other directions. She knew where she was, in the past and the present. In both cases, she was standing in the camera obscura, about to climb down the rusted old ladder into a dark, wet cave. No torch. No safety rope. Suze's instincts were screaming at her to wake up, to pull back the veil and end this. It was too dangerous. *But the ladder was safe, wasn't it?* She could climb it again, she just had to be careful. More than any risk, more than any fear of falling, she *wanted* to know. She had no option but to follow.

A sudden hammering at the steel entry door shook Suze from her thoughts. She felt her mother's fear.

'Emma, Emma! I know you're there. Open this door!' The voice boomed. A man's. Not Samuel's. It was a voice that carried assertiveness and rage: Henry Lacey's.

The black lodestones gleamed up from the hatch opening. 'We have to go now.'

Suze felt the shaking of her mother's legs. Perhaps her own were shaking too. She swung herself into the hatch entryway and stepped down to the landing of steel grating. It groaned. *A sound from the present, or the past?*

Samantha was already a dim shape far below, descending into darkness. Suze clutched the ladder and began her climb down, breathing evenly, releasing only one limb from the steel rungs at a time. Above her, the hammering and bellowing continued. The door was strong. It would hold.

Step by step, she climbed lower into the freezing dark. Her eyesight adjusted, grew accustomed to the lack of light. In time, faint glimmers of daylight danced across the wet rocks of the cave below. The shouting and hammering faded, replaced by the funnelling of the wind and the roar of the sea beyond the cave.

She reached bedrock and stepped from the ladder, taking a

huge lungful of air. Then she turned towards the high, slanting crack of daylight that was the opening of the cave. Samantha stood, a tiny silhouette, framed in sunlight, basket in hand, beckoning.

These rocks were familiar to Suze, although she still stepped with care over their damp, slippery surface. Samantha waited for her at the mouth of the cave. Joining, they held hands and emerged into summer sun.

The rock of Klegger Dhu looked less dangerous, less formidable in the bright sunshine. Its high cliffs still shone darkly, sea-wet and sparkling with black mica, but the savage waves that pounded its base were lulled to an unusual calm. The sea rolled in glossy, undulating surfaces of azure and sapphire. The wind blew from the west, mild and balmy, and the island and causeway were crowned with thick grass of verdant green.

With the basket swinging in her hand, Samantha stepped onto the narrowest part of the causeway alone. She moved briskly across, in one unfaltering motion, to the other side. Suze had crossed here before in a stiff breeze yet, despite her confidence at crossing under such calm conditions, she could feel the tremble in her mother's legs.

Together, mother and daughter walked the narrow causeway to Klegger Dhu and ascended the natural staircase of stone to the cell and altar of the hermit saint. Samantha waited, kneeling in the summer grass, the basket with its wrapped bundle at her knees.

Suze knelt too, as her mother once did, and looked on as Samantha lifted the bundle from the basket. 'You're wearing the dress we chose,' Samantha said. Her voice rolled, deep and sonorous, like a summer storm. 'It's perfect.' The black lodestones sparkled at Suze, at Emma, then flashed to the top of the cliff. 'They'll find us shortly, so let's begin.'

Samantha peeled away the folds of cloth. 'I searched so long to find the right means,' she said. 'Then I found something perfect for our needs.' She pulled the final fold away to reveal an ornate box of dark, close-grained wood.

Suze's heart was in her mouth. She knew this box. In contrast, her mother seemed to feel no fear, no sudden stab-wounds of panic.

Samantha slid the silver catch across and opened the lid. Inside lay two long, dark shapes cushioned in red velvet. 'Here are the instruments of our union.'

Words from the letter flew about in Suze's memory.

Our day approaches and it fills me in equal measure with both joy and fear.

I rejoice that soon we will stand before He who cannot deny us, the God of love Himself.

He will join us. And we shall be apart no more.

Until that day, and evermore.

From the top of the cliff came a shout, insistent, urgent. Two figures were running, scrambling down the path to the old pilchard hut. Henry and Samuel had given up reaching the ladder in the camera obscura and were now attempting the cliff path down to Klegger Dhu.

Samantha's dark eyes shot again to the top of the cliff. They returned to Suze, to Emma, and she spoke a little more quickly. 'The pistols are called the Crossley Twins. They're old but still deadly enough for our purpose.' She leaned close, fixing Suze with a look of dark entreaty. 'They're loaded – choose one.'

Suze did not move, yet somehow, against the command of her

own will, her hand, her mother's hand, moved towards the wooden case and lifted one of the long, dark shapes of steel and wood from its lining.

'They're called the Twins for a reason,' continued Samantha. 'It's because they're identical – so that neither duellist could have any kind of advantage. They say their maker couldn't even tell them apart.' The lodestones glowed. 'This is why they're like you and I, Emma. Without the other they have no meaning, no value, no purpose. They were created only to be together. To be the same, to be equals.'

Samantha Grey lifted the remaining pistol from the case and stood. She walked to the altar-stone and ran her free hand across its flat surface. Then she turned, and Suze could see a tear gleam in the corner of one dark eye.

'Come. They're almost here,' said Samantha.

The two men were skidding, sliding, raising clouds of dust in the middle of the path between the clifftop and Klegger Dhu.

Against Suze's will, her mother stood and joined her lover at the saint's altar.

Samantha raised her pistol and pressed its muzzle into Emma's chest, Suze's chest, above her racing heart. Then she clicked the hammer back, once, twice. *Half-cock. Full-cock.*

Emma did the same, placing the heavy, octagonal barrel of the pistol against Samantha's heart. Two women. In wedding dresses. Pointing duelling pistols at each other beside a ruined altar.

From the causeway, Suze heard more shouting. 'Stop! Enough!' bellowed Henry Lacey.

'On three,' commanded Samantha. 'One, two...'

Terror crawled over Suze like a plague of insects. She couldn't move. Physically, she couldn't turn the pistol away, couldn't lift the veil, couldn't put a stop to the madness. She thought of Henry Lacey striking her mother across the face, striking *her* across the face. Somehow the actions of this past life had an impact on the present. These visions could hurt, wound, perhaps even kill. If Samantha pulled the trigger now, then what?

But Emma Lacey didn't die here. The thought screamed loud in Suze's mind. *She died at the age of sixty, alone, on a cold, wet moor.*

The barrel of the Crossley pistol that lay against Samantha Grey's breast wavered, lifted free and was lowered. Suze felt her mother's arm drop to her side, the pistol with it.

The black lodestones of Samantha Grey's eyes speared her with hurt and confusion.

Her mother's free hand dropped to her belly, smoothing the silk, cupping the now-exposed mound.

Samantha's astonished gaze lay fixed on her mother's rounded belly, then flew to meet her own. 'You carry his *child*?' The words were both a question and an accusation.

Suze knew the child inside was herself. She was inside her mother's body in two ways now: as an unborn babe, and as a grown woman looking back from thirty years hence. She was within her mother both physically and spiritually. *Isn't this what she'd always wanted*? All those years spent wrapping herself in the dresses of other women, the embrace of other mothers, trying to recreate what she'd lost, what she should have felt, to touch the godhead, to finally *understand*.

After years of searching, she was here. The moment came at her like a bullet from a pistol.

Samantha shook her head in despair. The heavy pistol now hung slack at her side. 'This is no reason to stop. Emma, we must go on.' Her eyes flashed briefly to the figures on the cliff path. 'You cannot bring this child into the world, because you can never protect it. He'll never allow it to be yours, don't you see?'

Suze felt her mother step back, she disagreed. Her mother's hand cupped her belly more protectively. Suze felt emotion fizzle and spark. She had been loved, once. She knew that now.

Samantha's dark eyes brimmed with desperate tears. 'Why don't we take it with us? It will be our child, and we can love it together, forever.' She looked to the approaching men. They were across the causeway. Turning back, her voice became level, and Suze felt the black lodestones pull at her. 'Emma, this child will not be loved here. Not in this life.'

Suze felt her mother step backwards again. She could feel the tendrils of affection, of love and devotion that reached between these two women. They had been soulmates, they were meant to be one. And Suze knew in that instant that her mother loved her own unborn daughter, too. Her mother had loved *her*. The heart of Emma Lacey was being pulled in two directions and was in danger of being torn apart.

From behind, Suze felt rough hands upon her, wheeling her around. She turned and looked into the face of her mother's tormentor, his eyes scratched out in loathing, in fury. Shredded paper lay behind them, the score-marks shivered and vibrated, and the eyes were scratched out again and again.

Panting with exertion, Henry Lacey snatched the Crossley

pistol from her grasp and closed the hammer with a thumb. Then he cast it wide, towards the feet of Samuel Grey who bent, hands on knees, panting, a few yards behind.

'You persist with this depravity?' shouted Henry Lacey at Samantha. The veins in his neck and forehead bulged, raw with fury.

'Leave her be!' screamed Samantha, pointing at Emma, dark eyes flashing.

'I will not, she is *my* daughter...'

'Please Sam...' said Samuel, palms raised in placation.

'I said, leave her be!' Samantha was advancing now, pistol in hand.

Henry Lacey began dragging Suze, pulling Emma, back towards the causeway. He shouted over his shoulder. 'She is *my* responsibility and I will keep her from harm, beyond the reach of your perversions...'

'Let her be!' Samantha raised her pistol, aiming at Henry Lacey. He spun around, his face now fearful, and pulled Suze into the pistol's aim. Suze stared into the deadly blackness of the muzzle and heard a gasp of dread – *hers, or her mother's?*

'See how well you protect her now, by placing her in death's way to save yourself!' Samantha lowered the pistol, black fire dancing in her eyes. 'And don't talk to me of *perversions*. I know whose child she carries!'

Henry Lacey resumed his tugging and pulling at Emma, at Suze. Emma resisted out of fear, out of love for Samantha while Suze struggled out of anger at this man's hands upon her. He was fighting the combined strength of two women now.

Samuel Grey stared after Henry Lacey, aghast at his sister's accusation. 'Is this true?'

'For God's sake, Samuel, help me,' said Henry, struggling with his daughter. Samuel moved to help. Distracted, he helped Henry Lacey haul Suze and her mother, as one, back down the rocky staircase and across the causeway.

Kicking, fighting, Suze looked back to the isthmus isle of Klegger Dhu and saw the form of Samantha Grey, loping with unsteady steps to the edge of the cliff above the causeway. She held out her arms in a final gesture of appeal, desolate, weeping. 'Emma!' she called.

Inside, Suze felt Emma's voice rising to answer. A heavy hand was clasped across her mouth, silencing her, and she was dragged away.

The eyes of dark lodestone shone then with a different aspect, resolute and terrible. From the folds of her white dress, Samantha lifted the long shadow of dark wood and steel. She placed the barrel of the pistol to her breast and laced her thumbs across the trigger.

'Emma!' Samantha's voice lifted, plaintive above the sounds of sea and wind. 'Follow me!' she said.

Then she pulled the trigger.

A long, grievous howl went up, the cry of an animal in a trap. Suze realised its point of origin lay deep inside her, inside Emma.

The blast sent the pistol spinning from Samantha's hand. It clattered over rocks and dropped into the sea far below. Samantha fell backwards onto soft grass, the splash of crimson at her breast spread quickly, soaking the white silk. Black eyes were fixed on the sky. Death was merciful and had come quickly.

Suze felt the weight of her mother's grief now. The fight went out of her and her legs buckled. She fell to her knees, still howling. Henry Lacey tugged and pulled her, across rock, grass and soil. The dress tore against sharp edges. Samuel, seemingly caught between two imperatives, looked at Henry Lacey with brimming eyes and chose family. He ran back across the causeway to his sister's side. Suze could hear his shrill voice raised in lament.

From the edges of the blue sky crept the darkness. It rolled across the sea and cliffs, swirling like blood in black oil. It hid the sun and scaled the cliffs of Klegger Dhu, darkened the thick green grass and crawled across the body of Samantha Grey. It took her for its own then. Lightning flashed behind storm clouds.

She had no strength now. The weight of her mother's grief was like rocks in her pockets, dragging her down through cold water. Henry Lacey was powerful. A broad, strong hand was locked around her arm, wrenching her along, up the shadowed cliff past the old pilchard hut that was now the camera obscura. If she fell, his pulling continued, and she scraped and scuffed across rough ground. The dress caught and snagged. She skinned her knees and her hands all the way to the top. Her mother's tears were wet upon her face, her sobbing filled Suze's lungs. The wind lifted and whispered around them, a choir chanting its curses. At the crest of the cliff she saw the house, shrouded in tomb-like shadow. The Scots pine hung in the air, a dark shape revolving slowly like a dervish in some wild dance. Suze was exhausted, her mother, inconsolable. But still Henry Lacey dragged them on.

He flung the front door to Aeolus House wide and it crashed against the wall. Suze felt him hurl Emma inside, her ankles gave way and she slid across polished floorboards, outstretched hands burning against timber. She lifted heaving shoulders from the floor and watched him lock and bolt the door. Then he turned.

'Do you understand the harm you do?' he shouted. 'To yourself, and others?'

She tried to stand.

'Treatment will continue until such time as you see fit to embrace the cure.'

She made it to her feet and heard his thunderous footsteps approach. Looking up, she saw his shredded face, the scratched-out eyes, and one hand held aloft, as if in preparation for an oath.

The hand came down hard across her face.

The world went black.

⬩

Standing before her was a smiling woodsman. He was stripped to the waist, one foot resting on a felled tree, a hand on the haft of his axe. He stood in a clearing of other felled trees and his skin shone with labour. Through the veil, Suze could see no colour in the scene, just luminous tones of whites and greys. The woodsman was motionless, captured in time, smiling an eternal smile.

Metal moved against metal and the woodsman and his landscape slid from view, replaced by a monochrome scene beside a swimming pool on a hot, cloudless day. A male diving team posed for the camera in their bathing suits, displaying their musculature. The overhead sun cast glowing highlights on wet skin. Suze's eyes darted across the image, taking it in. She tried to move, but was constrained. Straps of leather bound her wrists, her feet. She felt hard rubber between her teeth, stopping her mouth. Another strap lay across her forehead, binding her head in place. Beneath this strap, two wires trailed from her temples.

The swimming team slid mechanically from view. Light flashed, then she saw two men, wrestlers in a ring. They grappled, smiling towards her, fixed in their contortion. She kicked now, trying to scream. She knew these images, knew where she was. She was fighting against her captivity, her binding. Inside her, something else rose. It was her mother's terror, soaring above everything, a foreboding that put all other thought to flight. Suze began to feel it too, it crept over her, and inside her like infection. She knew what was coming. They both did.

Another flash of light and the wrestlers vanished. Now a woman lay across a sofa, front down, naked, displaying her rear to the viewer. She wore stockings with garters of tied cloth and a coquettish smile. The image lasted only a moment.

Then came the pain.

It was sudden, and excruciating. Suze would have gasped, but could only draw in breath through her nose. She felt her eyes open completely. Agony surged in currents between the electrodes and her limbs snapped taut, her muscles convulsed, joints straining. Her body arched from the back of the chair. Through her head, the bolts of lightning seared and burned. Her brain fizzled and popped like frying bacon. In her fevered imagination she could smell it, wisps of black smoke rising. Striations of pain, viewed as light, flashed. A scream rose inside her, gagged and silent, unable to find release. Shadows crept into the corners of her vision. She was losing consciousness, her body's reaction to the torment.

When the pain stopped, when the electricity ceased, she felt as though she had been dropped from a great height, from high above the clouds, back to earth. She fell through the black and purple sky, through the roof of Aeolus house and into the hard, wooden chair, her limbs held fast inside its bindings once more.

Henry Lacey stood against the blank screen, washed with the harsh glare of the projector. The scratches across his eyes retraced themselves over and over. 'Is this what you force me to do?' he said. He pointed to a space beyond the dark and curtained room, to the island where Samantha lay. 'A woman died today. And her blood is on you.'

Suze felt the welling of her mother's despair. Deep inside, something was lost forever, the thaw of all hope.

'She was diseased, yes, but not incurable. She didn't need to meet her end like that,' continued Henry Lacey.

Her nose ran, she drooled from the gag.

He pointed at her now. 'This was your doing, your wilfulness, your insistence to follow a path to – to where? Some fanciful, unliveable way of life?' He shook his head in disdain, then snapped, 'Wake up, Emma!'

He began to pace in the light of the projector – actor, producer and audience in the spotlight of his own theatre.

'What you do, what you have *done*, is a sin and a crime.'

He turned to her, his eyes gouged to shreds of paper. He pointed again in the direction of the island. 'And you leave me to play janitor, to follow you around with a mop and bucket, forever trying to wipe away our shame, to clear our name again and again?'

His raving stopped. He ran a hand through his hair. Then sank to a knee beside her. 'Come back to me Emma, why don't you come back? This pain can stop. If you want it. We'll send the child away. We'll be together, the way we were, when you were a little girl. Remember?'

At this, Suze felt some of her mother's fight return. Emma wouldn't go along with this easily. She was looking down a road, a long journey of suffering but, if she could only hold onto her child, every step would be worth it. She wanted her daughter with her, she wanted Suze by her side. Something trembled inside the aquamarine suitcase. Her mother's feelings for her, the feelings she'd always felt denied.

'Remember?' repeated Henry Lacey.

Suze was now aware of his hand moving through the folds of the dress, a fumbling search, lascivious and wrong. His breath became ragged, harder, its staleness reached her nostrils. She screamed another silent scream. Drool dripped, her eyes clouded with furious, hopeless tears. Inside her, Emma grew listless and fell inwards, her resolve began to crumble and collapse. She was falling to pieces like a sandcastle in the face of an incoming tide.

'Come back to me Emma,' muttered Henry Lacey.

Suze could only fix those torn eyes with her own and hope he saw the hatred in them. It was her only weapon. She kicked and fought. The hand went deeper.

He stood then and seemed to regard her with a vacant, automatic look. Then his eyes steeled and he turned to the table with the machines.

The light on the screen flashed, then became a male gymnast. He hung from a set of rings, the veins and sinews in his arms corded and prominent. Suze drew repeated breaths through her nose, her eyes widening. With each breath her fear mounted, towards the inevitable, towards the pain she knew was coming.

'It can stop, anytime. Anytime you want. Just come back,' he shouted over the humming of the machines.

The projector clunked and whirred, the light on the screen flashed and became a naked woman, arms and legs crossed to hide her modesty, a flower pressed to her nose. Her eyes gleamed with invitation.

A red-hot poker lanced through Suze's head. It travelled from side to side, burning and cauterising in the space behind her eyes. Her limbs were racked to dislocation, pulled and stretched into new paroxysms of agony. She struggled to breathe. The space inside her skull was filled to bursting. Her brain, now swollen and on fire, threatened to rupture in gouts of hot blood. She felt her nose, eyes and mouth stream. Images she couldn't see continued to flash and change on the screen in front of her. She was looking through a waterfall now. And still the pain came. The edges of her vision blurred, grew darker and closed in. She was struggling to hold onto consciousness. She was grasping at a rope that dangled from a steel hatch into the impenetrable black of a deep cave. Her fingers slipped and she fell, tumbling, into oblivion.

$$30$$

THE PRODIGAL DAUGHTER

IN THE DARKNESS was a sound, earth-shaking and clamorous.

It thundered and rang around her like monstrous footsteps.

Was it him? Was he still after her?

In her stupor Suze felt panic seize her like a hand at her throat. She struggled through clinging layers of unconsciousness and fought for air.

Waking with a gasp, she found herself in the hard wooden chair. There were no straps at her wrists. She was wearing her jeans, muddied and rucked from the climb back from Klegger Dhu. Her knees hurt. Her muscles ached. In front of her the collapsible screen hung filthy and tattered.

She pulled back the veil and took in the dim, dusty room.

The thunder persisted.

Her reason seemed to hang by a thread, halfway between things, between worlds. She was back – so why could she still hear his footsteps?

Standing a little too quickly, she brought a hand to her temple. There was no burn there, although she'd witnessed every electron of her mother's torture, every molecule of pain.

The sound echoed through the house, clanging, banging, like a blacksmith at an anvil.

Stumbling from the secret room into the study, she looked about. In the murky light she could make out the decay, the desk with the photograph in the silver frame, the transistor radio, the box with the single Crossley pistol. It was all familiar, reassuring.

Passing the bust of Pavlov on his pedestal, she pulled the veil from her hair and placed it in his safekeeping. The sound seemed to come from the great hall, so she followed it. Emerging from the study, she saw daylight flash in time with the noise of the clanging. She peered around a corner towards the stormwatchers' gallery.

It was the storm shutters. They beat themselves against the window frames in the wild weather. Patches of drizzle blew horizontally at the glass and misted the view. Suze ran for the rear door and forced it open against the wind. Outside, it was wet and blustery. The sea pitched and rolled in foothills of white and grey. Squalls raked its surface in violent gusts. Below the cliff, mountainous waves would be arching over Klegger Dhu in spumes of white. She struggled with the shutters but the wind seemed to come from everywhere at once, gusting erratically from the north, then the west, ripping the shutters from her hands and whipping them about. She was in danger of being struck. Working methodically was the safest way. She moved from one end to the other, closing and bolting each shutter in turn, until the clanging stopped and she was tired and soaked.

The interior of the stormwatchers' gallery was dark now. She flung the rain from her hands and walked through the gloom into the great hall. The window above the staircase landing cast patches of light across the floor that ran wet with gathering rain. She stopped, glancing at the oval photograph of her mother and grandfather. Her mother, frightened and alone, a scarf around her head to hide the scars of suffering. He, boastful and cruel, eyes scratched out in retribution.

The veil had shown her all it could, all her mother wanted her to know. She had the truth, she knew which way her mother's heart had leaned, and she knew her own path now. She lifted her chin at the portrait, breathing in the knowledge. Then she turned and walked quickly to the new phone that hung from the wall. On the faded wallpaper she'd written a list of numbers in pencil. Her finger ran down the list and stopped at one. Lifting the handset she punched a number.

A matronly voice answered. 'Bosvenor Sanatorium.'

'Doctor Passmore please.'

'Who's calling?'

'Suze Newman, and please tell him it's urgent.'

The line went silent, then crackled and buzzed. Suze wondered if she was still connected. She waited. 'Hello?' came the eventual answer. A man's voice.

'Doctor Passmore?' She still didn't know if Passmore was in league with Ava Carfax, whether he was part of the scheme to pull down Aeolus House and carve up the land for profit. She didn't care, she'd ruined that little escapade and now Passmore would answer to her in his professional capacity.

'Yes?'

'My mother can't be cremated,' she said.

'I'm sorry, whatever do you mean?'

'You need to cancel.'

Passmore's words became indistinct, broken. 'Why?' was all she could make out.

'Just stop the cremation.'

The line went dead.

'Hello?'

She tapped the cradle a few times. Nothing.

'*Shit!*'

Suze slammed the handset back and turned to the house.

Storm Bay was about to live up to its name.

As would Aeolus House.

———◆———

Lundy north-westerly... backing northerly... gale force nine... heavy rain... very poor.

Suze lay in bed with her transistor radio. She'd tuned it to the strange chant of the shipping forecast just as Harlan had taught her. He'd explained how to decipher the odd pattern, what it meant, but the weather reporter read so quickly that it was impossible to understand. It was like listening to a foreign language. She didn't really need the forecast, she could hear what was happening outside. She'd taken the radio upstairs to her bed, then listened to it throughout the night. It was company more than anything. Another human, another voice.

She hadn't really slept, only dozed and dreamed of storms.

Storms she'd seen through the veil, purple and black, trees plucked from the soil and held suspended in air. Sounds woke her: shattered tiles blown from the roof, the howl of the wind in the chimneys, dislodged plaster falling from the ceilings. Glass broke, beams and joists groaned and the windows rattled.

By morning, the situation hadn't improved.

Fastnet... westerly... force nine... heavy rain... very poor.

Today her mother would be cremated. She'd be moved from that cold, dark room in Bosvenor Sanatorium to a place with an oven and a fireproof door. The end. A burning. Ashes to ashes. Tomorrow there'd be a service in an empty church. Hymns she didn't know the tune to. A eulogy she might read for no one to hear. Then, a locking away in a family vault, next to the people who'd never understood her, never kept her safe from harm, never allowed her to be the person she was supposed to be. Would the storm put an end to all this? She hoped so but she couldn't be certain. In her imagination the possibilities blew about like bad weather.

Sole... westerly... nine, increasing to gale force ten... heavy rain becoming sleet... very poor.

The murky light outside tricked her into thinking it was earlier than it was. She checked her wristwatch. *Eight fifteen.*

She crawled from her sleeping bag and got to her feet, eyes gritty from lack of sleep.

Turning off the radio, she pulled on her filthy jeans and damp sweater. Gazing round her mother's bedroom her eyes fell upon the bloom of secret words that covered the wall behind the bed and behind the dressing-table. She knew what they meant now, why they were there. They were a promise made by her mother over the space of a lifetime. An answer to her lover's own last words.

Follow me...

...I follow.

She collected the cardboard box containing the wedding dress then made her way downstairs.

The phone was still out. She remembered the complaining technicians from British Telecom holding up coloured wires and moaning about the connection to the exchange. Perhaps it was just Aeolus House that was affected? Perhaps it was the whole area.

Suze sighed and looked up at the window above the landing. The storm still raged, arrogant and destructive, like some meteorological version of Henry Lacey. She moved to the study, relieved Pavlov of the veil and folded it into the cardboard box with the wedding dress.

Could she ever tell Harlan what she knew? About her mother and his aunt?

She wouldn't need to tell him exactly *how* she knew, or what she'd seen through the veil. There was enough evidence in the real world to show him: a love letter in his aunt's hand, the entwined fingers of two women in a photograph, a broken book that diagnosed her mother's disease and catalogued her crimes. It was just as easy to reach the truth this way.

Her eyes fell on the box containing the Crossley pistol. *How many times had her mother raised it to her heart? Why had she not pulled the trigger and gone to her soulmate? Was it fear? Or, as Suze wanted to believe, was it because Emma Lacey knew she had a child somewhere in the world? A child who might one day return to her?*

The prodigal daughter had returned.

Here I am, Mum.

She'd never be able to tell Harlan how his aunt died, or what happened at Klegger Dhu. Henry Lacey would have cleaned away every shred of evidence. He would have bribed the Greys or coerced them into secrecy to protect his name. Then, when his grand-daughter was born, he'd place her in foster care, as far away as he could.

That's how you bury a family's shame.

She crossed the study and stared with contempt at the broken book on the floor. Lifting it between finger and thumb like a dead rodent, she recrossed the study to place it in the box on top of the dress and veil. Replacing the lid, she carried the box from the study and lowered it into the basket of her bicycle. Then she pulled on her raincoat and opened the front door of Aeolus House.

The wind struck her square in the face, blew back her hair and tugged at her coat. Twigs, leaves and debris rushed through the door like a home invasion.

Outside, long weeds thrashed about in the gale. Rain sheeted horizontally across the landscape.

Hands on the handlebars, Suze pushed her bike through the door. And into the storm.

31

'I KNOW WHAT SHE REALLY WANTS'

THERE SEEMED to be no shelter, even between the tall hedges of the narrow road that ran down to the village of Storm Bay.

Suze rode some sections, then was blown so violently off-course that she careened into bushes and thicket, thrashed by branches that left weals on her face and hands. Even downhill, she had to pedal hard against the wind. Trees had fallen across the road, roots exposed. Power and phone lines whipped loose from telegraph poles and an onslaught of branches and leaves flew at her, pushing her back. So she dismounted, pointed the bike's front wheel in the direction of the village, and pushed.

Near the junction with the main road she hopped back into the saddle. The road was wider here and the bike moved more freely downhill. As she reached the junction a car, headlights blazing, turned the corner at speed in her direction. She steered hard to avoid a collision as the vehicle skidded to halt. The driver struggled to wind down the window and shout through wind and rain. 'I was coming to check on you.'

Suze recognised the Land Rover. It was Harlan.

'I'm fine,' she shouted back.

'You shouldn't be out in this.'

'I need to get to Bosvenor.'

Harlan lifted hands from the steering wheel. 'How?'

'The bus…'

Harlan nodded to the passenger seat. 'Get in!'

Grateful for a little shelter, Suze dumped her bike and hauled out the wet cardboard box. With one hand she struggled to open the door against the wind and soon sat, panting, dripping, facing Harlan. He took in the soaking clothes, the weals across her face. A twig was lodged in her hair.

'There's no bus, Suze.'

She shook her head, eyes closed. This wasn't what she needed to hear.

'There's nothing. You should see the village. There's no power, no phones, the place is a mess.'

'I need to get to Bosvenor,' she repeated through clenched teeth.

'They're predicting sixty mile an hour winds.'

'I don't care.'

He searched her eyes. 'But why?'

'Will the cremation still go ahead today?' she asked.

'I've no idea…'

'Is there any chance it might?'

'Well, Bodmin's inland, it may be sheltered there…'

'So there's a chance it might?'

Harlan was flummoxed. 'I wouldn't think so, but...'

'Harlan, is there any chance it still might go ahead?'

Harlan's eyebrows were hidden high in his fringe. 'Well, I guess so – yeah.'

Suze looked about, her mind racing. 'Your Land Rover, could it get us there?'

'In *this*?' Harlan gestured to the raging storm.

Suze's gaze was unwavering.

'Suze, what's this all about?'

She pulled away the sopping lid of the cardboard box. Reaching inside, she pulled out her grandfather's book and slammed it against the dashboard. She thumbed through wet pages until she found what she was looking for and placed a dripping finger on a photograph.

Plate IX. Subject 53.

Harlan leaned close, expression sliding from confusion to horror. 'My God,' he whispered.

'That's why she can't be cremated,' explained Suze. 'I don't want her ashes placed in some family vault, next to *him*.'

Harlan searched her face. 'But there's no need to stop the cremation. We could place her ashes somewhere else?'

'I don't think she ever wanted to be cremated. I think I know what she *really* wants. I can explain on the way.'

———— ◆ ➤ ————

Making a three-point turn, Harlan steered his Land Rover back towards the main road. At the junction he stopped as a metal dustbin bounced and ricocheted in front of them from the direction of the village, spewing rubbish as it went. There was no other traffic. Harlan and Suze were the only ones foolhardy enough to take to the road in such conditions.

The wind continued to batter the landscape. Trees were bent to breaking point, crops of yellow rapeseed were torn from the fields and clouds were hurled across the lowering sky. The rain came at them horizontally, like bullets. Harlan switched the windscreen wipers to full speed. It made little difference. Between each sweep of the rubber blades, the wind-driven rain pummelled the glass, reducing visibility and forcing their progress to a slow, infuriating crawl.

They crested the long hill out of the village, the storm beating at their rear and shaking the Land Rover on its suspension. In the lee of the hill they were a little more sheltered. Harlan increased speed, spurring the Land Rover forward, but in the low of the valley he was forced to slow to a stop. In front of them a broad swathe of floodwater surged across the road, muddy and filled with silage from nearby farms. Harlan gazed over his knuckles at the fast-moving torrent of brown and green.

'There's no telling how deep it is,' he said. 'We could get swept off the road, or stranded. We could lose the vehicle.'

'Can we walk?'

'You'd get swept away for sure.'

Suze simmered. They couldn't stop now.

Harlan shook his head at the situation.

'Can we try driving through it?' urged Suze. 'If you lose the car, I promise I'll buy you a new one.'

Harlan shot her a searching look, as if trying to figure out whether she was joking, or as reckless as he'd always suspected. He seemed to settle on the latter and turned to the road ahead. He selected four-wheel drive, pulled on the low-range lever and punched the Land Rover into first. They trundled towards the ominous stretch of water, gathering pace.

The river of brown rose around them, there was a shudder as one of the wheels found a hole. Water began to slop in the foot-wells. Harlan drove on, knuckles bone-white on the steering wheel. The surge of water threatened to push them sideways and off the road. 'Come on girl,' Harlan exhorted the ageing vehicle. Suze felt the road rise, the tyres gripped more surely and soon they were emerging from the floodwater. Harlan slapped the wheel and grinned.

A mile or two later, the wind dropped and the visibility improved. Chased along by low clouds, they drove more quickly through the pelting rain. The road seemed clearer, less strewn with debris. Harlan turned the Land Rover through granite gateposts and Suze saw the flash of a white signpost and heard the crunch of gravel beneath the tyres. Bosvenor Sanatorium.

Harlan yanked on the handbrake and turned to her. 'Let's hope they haven't left,' he said. 'You wait here.' Then he pulled his coat collar round his throat, opened the door, and dashed towards the building's grey silhouette. Suze waited, listening to the drumming of the rain on the Land Rover's roof. It seemed to take Harlan an eternity to emerge. She felt a surge of hope at seeing him running back to the car, splashing clumsily through puddles. He threw himself inside, panting, and reached for the ignition. 'They've already left,' he said, starting the engine. Suze felt hope seep away like rainwater down a drain.

The crematorium was only few miles further but their progress through the storm was slow. After what seemed like an age battling the weather, they pulled to a stop under the awning of the crematorium's main entrance and jumped out, bolting through the entry doors.

There was a foyer with flower arrangements and a noticeboard with plastic reusable lettering Suze had no time to read. Ahead of them stretched a corridor with the chapel beyond. She saw a casket sliding away from her on its dais, through a parted curtain where the fires of the hereafter burned.

'No!' she screamed, pitching herself headlong down the corridor and into the chapel. A small gathering looked up in shock, some nurses and staff she recognised from Bosvenor. The funeral director stood at a podium, operating the machinery of her mother's incineration. He gawped at Suze, open-mouthed, the casket continued moving. 'Stop!' she shouted, reaching the casket. She laid the flat of her hand upon it, as if claiming it. 'Stop this cremation now!'

The funeral director came to his senses and looked down to the controls. The casket came to rest on the dais, poised between this world and the next. He looked up. 'What's the meaning of this?' he demanded.

Suze slapped the casket. '*This* is my mother,' she declared. 'And she's not going to be cremated.'

A tape recording of organ music played softly in the background. Everyone remained silent.

'This is Susanna Newman,' said Harlan, pointing at Suze in

explanation. 'The deceased's daughter and only relative.'

The funeral director blinked.

'Well, back it up!' demanded Suze, indicating the conveyor on which her mother's casket rested.

'It's not that simple, there's no *reverse...*' protested the funeral director.

'Then help me pull.' Suze had her hands through one of the casket handles, straining against it.

Together, they hauled Emma Lacey back into the world of the living. The crematorium chapel cleared, leaving only Suze, Harlan, the funeral director and his assistant. Trying to appear calm and in control, Suze explained what she wanted of the funeral director. She apologised for the inconvenience, put it down to misunderstanding and the weather. She even offered to pay for any further expenses and the funeral director's time. The memorial at St Carras would take place tomorrow as planned but now they'd need to transport her mother in her casket. Not as ashes in an urn. The funeral director seemed professional enough to overcome his indignation. After all, there was no real change to his schedule. But his hostility flared again when Suze went back out to the Land Rover, and returned with the sodden cardboard box.

'And one last thing,' she said, pulling out the worn, grimy wedding dress. 'She's to wear this.'

The casket was wheeled into a service room beside the chapel.

Suze oversaw the operation. The funeral director moaned and complained that reopening a casket at this stage was unorthodox and disrespectful. Suze didn't care. Her mother had endured far worse in life. What happened to her now would hardly matter. Besides, she knew that this was what her mother would want. Suze watched them gently strip her mother's stiff, wizened figure bare, then pull the old wedding dress over her. They placed the veil with its silver-wreathed crown across her brow and Suze stepped close for one final look.

Then she pulled the veil over her mother's face.

And the casket was closed for the last time.

———◆———

Suze returned to the chapel to find Harlan sitting alone on a pew.

He looked cold, damp and wrung out, but offered his unsure smile at her approach. She sat beside him. 'Thanks – for today,' she said. She meant it. Despite the storms and fair weather of their friendship, Harlan Grey had proved to be the only soul who'd stood beside her when she needed it most.

'What you said earlier about buying me a new car – does that mean what I think it means?' he asked.

'What do you think it means?'

'That you'll take Hislop's offer?'

'I don't have much choice,' she said, eyes on the floor. She looked up. 'But it's a good offer. Thanks for sending him my way.'

'Welcome.'

'One of your farmer contacts will buy the land. I'll avoid tax and Hislop has promised to renovate the house. It's the best outcome for everyone.' She let out a sigh. 'Best of all, there'll be no housing estates and nothing in it for Ava Carfax.'

'You'll still have to pay her, and Bosvenor.'

'I know. I'll manage.'

Harlan wiped his wet fringe from his eyes. 'Will you go back to

London?'

'Think I'll stick around.'

Harlan's mood brightened. 'Oh?'

'Hislop promised something else...'

'Ah, he agreed to your *condition*?'

Suze nodded. 'I agreed to give him the house if he gave me a job.'

'A job?'

'Working with kids. It's what I do, remember?'

'So you'll work at Aeolus House, looking after orphans and foster kids?'

'For now. If it works out.'

'You'll be good at that,' said Harlan.

She searched his eyes for any trace of playfulness or mockery but found only sincerity.

'And you'll live up there too, at the house?' he asked.

Suze shook her head. 'Think I'll look for a place in the village,' she said. 'Something less old – less *windy*.'

Harlan grinned.

32

A TIME TO WEEP.
A TIME TO LAUGH

SUZE AND HARLAN followed the casket of Emma Lacey through the heavy oak door of St Carras' church into the parade of headstones outside. The storm had blown itself out overnight, leaving in its wake a trail of damaged roofs, broken chimney pots and cracked windows. Above, the sky was streaked with high clouds that trailed in curls and wisps against the blue. The wind had dropped, becoming an even-tempered westerly. In all respects it was a fine day. The calm after the storm.

The pall-bearers' footsteps crunched on gravel. The funeral director had arranged everything just as Suze had asked, although he'd sent only four men to carry her mother. There was no weight to the casket. Any more would have been unnecessary.

The service had gone just as Suze expected. She and Harlan were the only mourners. Suze had mumbled a few unrehearsed words. She admitted to never knowing her mother in life, but had come to understand her a little better in death. The comment caused Reverend Tonkin to raise a questioning brow. What she said would make no sense to anyone else but, in every way, it was true.

They walked behind the casket along the white gravel path to the lychgate, then the procession swung out into the road. Following the low stone wall of the church, they made their way to an opened farm gate. The funeral party slipped and slid across pasture still wet from the storm to the corner of the field and the patch of ground beneath the crab-apple tree. The tree had been cut back and the bracken cleared away to expose the little wooden cross and the mound of soil. The damp earth had been easy to dig. A fresh grave was opened beside the old one. Suze decided that, in time, she'd commission two new headstones. Apart from the lovers' names, they would carry two simple dedications.

Follow me.

I follow.

Now Emma Lacey would make good on that promise. Her life had been a short detour, nothing more. She'd fallen behind, waiting for a daughter to come home. *You go ahead, I'll catch up.* This was the place she'd always been travelling towards: to lie dressed in white, joined with the one that held her heart.

Reverend Tonkin gave a short graveside reading. 'For everything, there is a season,' he began. 'A time to be born and a time to die. A time to plant and a time to uproot...'

Suze watched as her mother's casket was lowered into the welcoming earth. She thought of her own uprooting, and where she would plant herself next. Winter would arrive soon, then spring. She should be settled by spring. New life, new possibilities.

'A time to tear down and a time to build...'

She thought of all she'd torn down: a family's lie, the barricades of bureaucracy and pride that had separated her from her mother, separated her from the truth. She'd dismantled the conspiracies of Ava Carfax and her accessories. In place of all this she was building something, too. Something lasting, something meaningful. She was helping build a home for children – the kind of children she'd once counted herself among, the kind of children she'd be among again, only this time as guide, mentor and friend.

Suze could feel Harlan watching her. She turned to meet his eyes.

'You're crying,' he said, in wonder and disbelief.

He was right. Tears now coursed freely down her cheeks to her chin. She sniffed and reached for his hand, squeezing it so tight that he winced.

'A time to weep and a time to laugh.'

Through her tears she smiled at him. If it didn't suit her she didn't care.

In her mind the aquamarine suitcase of her childhood began to split and tear at the seams. The silver locks and hinges, freckled with rust, buckled and burst. The scuffed, turquoise cardboard ripped, the lining of grey aeroplanes and ocean liners tore into little pieces and blew away. She cried openly now, in great, heaving sobs. She cried like a child without thought to guard her emotions. It felt good, a release. She cried for every little hurt that now tumbled from the suitcase, every little hurt she'd locked away. She cried for her mother, for her short, tortured life, and the fact she'd loved her daughter enough to deny her own heart. She cried because once she'd been loved. She cried for Samantha Grey. She cried because her grandfather was also her father. She cried because her mother was also her sister.

Most of all she was crying because of *this moment*, caught up in this strange little ceremony of promises and prayers. She was crying out of a feeling that had lain hidden for so long at the bottom of the aquamarine suitcase. She'd never even known it was there. Now it was free – and it rose up to greet her.

She looked to the lovers' graves as the first clods of soil fell. This wasn't a funeral. Not really.

And Suze Newman was the kind of girl who cried at weddings.

A Thank-You

If you enjoyed this book, you can help other readers find my work by leaving an online review with the retailer you purchased it from, or at Goodreads.

Many thanks,

Jeff

About This Book

BACK IN 1998 I was walking past a Sydney charity shop when something caught my eye.

It was a wedding dress, complete with veil, draped over a mannequin in the front window. The dress was old and careworn but stunning in a yesteryear kind of way.

My immediate reaction was to chuckle – quietly to myself. What were they thinking? It would never sell. What bride-to-be would consider a charity shop hand-me-down to wear on the most important day of her life? It wasn't fashionable or modern, it may not fit and it would never be truly *hers*.

So why was it here?

My grin was reflected back at me from the shop window. It faded. There was a deeper question here, I could feel it.

I like to think that writers have a kind of radar, sweeping continuously, whether consciously or unconsciously, for ideas, for stories. My radar was active, scanning, probing. I paid attention and suddenly felt a colossal blip.

It occurred to me that most women hang onto their wedding dresses through thick and thin, my own partner included. The gowns are stashed away like treasure, as heirlooms to be handed down to daughters, granddaughters and nieces. More than just garments, they are symbols of happiness, love, family, and a moment of great change in a woman's life. You'd think the same might be true of a man's wedding suit, tie and waistcoat. But it just *isn't*.

Wedding dresses are special.

Wedding dresses are sacred.

So why did this woman give hers away?

Did she still live?

Was there no one to cherish it, no one to hand it down to?

Was this a marriage best forgotten? Did she marry a second time?

The questions roiled inside me. I looked up at the veil and wondered what this bride had seen through its silk all those years ago.

Then it landed. An idea for a story. The idea for *this* story.

My first attempts were short stories. *Bad* short stories.

From a genre standpoint they were confused.

So I hid them away.

Soon after, our children were born and writing became less important. A few years later I accepted a job offer in Hong Kong. We moved as a family and I dedicated myself to my career.

But the idea for 'Veil' never left me.

I began rewriting. The story became longer. Darker. With each new draft it drifted closer to horror, towards something gothic. We don't get to choose our stories, or our genre. The stories always know more. They know how they want to be told. All a writer needs to do is interpret the clues we are given. This is the story revealing itself. Our only job is to act as mediums and usher these stories into the real world, to get them down on paper.

While meditating on this story's meaning, an image surfaced in my imagination. It was unbidden and dreamlike. I visualised two women on a clifftop, clothed in long, white wedding dresses like the one I'd seen in the charity shop window. The two brides were aiming pistols at each other as if taking part in a duel. It was like a movie poster, a freeze-frame of a critical scene. I knew that if I could only understand what it meant, the story would unlock for me.

It took several more years for that to happen.

By 2017 I was back in Australia with my family and the nation was locked in debate: should same sex marriage be legalised?

I clearly remember the televised arguments for and against. Some were infuriating but most were moving, inspirational. While politicians harangued each other, the decision-making process moved from a compulsory plebiscite to a voluntary postal vote. Posters were fixed to doorways and windows as households made their position known. The posters were simple: the word 'Yes!' emblazoned across a background of rainbow colours. The nation voted and same sex marriage became legal in December 2017. Within a week of its passing, the first same sex couple was married.

Perhaps it was the euphoria of that time, the celebrations and rejoicing at that final decision. Whatever it was, the vision of the two women in white re-framed itself for me.

I saw then that it wasn't a duel, a conflict. It wasn't two women fighting over a man – nothing so trite. The vintage of the wedding dresses helped me understand that the vision was a window onto a bygone age. Then the story revealed itself like the drawing back of a wedding veil. It was a joining, a marriage. It was an act of love at a time when such love was outlawed. A suicide pact.

I buried myself in research, attempting to understand the difference between a time when same sex relations were illegal and our more liberal society of today. My story, I'd decided, would be set in the 1980s. This allowed me to contrast a more progressive period in history with a less tolerant one only thirty years earlier: the 1950s.

Researching this earlier period made for some harrowing reading. Particularly with regard to the assumption that homosexuality was a mental disorder. This was also accompanied by the theory that, as a disorder, it had to be curable.

Pavlov was one of the first scientists to understand the connection between environmental stimuli and behavioural response. In 1901 he accidentally stumbled into the field while measuring the salivation of dogs in order to better understand the workings of the digestive system. He published his findings in 1903.

Pavlov only ever presented his findings as concept. But the world of psychotherapy saw it differently: as a way to *modify* behaviour. And so Pavlov's *Conditional Reflex* became a new methodology: *Classical Conditioning*.

Psychotherapists of the day pursued a range of treatments. By the 1940s gay men and women around the civilised world were being institutionalised without consent and subjected to *Behavioural Conditioning* and *Aversion Therapy*. The treatments included electric shock therapy designed to inflict agony while viewing images of 'abnormal' sexual orientation. Electrodes were attached to the head and often, directly to the genitals. If behavioural conditioning failed, then castration or lobotomies were a possible recourse.

By the 1970s, the Farrall electro-therapy device featured in this novel was widely adopted. It famously became the centre of a campaign to 'Shock the Gay Away'. This device and its use in aversion therapy became responsible for PTSD, depression and even suicide. Aversion therapy was also directly responsible for a number of deaths. In 1973 America declared that homosexuality was no longer a mental disorder. Britain followed a year later. The torture stopped.

Learning all this made my blood boil. I felt a need to draw readers' attention to this shameful period of medical malpractice.

I started work on a fresh draft and the story grew to a novella of 38,000 words.

But I was so caught up in the larger humanitarian issues and the idea of my main character witnessing the atrocities of the past through a wedding veil that I missed something.

I hadn't made my main character believable.

She moved through the plot without making her own decisions, like a dull automaton. She wore the veil time and time again because I needed her to, for the story.

This is the tricky thing about writing horror. How do you convincingly make your protagonist face their fear again and again? Sure, you can have them trapped, fighting to escape. You can make them subject to external forces, have them pursued by monsters. But this story wasn't going to be so easy. Ask yourself, if you looked through a wedding veil and the world changed into another person's mad dream, would you do it a second time? Thought not.

My protagonist needed a motive. She needed to face her fear over and over because it was the only way to get to something greater.

It was then that Suze Newman shuffled into the story – lost, damaged, unsure of herself and beset by mummy issues. The veil would be her way to find out where she came from and who she really was. She'd endure the horror because she'd choose to learn the truth. The decisions would be hers.

It's a crying shame she came to the party so late. If I'd only understood how to craft my central character from the outset I could have saved myself years of writing.

But that's where writing a novel is so rewarding. It teaches you how to write the next one.

When people ask me what this story is about I tell them it's three stories in one.

The first is a love story lost in time.

The second is a story of self discovery, set in the recent past.

The third is a story of change. It marks the corner many of us have turned in our attitudes to same sex relations. We've moved from fear and intolerance, closer to acceptance and understanding. We've still a long way to go in this and heterosexual thinking still dominates our societies, but many of us now realise that the world is more wonderful for its diversity, and that love is love, in whatever form it walks.

Jeff Clulow – Sydney 2025

About the Author

Jeff Clulow is a prizewinning author of romantic dark fiction and horror. Born in Cornwall in the UK, Jeff now lives and writes in Sydney, Australia. Jeff's writing leans towards the lighter end of dark fiction, exploring themes of family, childhood, love and loss. He's inspired by folktale, mythology and the notion that the old gods still walk among us.

His stories have reached the finals of the Aurealis Awards, the Shadows Awards, the American BookFest Awards and the National Indie Excellence Awards. He has been awarded an 'Honourable Mention' in the Robert N. Stephenson competition for short fiction in horror and is the winner of the 2023 Asylumfest Mayday Hills Ghost Story Competition.

Find out more about Jeff and his work at www.jeffclulow.com

www.ingramcontent.com/pod-product-compliance
Lightning Source LLC
Chambersburg PA
CBHW050553190726
48283CB00007B/2129